THE BERLIN EMBASSY

Also by Michael Shea

SPIN DOCTOR
THE BRITISH AMBASSADOR
STATE OF THE NATION

THE BERLIN EMBASSY

Michael Shea

HarperCollins*Publishers*

This novel is entirely a work of fiction. The names,
characters and incidents portrayed in it are the work of the
author's imagination. Any resemblance to actual persons,
living or dead, events or localities is entirely coincidental.

HarperCollins*Publishers*
77–85 Fulham Palace Road,
Hammersmith, London W6 8JB

Published by HarperCollins*Publishers* 1998
1 3 5 7 9 8 6 4 2

The Author asserts the moral right to
be identified as the author of this work

A catalogue record for this book
is available from the British Library

ISBN 0 00 225472 7

Typeset in Sabon by Palimpsest Book Production Limited,
Polmont, Stirlingshire
Printed and bound in Great Britain by
Caledonian International Book Manufacturing Ltd, Glasgow

To Mona, Katriona and Ingeborg

'No one in authority believed it could or would happen. Not on such a vast canvas nor on such a gigantic scale. Those who had, in the past, prophesied that worst scenario, were branded as way-out prophets of doom. It was impossible. Governments, international organizations, the common sense of Europe's peoples, would prevent it. But, as chance would have it, the leaders of the major western democracies were looking the other way at the critical moment. Too much was left to the professional diplomats, the generals, admirals and air marshals of NATO, in making the crucial assessment of risk. These officials had at their disposal all the intelligence they needed: it came from the military attachés in the capitals of eastern Europe, from undercover agents of Britain's MI6 and the CIA, from communications intelligence out of GCHQ and the NSA. They monitored, with great efficiency, the Kremlin scene, the discontent in the Russian armed forces, and were alert to the dangers of eastern Europe's rotting nuclear defence installations.

'But, as always in international life, diplomats spend too much time watching the nuances of behaviour of other diplomats. Armies watch other armies. That is their job. But this time, neither politicians nor generals nor ambassadors paid attention to the mood of the eastern masses, those ordinary millions who had drunk that heady cocktail of envy and anarchy. All that was lacking to light their fire was a leader. And then he came.'

Leading article, Newsweek

PROLOGUE

The lone woman stood profiled on a bleak headland. Despite her threadbare raincoat and an unfashionable headscarf knotted over prematurely greying hair, she had a stateliness about her as she stared out across the wild North Sea. By her feet, fine white sand took turns with the harsh rye grass of the dunes in whipping at her ankles. But she was oblivious to all that.

After some time, she pulled her thoughts back to the present and gazed down towards the shoreline to where her two sons played happily by the water's edge. One, five years younger than his twelve-year-old sibling, always seemed to have more boundless energy and verve in building their magnificent sandcastle; it was he who, with shrieks of excitement, was frantically fortifying it with pebbles and seashells against the advancing tide. Eventually his older half-brother, tousle-haired and contemplative, gave up any pretence of helping with the unequal task. He stood to one side, hands on his hips in the manner of a more mature person, and watched with superior wisdom the futility of trying to forestall nature as each successive wave further eroded the structure. Yet, to the last, the younger boy feverishly continued to defend the central keep, where a tiny paper flag fluttered boldly from its crude flagpole. Then came a huge wave and the younger boy's screams of frustration, as their efforts slid into an anonymous pile of wet sand. After a while, chattering excitedly, the two made their way up the steep sandbank towards where their mother benevolently stood.

Her attention wandered away from them again as she turned to look inland for an instant, thinking, for the thousandth time, how different each was. She saw nothing of herself in either;

only of their fathers – one so strait-laced and conventional, one so passionate. How she longed for them both.

The idyll vanished. When she again looked down at her sons, everything had blackened. She would never know the whole truth. She did not see the blow struck. Probably no more than an unthinking jibe had triggered the latent violence that was always there below the surface. The younger boy looked up at her aghast, and, realizing what he had done, threw away the little wood and metal spade that had been his weapon and, in fear and remorse, ran off along the shore. He would be found only much later that night by the police, huddled cold and frightened in the lee of an abandoned beach hut. The older boy did not once cry out, despite the savage, gaping wound that ran deep and bloody from his forehead down the whole of his left cheek. The scars, visible and invisible, would remain with them all for ever.

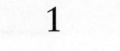

1

No more than a hundred metres separated the two worlds, so close, yet so far apart. On this side of the electrified razor wire, neat young men in cleanly laundered NATO uniforms, protected by their modern, all-weather anoraks, monitored the other, unbelievable existence. On the hour, they reported routinely to HQ up the line. They were fortunate; their tour of duty at the border was a short six months: tonight, it was eight hours on watch, then back to bright, centrally-heated barracks and good warm food.

The foot patrol of six soldiers halted at the base of the tall, sinister watchtower. Staff Sergeant Brace stood his men down and they shuffled off through the snow to light up or pull a warm drink from their Thermoses.

One young private, hair shaved down to his skull, paused where he was, then slowly raised and aimed his FK47 at something unseen across the floodlit fence. 'I could pick one off easy-like,' he said, half smiling. 'Wouldn't hear no sound in this wind.'

Staff Sergeant Brace looked at him sharply. 'Don't like that talk, Private Finney. They're humans too. This ain't no joke.'

The private sighed, slowly lowered his gun, and yawned. He was not evil, just very bored.

The watchtower had stood neglected for a decade and a half, ever since the Warsaw Pact troops had relinquished their waning control. Recently, however, the badly corroded metal ladders had been replaced, the glass in the windows renewed, and the wind no longer whistled round an ill-fitting door. Staff Sergeant Brace climbed up the twenty rungs to join Corporal Tate, newly come on duty, ready for the night's task.

That task, or the definition of it, immediately became the subject of their latest small altercation. 'You've been bloody thinking again, Corporal. Those books. I've warned you before,' said Sergeant Brace with good-natured resolve. He had taken to the younger man despite the latter's tendency to insubordination.

'Stop thinking, stop living,' came the low-muttered reply. Corporal Tate was an army oddball. He had never done anything particularly out of step, but on the other hand he had never quite fitted in. Even his uniform, smartly creased though it was, never seemed to fit his gangling frame.

'Now then, Corporal,' the sergeant glowered momentarily.

'I asked . . .' Tate paused, sucked his teeth, and peered through a slit-hole towards the east, 'exactly what the fuck are we meant to be doing here, Sarge?'

'Duty, Corporal. Wait, watch, observe, report.'

'That's what the orders say, Sarge. What d'they mean?'

'Don't come the philosopher with me, Corporal. Oughta be proud, you, serving NATO's front line.'

'We've done that together in Bosnia and Northern Ireland, Sarge, remember? Knew what we had to do then, didn't we? Some success we had. Here . . . well . . . must be the first time in history . . .' the corporal paused again, wondering how far to wind his sergeant up. He liked the other man too, for all his lack of imagination. Brace was a good name for someone so disciplined, so loyal, so full of a blinkered sense of duty. Unlike Tate, Brace did not know what cynicism or self-doubt were. Tate had been born with self-doubt, a childhood failing catered to by his brute of a father.

'What you getting at?' came another expected growl.

'Who's defending what from whom, and for why, Sarge?' Tate asked. He had thought about it. He genuinely did not know the answer.

'Just do your effing duty, Tate. No more bloody questions.' Sergeant Brace turned his back to hide his irritation at his lack of an answer, and started adjusting his night-vision binoculars.

'Goes for the whole NATO thing, Sarge. There's no point no

4

more.' He'd recently picked up an old copy of *The Economist* abandoned by the press liaison officer, and had read it from cover to cover. It had helped to crystallize views he already held.

'You'll get court-martialled if you don't belt your mouth, Corporal. You know what I know. NATO exists to defend western democracy.'

A long time passed, empty of words but filled with the whistling of the sharp wind outside. It had begun to snow again.

'Christ, it's bitter. Them folks over there,' said Corporal Tate after a while. 'Is it them, Sarge?'

'Is what them?'

'Defending western democracy, you said, but who the hell from? The Russians? No way! You know that. See that intelligence film of their army in training? Weapons so old and rusty that any scrapyard would reject them. Couldn't fight their way out of a bowl of cold borscht. The Emperor's clothes, Sarge . . .'

'What are you banging on about, Corporal? What Emperor's clothes?'

'Old fairy story, Sarge,' said Corporal Tate softly. He had left school when he was sixteen, but that was more to get away from his old man than from the teachers. He liked reading, and not just fairy stories.

Sergeant Brace hated it when Tate displayed too much knowledge. 'I'll give you fairy stories, if you don't get your binocs out and start scanning that fence. We don't want no more incursions while we're on duty.'

With a scarcely audible sigh, Corporal Tate unzipped the case, eased out the sophisticated infra-red equipment, clipped it on to its tripod, adjusted the focus, and peered into the snow-flecked gloom. He swung the powerful lenses to left and right, then back again.

'Nothing out there, Sarge,' he said eventually. 'Nothing, just nothing at all.'

Those two NATO soldiers experienced something of the cruelty of the unforgiving wind that blew the new snow horizontally across the bleak, featureless fields. But that was all they shared. That egalitarian wind roared on across the wire and only when it reached the huddle of roofless buildings that clustered around the ruins of a once-proud Orthodox church, did it find any barrier to its progress. In the partial shelter of the holy walls, dense black shapes revealed themselves, on close scrutiny, as another form of human being, desperately seeking shelter from the violence of the storm. Yet even those were fortunate in their way, packed as they were like sacks of garbage around a blazing fire that was fuelled by wood panelling stripped by sacrilegious hands from the church itself. Some planks still showed glimpses of gold leaf, while there, burning away, was an ancient icon, survivor of centuries of wars and purges, a candle-soot-blackened depiction of Christ crucified, burning its last, to give warmth to the living.

The bearded stranger sat well apart, restless with his thoughts. What was he doing here? Why was he not where he belonged? Why was he not now in some prosperous City boardroom, at his London club, or in his current passion's, scent-soaked bed? Why was he here, on the wrong side of this anonymous stretch of Russia's western border, surrounded by a scene that recalled for him some dimly remembered, black-and-white film drama of Napoleon's limping, frozen retreat from Moscow, or hideous, Solzhenitsyn replay of life and death in a Soviet gulag. But this was none of these. This was in sight of high-living western civilization, on a late December day, at the very climax of the twentieth century. Here was absolute destitution. Over there, only a short walk across the wire, beyond where the NATO soldiers patrolled, was an obscene abundance of food and warmth and plenty.

With the numbers that lay in shelter around him, the stranger would have expected, despite the constant whine of the wind, to have heard at least some human noise: the crying of a child, the weeping of widows, the angry voices of frustrated men. But there was no such sound. It was then that he realized, with a mind-numbing shock, that only one thing was crucial to those abandoned souls: to conserve their strength for the single purpose of keeping alive. Those were people waiting, not to be stood down from some brief military duty, but waiting for food, waiting for deliverance, waiting for something other than empty promises of a better life that had come in the bitter aftermath of the post-communist revolution.

What was he doing here? The stranger sat as close as he could to the fire but as far as possible from his evil-smelling, verminous neighbours. He knew why. He knew what he had been ordered to do. He knew he must act. Eventually, having checked the precise time on his solid gold Rolex, he forced himself to stand up among those huddled, frozen shapes. He towered above them, a clean, recognizable human being, well-dressed in a long, tailored, fur-lined coat, and with new-shod boots and warm Cossack cap. Who from his other life would recognize him now? He was bearded; contact lenses had been replaced, for convenience, by a pair of round, rimless glasses wired close to his face, giving him the appearance of some driven, revolutionary commissar. But he was no communist; no nameless party worker. When he spoke he made no reference to comrades nor to world brotherhood. His was an heroic, blood-red, nationalistic battle cry. He called them *my fellow Russians*.

'My fellow Russians . . . for too long you have been treated like cattle. With the collapse of the old regime, those Gorbachevs and Yeltsins, so-called democratic leaders, promised you the world. All . . . all of it this past decade, has proved empty lies. You know that. You see them daily, posturing, vacillating, corrupt, as they sweep past you in their gleaming Mercedes. They have forgotten, in their rotten, vodka-sodden lives, that we ordinary Russians are proud. We deserve to live well, to succeed, to conquer. That is our destiny.'

He paused and looked around him, his well-practised words carrying easily, even against the numbing wind. 'To do so,' he shouted even louder, 'we must have food, warmth for ourselves and for our children, a proper future for this great country of ours. That is why, when the moment comes, we must be ready to move westward, march peacefully and unarmed, to where the bloated nations of Europe sit gorging at their tables. Why should we, with our Ukrainian and Belorussian brothers and sisters, starve, when the European Community is overwhelmed by its food mountains? Are we not part of Europe too? Why should we not share . . . or *take* . . . that prosperity? My fellow countrymen, when the signal comes, we *will* move. We *will* break down, with our bare hands, the barbed-wire barriers that have been erected between us and that future which is surely ours to share. Prepare . . . Prepare . . .'

As the bearded stranger spoke on, he was inspired by the effect he was having. He knew he was good at being sincere, at being passionate, at rousing the emotions of the people. He knew what he was doing, why he was there. In front of him, the huddled shapes had gradually formed up in a semi-circle, a throng of recognizable human beings. One by one they stood, and came closer, gaunt faces revealed. Then they began shouting their applause. There was a terrible excitement in the air.

Later that day, despite the driving snow, several hundred men, women and children, with the help of a commandeered lorry which was backed into the border fence at speed to break through the lacerating razor wire, did not wait for any signal, but broke out from Belorussia and began their march through Poland towards the ever more affluent West. They were weak, undernourished and ill-prepared, and were rapidly rounded up by the army and police and forcibly driven back to where they had come from. The combination of a NATO-inspired news blackout and a major aircrash in southern France meant that no coverage whatsoever was given by the world's press to that minor border incursion.

Her Majesty's Government had, over the previous years, re-injected some of the old imperial splendour into the halls, stairways and offices of the Foreign and Commonwealth Office in Whitehall. Approached from Downing Street or King Charles Street, the building, designed by the Victorian architect Sir

George Gilbert Scott, had more of the air of an Italianate palazzo about it than the home of British foreign policy, which was why, when he came there for briefings between his foreign postings, Alex Murray always felt something of an alien in that setting of ornate grandeur. It was many years since he had served in the Office itself; as he had progressed up the slippery promotion pole, the personnel department had made it all too clear to him that his superiors considered him to be too angular, too tricky – they never actually said too blunt and middle-class – for a safe-pair-of-hands, domestic posting, working with government ministers and the smooth mandarins in the rest of Whitehall. He was, they said, better suited to being out in some foreign field, ruggedly fighting his corner for British interests. 'Horses for courses' they would add, with kindly condescension. He had always shrugged, accepted this assessment of himself, and got on with his life. He preferred the comparative luxury of being overseas in any case, where a salary and allowances went so much further than they did back in London. If personnel's attitude occasionally made him think about the downside aspects of his character, particularly about how he got on with other people, he was a fatalist: human existence was too short to worry about small defects like that for long. Friends and critics alike put his occasional abrasiveness down to his wifeless state. Even his closest friends shied clear of telling him that what he intended as light-hearted repartee often gave offence. He did it without meaning to, and when he went home at the end of a working day or social evening, there was no one to nag him about those defects in his manners. It was not too serious a blemish, but it had hardly helped his career prospects. Because he seldom referred to it, only his closest colleagues knew that he had once been blissfully, wonderfully married to a pretty, delicate Scots girl of twenty-five, who was diagnosed as having a rare form of cancer even before the wedding. It had not stopped them going forward with the ceremony, but she had died in his arms only a few short months thereafter. He had found no emotional solace, no person to replace her in the decade and a half since her death. His sexual and emotional life had, with casual physical flings in between, been an empty hell.

Murray's appearance belied his reputation. He was well-built, with a comfortable rather than handsome face and furrowed lines round his eyes that were etched even deeper every time he smiled. A thatch of reddish, turbulent hair added to the uneasy impression he always gave. Something about his whole body language suggested that he might be difficult to live with. That was not an inaccurate assessment, but he could, on the other hand, be generous and extremely understanding of the problems of others, where compassion or kindness was required.

His final briefing at the Foreign Office the day prior to his departure for the Berlin Embassy was with Nick Pearson, the larger-than-life head of the West European department. For the whole of the previous month, indeed from late October when Murray had finally left his political counsellor post at the UK Mission to the United Nations in New York, he seemed to have done nothing but attend briefing sessions, devour background files, brush up on his rusty German, all in preparation for his posting as Number Two at the new British Embassy in the new German capital. *New* was the operative word. Berlin had, until the outbreak of the Second World War in 1939, been home to a British Embassy for generations. Now the embassy was back once again, having reluctantly moved, section by section, from the grey, fifties, concrete building on Friedrich-Ebert-Allee in Bonn, following the Federal Government's equally dilatory decision to relocate itself back in the heart of the old Prussian empire.

Nick Pearson was of the old school, a jovial diplomat who dressed impeccably in the best Jermyn Street shirts and well-tailored Savile Row suits. He and Murray had joined the service in the same intake some twenty-five years earlier, and today he was at his bonhomous best as they sat together in his high-ceilinged office, chatting about the political and administrative problems Murray would face when he arrived in Berlin. Very different though he was from Murray both in background and in attitude to life, Pearson openly shared his thinking with him; there could be few secrets between them. After all, they would constantly be talking on the telephone, faxing and e-mailing back and forth over the months and years ahead. They were largely agreed on the basic issues: the solutions were another matter.

At twelve-thirty, by arrangement, they collected their coats and strolled together across a snow-flecked St James's Park to the Travellers' Club in Pall Mall where, over a leisurely lunch, they plotted the parameters of their future working relationship. Murray was as cooperative as he could ever be. He knew he would need Pearson's backing and support since his future ambassador, the aristocratic Sir Edward Cornwall, was known as a martinet, a pedant and a stickler for protocol. From bitter experience, Murray somehow always expected to be in conflict with his superiors, even when they were less rigorous than Sir Edward was reputed to be. He smelled danger ahead.

Their discussions further defined Murray's character. At one level he was sincere and open: any reading of his face declared his intellectual honesty. At another level, after these first impressions had worn off, those who got to know him better came face to face with a conundrum, a paradox. Sociable yet often anti-social, engaging yet self-contained, even reclusive, his seeming openness at one level hid uncharted depths away below, which was why he had so few whom he called friends.

Over an alcohol-free lunch – he and Pearson wistfully recalled how, in the old days, they would think nothing of sinking a bottle of claret or downing a few pints of beer during their midday break – they reviewed the politics and logistics of modern Berlin. Ever since the destruction of the Wall in 1990, the new united Germany had gradually implemented the move of all its major government functions, including the Department of External Affairs, from the sleepy little town on the Rhine. It had taken them almost a decade; the British Embassy, one of the last to follow suit, had also been in the vanguard, since, from the postwar days of military rule, Her Majesty's Government had retained a substantial diplomatic presence in Berlin.

Behind the scenes, there had also been the inevitably bitter and long-drawn-out battle with the Treasury over the costs of the move. But now, at last, the British had returned to the heart of the reunited nation in a united Europe.

Dubbed Europe's centre of gravity, Berlin was, after all, the way-station between London, Warsaw and Moscow. The capital first of the electorate of Brandenburg, then of the kingdom of Prussia, for most of its history it had looked east, since that was where its territorial ambitions lay. But Berlin also looked towards the civilized west: London, Paris and Vienna; it had always suffered from this severe internal schizophrenia. It monitored many turbulent nationalisms and a whole range of international conflicts, hopes and fears. It was a boom town, where, with all the building and rebuilding, it was said that the mortar never dried, while its resilient citizens were, once more, pushing at the frontiers of every experience as they had done throughout their history. Berlin was a hyper-modern city, but there was a perpetual overhang of shadows, from Weimar, from the Third Reich, from the desolate ruins of the aftermath of 1945. Even today, a flavour of the decadence that the film *Cabaret* had so vividly projected, still lingered on.

To report on this city and this Germany reborn was the task of the British Embassy. That was why, as Pearson unnecessarily emphasized as he supped his soup, it contained some of the most able, ambitious, charming and duplicitous members of the entire British diplomatic service. The Berlin Embassy, with Washington and New York, was in the front line of global diplomacy, representing every interest of the United Kingdom, reporting on Germany to the Foreign Office, protecting British citizens, and encouraging British economic and trading ventures.

'Thanks for the commercial,' responded Murray, cynically dismissive. 'You're trying to tell me I should be honoured to be going.'

Pearson shrugged, then turned to talk with surprising indiscretion about the way the embassy was dominated by the attitudes of the ambassador, with his elitist, old-school beliefs. 'We've had more than a few teething problems with him over the move,' he said wearily. 'The Foreign Secretary got very angry at the delays. You've seen the files full of letters of complaint. We're sending out an inspection team. His Excellency will bitch like hell when we cut his staff . . . and his allowances.'

'I'm behind you on that,' said Murray, incautiously. 'Never believed in big numbers. It makes for conflict in any embassy if too many clever people chase too little work. I like a tight team with too much to do.'

'Wouldn't put that in writing if I were you. Sir Edward'll explode if he hears that sort of talk,' Pearson warned.

'I've promised myself I'll play it cool . . . least at the start. But . . . there are going to be conflicts.' Murray looked away.

'You'll handle it OK,' said Pearson beaming warmly. He knew from personnel's files too much about Murray and his personal defects to believe what he was saying. But it had been a difficult post to fill at short notice, after Douglas Young, Murray's predecessor, had departed so rapidly and in such unexplained circumstances. Privately, Pearson was also only too well aware that Sir Edward had made his strong objections to Murray known at the highest levels in the Office. He had been overruled.

It was as if Murray had been reading his thoughts. 'What went wrong with Young?' he asked.

'Personal problems,' murmured Pearson unhelpfully. 'I wasn't consulted directly, but . . . picked up some of the gossip.'

'Tell me,' Murray pressed. 'Sex, drink or fraud?'

'Don't know the details. Financial troubles, I gather. Spent too much time at Berlin's gaming tables . . . On the political front,' Pearson went on, deliberately changing the subject, 'on top of all the major issues you've read up about, you'll unearth a clutch of other nasty little problems. For a start, diametrically conflicting views reach the Foreign Office daily out of the embassy itself. The ambassador thinks that the move to the right in German politics, despite the voting into power of extremist leaders in Budapest and elsewhere, is a transient phenomenon, and not something for the UK to get too steamed up about. The contrary view we get via MI6 intelligence reports: the extreme right, led by that bearded iconoclast, Professor Krauss, is a real throwback, a dangerous breed that could easily get out of hand. It's not just the skinheads in the streets, the neo-Nazi thugs. MI6 sources, particularly their man in Berlin, Anthony Fox, who's as shrewd as they come, have identified a growing intellectual cadre of thinkers who've begun to believe that such right-wing ideas – Germany for the Germans and so on – are fashionable and chic once again.'

'All that vanishes into insignificance set against what's happening inside Russia and the Ukraine,' Murray countered. It was towards the end of their meal; he was playing with a wedge of ripe Stilton and desperately wishing he had a glass of claret to wash it down. Cheese and sparkling mineral water never did go tellingly together. 'What's your latest thinking on these food riots?' he asked Pearson. 'NATO and the European Community seem to be pussyfooting around as usual, not knowing which way to jump. Whatever happened to that brave idea of a new Marshall Plan?'

'Too brave. Politicians don't like bravery. Ran out of steam because nobody's willing to put up the huge amounts of money that would have been required.' Pearson pushed an empty plate away from in front of him.

Murray paused and studied his companion for a moment. 'The Armageddon Scenario,' he said suddenly. 'I sometimes wake up in a sweat when I think about it. What if those millions in Russia, the Ukraine, Belorussia, all those starving have-nots, suddenly decided to march westwards. How much would we help Poland?' Murray paused again, then went on relentlessly. 'We've built a new Iron Curtain to stop these economic migrants engulfing us. We reassure ourselves, and our consciences, by feeding them like monkeys through the fence. What would we do if they all suddenly decided to push down the barbed wire? Shoot at them, would we? How would that look in the world's press?'

'Look, we've got to handle the Poles particularly carefully

14

over all this,' Pearson said. 'They've been hellish frustrated by their relationship with NATO. Enlarging the Western Alliance to include them and Hungary wasn't without its difficulties. The Poles have been the most committed, fully prepared to put their military resources at our disposal. They're extremely effective fighting partners.'

'But who are we guarding them against?'

'That answer's dead simple, Alex: their old enemy, Russia and its allies in Belorussia and the Ukraine.' Pearson shrugged, as he summoned the waiter for the bill.

'You're not advocating, are you, that we let more economic migrants come across . . . as some sort of safety valve?' Murray asked.

Pearson's smile was fading fast. He guessed he was being baited like the Russian bear. 'Course not. We'd be overwhelmed.'

'That nightmare of mine, a huge army of starving men, women and children, tearing down the barriers with their bare hands, moving westwards like locusts . . . it could happen.' Murray was staring intently at him. With a slight shock Pearson realized that his companion was being deadly serious.

'Seeking the Apocalypse, are we, Alex? I dunno. We'd get round to setting up an extensive chain of soup kitchens or something.' Pearson sighed uncertainly. He always tried to keep emotional images out of his decision-taking. It was cleaner that way. 'Most western European countries have too many domestic issues of their own to worry about that. Sure, the Germans, the Poles, the Hungarians, wake up screaming just like you. You'll get your ears bent by the German Foreign Ministry on similar lines.'

'And the border situation at the moment?' Murray asked intently.

'Depends what border, Alex. The Polish–Lithuanian, the Belorussian, the Czech, the Slovak, the Ukrainian borders, Romania, Moldavia or with Russia itself? They're all tensed up to a greater or lesser degree. Each one, from the old West Germany eastwards, has its own problems. Hundreds of prostitutes line the roads out of the Czech Republic, at the German frontier in Bohemia. Think of that, Alex! The region is the toyshop of East–West sex tourism! Seedy as that may be, it helps process the flow of hard German currency into the pockets of east European entrepreneurs. Further east, however, the problems get really cataclysmic. One side of the border: near starvation; the other: a land of plenty.'

'Which worries you most?' asked Murray.

'More of my lecture, Alex? OK, you asked. You can have it. They all do, that's what. We've lost the old certainties: NATO versus the Warsaw Pact. For decades, the Iron Curtain, concrete and razor wire, floodlights and anti-personnel mines, stretched from Stettin on the Baltic to Trieste on the Mediterranean, and antiseptically separated us. We didn't have to think about it. It was there. Eventually, NATO was a victim of its own success. It won the Cold War without having to fight that big nuclear war it was so expensively equipped to do. The Truman Doctrine assured the free world that the United States would stand firm against communism no matter where it reared its head. NATO knew its enemy. After communism collapsed, an expansionist NATO swept into its comforting embrace the "good", free nations of central Europe: Poles, Czechs, Hungarians. That wasn't very clever. We simply pushed the old jealousies and divisions further east. The new boundaries, like the old, are drawn and defended between poverty and prosperity, between the have-nots and the haves. Most of the other former Soviet satellites, to protect themselves from the ice-cold attentions of Mother Russia, clamour to join us. Only a few are chosen.' Pearson paused. 'You want me to go on?' he asked. When there was no response, he continued, 'You know only too well, Alex, that successive Washington administrations and us Euro-poodles have, in consequence, had to spend inordinate amounts of effort assuring the Russians from Yeltsin on, that new NATO is not aggressive, that it's not trying to isolate Russia. Empty words, fruitless gestures. Everyone knows that's exactly what's happening, despite the creation of window-dressing organizations like the so-called Partnership for Peace.' Pearson signed the chit the waiter had presented him with and kept on going: 'The key borders have moved east. Prosperity guarded from penury; our Europe protected from Belorussia, the Ukraine, Moldavia, Romania, and, beyond these, the corruptions and conspiracies of modern Russia, which begs the next question. Ask any Russian what it means to be Russian and you listen a long time. Slavic roots and the Orthodox Church have played their part in traditional Russian nationalism, but among the twenty or so ethnic republics of today's Federation, few are either Slavic or Orthodox. What unites them is poverty, indiscipline, and lust for what they don't have.' Pearson paused, then, almost as an afterthought, added: 'I take these threats very seriously too, Alex.'

'Well, I asked for that, didn't I?' said Murray. 'The Germans seem to see the problem far more clearly than we do. Why don't they insist we share the solution?'

'You always were too good at asking questions to which you already know the answers,' said Pearson irritably, glancing down at his watch, and making to leave the table. 'You know precisely why: because of international opinion and their own right wing, that's why. It would be dead easy for the Federal Government to take extreme action to please the neo-fascists. Ban all further immigration, from anywhere – east Europe, Turkey, north Africa, the lot. That would hand a splendid weapon to those who are constantly on the lookout for signs of a resurgence of nasty old German habits. The Chancellor's got that dilemma and hasn't a big enough majority to ignore it. He's got to play the balancing act. And he's not doing too badly.'

'Sitting on the fence gives a good view of both sides of the game, but it's bloody uncomfortable after a while.' Murray picked at a last fragment of cheese on his plate. 'All those anti-immigrant demonstrations: are they coordinated?'

'Course. They've more or less stopped burning down refugee centres and all that. The worrying phenomenon is that a lot of middle-class intellectuals, once terrified of being thought politically incorrect, are queuing up to agree that enough immigration is enough. The Chancellor's having to listen.' Pearson stared hard at the other man.

'My solution is simple,' Murray volunteered lazily.

'Yes?' Pearson was wanting to go. Murray was beginning to irritate him more than a little.

'Get rid of the Community food mountains by setting up a direct supply line to eastern Europe. Kill two birds with one stone. See the east Europeans through this winter at least. Gives us more time to think.' Murray knew it was too simple, too short-term, but . . .

Pearson sighed. He knew he was being provoked. 'Remember that aid-workers' slogan: "Give a man a fish and he'll eat for a day. Teach him to fish and he'll live a lifetime." Hand out food aid and they won't do anything about improving their lot. I tell you what would happen. The Russian Mafia bosses would syphon off most of it, and continue to grind the peasants into the ground exactly as the communists and the Tsars did before them.' Pearson again looked at his watch. 'Sorry, must be getting back. Meetings all afternoon. Foreign Secretary's got a bunch of parliamentary questions, and I've got to coordinate all the bloody answers. Late-night sitting for me, I can tell you. Wife won't be best pleased.'

'Thanks for lunch,' said Murray as they stood to leave. 'By the way, you didn't answer my question. I asked personnel too but they weren't letting on. Precisely why did Douglas Young leave so rapidly? You do know, don't you?'

Pearson looked away. 'Don't be difficult,' he said.

'In the old days it was sex or spying,' Murray kept pressing. 'Can you find out? Let me know?'

'I mean it. I've nothing more to say,' said Pearson, rapidly leading the way to the door of the dining room.

Some time later that same afternoon, a secretary in personnel inadvertently pressed a wrong digit on the machine and so the fax which Alex Murray sent to the British Ambassador in Berlin did not arrive. It would have told Sir Edward Cornwall, had he received it, that Murray was arriving early, on the BA 986 flight at Berlin's Tegel Airport at 18:15 on Tuesday the thirteenth of January. Murray indicated that he would be grateful to be met by an embassy driver.

In the event, dragging two very heavy suitcases – he could not find a luggage trolley – he found no one to greet him and, cursing under his breath, had to struggle his way to the end of a long taxi queue. It was snowing heavily, taxis were few, and it was almost half an hour before he climbed into the back of a battered Mercedes. Another twenty minutes and he was deposited, tired and increasingly irritated, outside the front door of the new chancery in Wilhelmstrasse, a building of much criticized architectural dullness.

The original British Embassy, built in 1868, had once been the palace of a German railway magnate. When that individual lost all his money, his vast house, with its splendid Corinthian pillars, was bought by the British government in 1884, but the Treasury of the day insisted that the large landscaped gardens should be sold off to help cover the costs of maintaining it. It was thus that a glamorous hotel was built on the embassy lawn, which provided those languid British diplomats of that past age with both restaurant and café where they could meet and conspire with their contacts from the Foreign Ministry, which was only a short walk further down the Wilhelmstrasse. In reality the pre-war glamour was not as gilded as it might seem, as Sir Nevile Henderson, the last Berlin-based British Ambassador, described with trenchant feeling in his diaries. In 1938, the embassy was cramped, dirty and dark, but Sir Nevile's main problem was that the would-be palace had to serve a dual function as both ambassadorial residence and embassy chancery. It was ironic that British bombers flattened the building during the war along with most of the rest of Wilhelmstrasse, because the German Air Ministry, the Propaganda Ministry, as well as Hitler's own Chancellery and bunker were in the same area. Yet in 1945, the gates of the embassy stood complete with the proud British coat of arms still intact. Another British presence existed in Berlin in the years after the Second World War: the British Embassy to East Germany was an ugly modern building situated on Unter den Linden, but all that had been rapidly forgotten.

All that was in the past; tonight was tonight. With the exception of one solitary light in an upstairs room, the chancery looked closed and shuttered. It was almost two hours after close of play, there was no particular crisis on the go, and the diplomatic staff would have gone home long ago. Momentarily distracted, Murray made the mistake of letting the taxi go, only realizing his folly as it disappeared in a flurry of snow.

After several minutes of ringing doorbells and banging, Murray managed to attract the attention of a security guard who unlocked the door and cautiously peered round it. 'Consulate's closed. Embassy's closed. Come back at nine tomorrow morning,' said the guard mechanically, first in English and then in far from grammatical German.

'I'm Alex Murray, your new counsellor.'

'Yes, sir. Are you, sir? Don't know anything about that, sir.' The man was understandably suspicious.

'Can you ring the ambassador or the duty officer . . . or get me an office car?'

'Embassy cars are all out, sir. Senior staff are at the residence. Ambassador's throwing a big party. Why don't you go there?'

'Can I dump my suitcases here?'

''Fraid not, sir. Don't know what's in them and all that. Couldn't be held responsible. You do understand, don't you, sir?' The voice was less aggressive, more uncertain.

Murray's tolerance was strained as he made a final plea. 'Remind me of the address of the residence will you, and ring for a taxi. Please . . .'

The security guard hesitated, then thought that if the angry man on the chancery doorstep was, by any chance, speaking the truth, it might be better for his career prospects to do as he was bid. Leaving Murray standing in the cold, he shut and locked the door, with the reluctant promise that he would return once he had contacted the duty officer. More freezing minutes elapsed. *The bloody man at least could have let me come in and stand in the warmth. I'll sort him out later*, thought Murray, though he knew perfectly well that the guard was only doing his duty, and that if some stranger had turned up unannounced on his doorstep, he would have acted in exactly the same way.

A few minutes later the chancery door again opened. 'Can't raise the duty officer, sir,' said the guard apologetically. 'I've called you a cab, though. Should be here any minute. Here's the address.' He thrust a scrap of paper at Murray.

'Thanks. Can I wait inside?'

'Here comes the cab now, sir,' said the security guard with relief, unwilling to take the risk of admitting him. Murray turned and, unaided, lugged his suitcases into the back of the second taxi and, with the guard watching from the partly open doorway, was driven off towards the residence.

The British Embassy Residence is a spacious if not particularly handsome building which had once housed one of the generals in the British military government in the days when Berlin had been occupied by the Allied forces. It stood grandly in its snow-covered grounds. Lights glittered in welcome from its windows, while, by the front door, official cars, chauffeurs sitting in steamed-up warmth inside or standing around in frosty-breathed clusters, were parked waiting for their masters and mistresses to emerge. Again no one offered him any assistance, so Murray paid off the cab driver and, suitcase in each hand, staggered and slipped his way up the icy path to the door.

He rang the bell. Almost immediately a neat, steel-grey-haired woman opened the door. Pushing his way past her he dumped his suitcases down angrily in the front hall and began pulling off his coat. 'And who, may I ask?' began the woman, a look of intense disapproval crossing her face.

'Name is Murray. Alex Murray. I'm the new embassy counsellor. I should have been met. Not the best welcome!' he exploded, bundling up his wet coat and handing it somewhat ungraciously to the reluctant woman. 'Where's the ambassador?' he demanded.

'I'm not sure . . .' she began, staring coldly back at him. Murray, tired from his journey, pushed past her unthinkingly; despite the fact he was in a scruffy, heavily-crushed tweed suit, and had a build-up of dirty snow sticking to his brown leather brogues, he stormed impatiently down the grand hallway towards the noise of the reception.

It was an opulent black-tie occasion: a concert given by a world-famous, London-based string quartet, followed by a buffet supper, all part of the British Council's current cultural offensive. The glitterati of Berlin were all there, and the British Ambassador, His Excellency Sir Edward Cornwall, KCMG, and, more especially, his wife, Lady Cornwall, had taken the greatest personal care with the arrangements. The flowers, the drink, the food were the best that his *frais* could afford. He had even supplemented the costs of the evening from his not-inconsiderable private income. The embassy had so recently removed to Berlin from Bonn, and he was determined to make as big a splash for Britain as he possibly could. Sir Edward was, therefore, less than pleased when he suddenly spotted an uninvited, scruffy, russet-haired man in old tweeds, standing in the doorway glaring accusingly around at the assembled throng.

Sir Edward beckoned to a supercilious young First Secretary, Paul Fawcett, and ordered him to investigate. Fawcett paced languidly across the floor to greet the new arrival, the ambassador watching from afar, a mix of curiosity and irritation on his face. Doubtless some distressed British subject had discovered his address, or, just as likely, a drunken businessman from Wolverhampton or somewhere, claiming his rights as a taxpayer, was out in search of a duty-free diplomatic drink. But then Sir Edward noted with interest the genuine show of surprise on Fawcett's face as the two men grudgingly shook hands. Fawcett turned and walked rapidly back towards the ambassador.

'It's a . . . it's the new counsellor, sir,' Fawcett stuttered. 'Alex Murray, sir. Arrived early.'

'The hell it is,' said the ambassador, taken aback. He walked over to the door. 'Goodness gracious. Are you Murray?' he asked, unnecessarily.

'Sir Edward.' Murray hesitated, attempting a partial smile. 'Sorry, sir, arriving here like this.'

'What are you doing?' responded Sir Edward, less than graciously. He was a man who liked order and disliked surprises intensely. 'I knew nothing about your arrival.'

'I sent you a fax, sir.'

'I received no fax.'

'Something must have gone wrong,' Murray responded weakly.

'Something has indeed gone very wrong. Now, if you don't mind, Murray, as you can see, we have a rather special party on here tonight, so why don't you go and . . .' He paused as the neat, grey-haired lady arrived and placed herself four-square beside him. In that instant Murray knew that he had already made one fundamental mistake. The woman on whom he had so cavalierly bestowed his wet coat was, he realized in a blinding flash of the obvious, none other than the imperious and much-feared Lady Cornwall herself.

Her eyes and body language said it all. Ice-cold and contemptuous, while her lips moved into something resembling a smile at his profuse and gabbled apologies, no warmth of greeting was transmitted by any other part of her.

'Ah. You've already met,' began Sir Edward, glancing anxiously at his wife. Murray had heard tell, back in London, that the ambassador was much in awe of her.

'I don't think we have,' said Lady Cornwall distantly, clearly indicating that she had no desire to do so either.

'I'm so sorry,' Murray vainly repeated.

'So I should think,' said Lady Cornwall, and without offering to shake his outstretched hand or looking at him again, she turned on her heel and walked away across the crowded room.

'I couldn't have guessed that Lady . . . that your wife would open the door herself,' Murray struggled feebly.

23

'Staff are all fully occupied in the kitchen,' the ambassador started to explain, then, alert to his wife's reaction, went on: 'Bad beginning that, Murray. You've upset her. Doesn't forget easily, I'm afraid. Look, I think the best thing would be for you to go off and find a hotel somewhere and let's sort all this out in the morning. I'll get Fawcett to look after you. Good night, Murray. Let's hope things improve from now on.' On that the ambassador returned to his guests, leaving Murray angry, humiliated, and embarrassed in equal doses. He was left standing, without even being offered a drink, until the arrogant Fawcett appeared once more, and, with little show of charity, further undermined by the latter's irritation at having been dragged away from what was a rather enjoyable evening, led him out into the night. As he escorted Murray from the reception room, he offered the chill remark, 'Bad luck, eh! Ambassador's such a stickler for protocol. To him, the little things in life are all-important. "Etiquette, dress and courtesy", he keeps repeating. But I'm sure you'll be able to make it up with him in due course.' Fawcett sighed. 'Lady Cornwall's another matter,' he added, with just a hint of a sneer in his voice.

2

Corporal Tate had a baby daughter and a wife, Betty, who lived in married quarters back in Britain and taught at an infant school just outside Colchester. Betty, better educated but no more intelligent, loved her husband dearly but simply could not understand why he had ever wanted to join, let alone to remain in, the British army, an institution she believed had long passed its sell-by date. She knew his excuse of having been prepared to do anything to get away from his father and an unhappy home life, but surely there were other ways. Tate himself shared something of this view, but felt he needed the challenge of military discipline for a little while longer, before he released himself to the self-discipline he believed he would need to cope with civilian life. He was not a particularly physical man, but liked being fit, and felt that left to his own devices he might run to fat. Staff Sergeant Brace, by contrast, had no such self-doubts. He had had numerous girlfriends, all of whom had failed to stay the course because he was so very firmly married to his military career.

Outside the mechanics' workshop on a cold winter's morning, Sergeant Brace stood back, hands on his hips, watching as the corporal carefully applied grease to a metal gun clip on the side of the armoured personnel carrier. He liked working with the younger man despite being unsettled by his ideals and his musings. Brace was a simple soldier; it did not occur to him to question what he was ordered to do. A command was a command. But the corporal did have a point; when he, Brace, had joined the regiment all those years ago, he had known his enemy, whether it was Saddam, the IRA, or the Evil Empire controlled from Moscow. In Bosnia there had been the brutal Serbs, though, even there, his confrontations had too often been with their bitter-mouthed women and children who had blocked the emergency supply routes to starving Croats and Muslims. Did he think of them as 'women'? Harpies more like – evil, screeching harpies, and their war-criminal men.

'OK, Corporal. Time to go,' said Sergeant Brace, looking at his watch. 'Briefings begin in ten minutes.'

'There's more intelligence in that grease gun,' said the corporal softly as he wiped his hands on a bundle of rags.

'That's enough of that, Corporal,' said Brace with resignation. Come to think of it, this time he agreed with Tate.

If, as some military strategists along with Mrs Tate were arguing, the British army in its present form was past its sell-by date, Major Oldfield was positively rancid. Sergeant Brace and Corporal Tate were at one on that. The man did not have the breeding for the airs he affected. His commonness and lack of grasp of what was expected of him were revealed every time he opened his mouth. His fellow-officers shuffled at the back of the briefing room with barely concealed contempt, as he stood at the front, pointing with a thick, flabby finger at the red arrows and green marker flags on the big mapboard. Try as he might, however, the mediocrity of the major's performance could not camouflage the seriousness of the facts he was imparting. According to eye-witness accounts and telecommunications monitoring reports, thousands of homeless, starving men, women and children had been encouraged to move west by political rabble-rousers, and were now temporarily camped all along the Polish/Belorussian border in a perceived attempt at massive international blackmail, to force more charity out of western governments. Blackmail was the correct word, but the major, reading badly from his Ministry of Defence brief, spoke only of military containment, and of the army acting in support of the civil authorities, as if it was some form of crowd control after a demonstration in Hyde Park.

As the major droned on, Corporal Tate, who was seated beside Sergeant Brace at the back of the briefing room, turned and whispered: 'Human locusts. That's what it'll be like. We've laughed at the drunken antics of people like that Russian demigod Vladimir for too long. He is devious and clever. He'll do anything for power, that rabble-rouser.'

'Shut up and listen,' Sergeant Brace whispered back.

Tate ignored him. 'Trouble is the UK and the US governments have failed to confront the watery liberals in Holland, Belgium and Scandinavia. They don't want their media to accuse them of being heartless. They could have nipped all this in the bud before it got out of hand – aid programmes for the Ukraine and the worst-affected Muslim republics like Uzbekistan.'

'Shut up, I said,' Sergeant Brace hissed. 'Bloody barrack-room politician. You ought to stand for parliament.'

'Thinking of just that, Sergeant. Then into government. Me as Minister of Defence. What do you think, Sarge? Like a job as my official driver?'

The resultant snort from Sergeant Brace caused Major Oldfield to pause in irritation and stare at them, while a few of the other NCOs in the rows in front turned round curiously. By that time Corporal Tate and Sergeant Brace were staring attentively at the mapboard, as innocent as any child.

'Containment,' said Major Oldfield. 'That is the task Supreme Headquarters in Brussels has set us. We are the front line, the only line . . .'

'Between now and world catastrophe,' whispered Tate. This time, Sergeant Brace totally ignored him.

After he had checked Murray in at reception and then left him to his own devices at the soulless hotel, Fawcett offhandedly suggested that it would be best if he ordered a taxi and turned up at the embassy at around nine the next morning. Murray controlled his well-brewed fury at this additional discourtesy by the young diplomat, and said nothing. In the event, after a sleepless night, not helped by a bout of indigestion from eating a room-service hamburger and having two large whisky nightcaps to anaesthetize his fury, Murray turned up at the chancery shortly after eight the next morning. Fawcett had pre-warned the early-shift security guard who manned the reception desk and he was greeted warmly enough and politely shown up to his office. As he approached the room, two men in overalls were blocking the doorway, in the process of moving a large desk.

'What's going on?' asked Murray genially.

'Last-bloody-minute furniture shifting, that's what. Could've given us a bit of bleeding notice,' said one of the workmen, wiping sweat from his forehead. Just then a flustered Fawcett appeared round a corner, looking decidedly uncomfortable.

'Oh, hello, Alex. Didn't expect to see you until nine,' he said breathlessly. 'Had a good night?'

Murray noticed he too was obviously on the move, since he was carrying an unwieldy bundle of office files. 'No. But thanks for looking after me last night,' he said routinely. 'Once I've settled in, I'll have to go try and put right the damage with H.E.'

'Ambassador will be OK, I guess,' Fawcett muttered. His mind was elsewhere. 'He was on edge, that's all. Always is with her ladyship around. Last night was a big event for him, even by our standards. Showing the cultural flag and all that, eh,' he added uneasily, at the same time nervously watching out of the corner of his eye as the workmen moved the desk into its new place by the window, then departed, still grumbling.

'What's going on?' asked Murray, with an enquiring sweep of his arm.

'Putting your room in good order, that's all. If we'd known you were coming early, we'd have had it freshened up for you. By the way, the ambassador rang me at home first thing this morning. Wants to see you at ten prompt, if that's all right. Let me know if there is anything else you need,' Fawcett added, obviously desperate to leave. 'I'm just along the corridor on the right. Leave you to get sorted out, shall I?'

Left on his own, Murray started sorting out the few papers he had brought with him in his briefcase. The office was spartan and gloomy, the desk battered, the other furniture tired, the walls a plain, official cream. The view from the window was of a neighbouring wall, a parking lot, and a busy roadway beyond. He would have to change all that. He sat down at the desk, dusted the top with his sleeve, produced a pad and pen, and started writing out a list of all the things he had to attend to. First and foremost, if he was going to have a successful posting in Berlin, he would have to build social bridges with the ambassador and his wife.

At nine o'clock, his PA, Samantha, a bubbling, debby type matching her name, appeared at the door and introduced herself. She came bearing a welcome mug of coffee which cheered him up a little. She was immediately familiar and very chatty.

'Milk? Sugar?' she beamed, looking round the room disapprovingly. 'I had no idea. If I'd known, I'd have got this dreadful little dump into some sort of order for you. I'm not quite sure why there was the change. Probably the fire damage . . .' She paused reflectively, then bustled over to the window and stared out. 'God, dire view.'

'Change?' Murray prompted cautiously, a first faint flicker of suspicion building within him.

'Nobody tells me nothing. I'm just meant to be your PA, that's all. I didn't know this was going to happen . . . you and Paul Fawcett swapping rooms. And desks too, I see,' she said, looking down with distaste at the one at which Murray was seated. 'Expect he consulted you.'

'Consulted? Who arranged what?' queried Murray, maintaining a deliberately low-key approach. He suddenly realized what might have been going on. 'What fire damage?'

'Douglas Young's room. Bit of a blaze, just as he left. Didn't you know? Lot of files went up. So doubtless Paul . . . well, I presume he cleared it with the ambassador at least, but, then . . . I'm speculating,' said Samantha, then stopped short as she noticed the expression on Murray's face. 'God, have I put my foot . . . ?' She flashed him a quick lopsided grin. 'Damn. I'm always doing it.'

'Not at all, Samantha,' he said, smiling up at her. 'Thank you.'

29

'Is your coffee all right?' she asked.

'Fine. Absolutely fine,' he responded, his mind on other things. 'I take it black in future, if you don't mind. One sugar.'

'Biscuits? Yummy chocolate biscuits? Have a supply some-where,' she burbled on nervously.

'No biscuits, thanks. Problem with the figure already,' he said, benevolently patting his stomach.

'Want to dictate or anything?' asked Samantha, ready to please. 'I'll go get my pad.'

'Not yet,' he responded. 'Better wait until I've seen the Old Man. Get that one over with.'

'Heard you made an old booboo last night.' Samantha giggled gaily. 'Tut, tut. Naughty you.'

'News gets around.'

'Paul told me,' she said.

'Surprising then that Paul didn't tell you about moving offices too,' he prompted gently.

'Oh, my God! He wanted to tell me something else, but he got a phone call as he was speaking to me. Perhaps I shouldn't have said anything. You won't let on, will you? He might be annoyed.'

'I won't let on, Samantha. I promise you,' said Murray with a further reassuring smile.

Just then the solitary telephone on his desk rang. A fierce female voice at the other end announced, 'Mr Murray? This is Sylvia Watt, H.E.'s PA. I know it's well before ten but he'll see you immediately, if you're free. Can you find your way here, or shall I come and fetch you?'

'Thank you. I have er . . . Samantha's here. I'm sure she'll show me the way.' The phone went dead.

A few minutes later, Alex Murray was ushered into Sir Edward Cornwall's spacious office.

The ambassador stood up grandly behind his great rosewood desk and stretched across it to shake Murray's hand. He smiled a thin-lipped, empty smile. Murray was able to focus on him properly for the first time. He was tall, angular, with a hooked

30

nose and cavernous cheeks. His mouth had a downward turn at the edges which made him look as if he felt continuous contempt for everything he saw around him. In this he was a fitting match for his wife.

'Unhappy beginning,' the ambassador hissed. 'But I'm sure if you drop Lady Cornwall a note, all will soon be forgotten. Almost understandable in the circumstances.'

'Thank you very much, sir. I'm so sorry,' Murray muttered. He felt surprisingly ill at ease.

'Enough said. Do come and sit down.' His Excellency waved in the direction of a pair of deep, fabric-covered armchairs. 'Coffee?'

'Thank you. Yes. Black, one sugar.' Murray turned in the direction of Sylvia Watt who was hovering in the doorway.

'Don't drink it myself. Bad for the health. Wife got me out of the habit. Haven't touched it for two years now. Feel great.' The ambassador lowered himself carefully into the chair opposite.

The formidable Sylvia reappeared almost at once, bearing a single cup and saucer and put it down on the low coffee table in front of Murray. She handed Sir Edward a tall glass of mineral water. 'Met Sylvia, have you?' waved the ambassador vaguely.

'As we came in, thank you.' Murray half rose from his chair.

'The source of all information inside the embassy, is Sylvia,' said the ambassador in a condescending voice. Murray immediately sensed a potential ally: Sylvia Watt was, at a guess, not someone who liked being patronized. 'Shut the door after you, Sylvia, there's a good girl,' the ambassador called after her as she was leaving. It was the way that he said it that jarred, as much as the words.

The two men sat facing each other across the low table. 'Well, Alex,' said the ambassador in a thin, reedy voice, 'welcome to Berlin. You've come to an exciting city at an exciting time.' Murray noted that the brusque 'Murray' of the previous evening had been replaced by his Christian name. Were things looking up?

'Sir. Here fifteen years ago, as you probably remember from my file. Attached to the military government.'

'I recall . . . But you have to realize it's all changed. Very changed. Very different. Admittedly, the German Foreign Ministry is still run by stolid Rhinelanders, who don't move easily. They've come to Berlin reluctantly. We mustn't forget that, Alex. We're not the occupying power any more, you know,' he added unnecessarily.

'Aware of that, sir.' Murray stared politely back.

'One of the reasons why, as you probably picked up, I wasn't too keen on having you. Nothing personal. Mean that. Better to be honest. Sorry if it sounds a bit blunt, but you know what I mean.' Sir Edward folded his hands carefully in front of him.

'Personnel department did explain.' Murray sipped at his coffee.

'With this new Germany, we don't want any lingering, old-fashioned attitudes.'

'I shall try to repress them, sir.' Murray bit his lip.

'Glad to hear it.'

As the exchange developed, Murray increasingly had to force himself not to explode. The insufferable pomposity of the man! Sir Edward Cornwall was widely known as one of the diplomatic service's most old-fashioned, unbending, cold warriors imaginable. Intelligent people in the Foreign Office had been horrified when he had been allocated to a highly sensitive post like Berlin. But Sir Edward had allies in high political circles, which was how he had been given this job rather than one for which he was more suited, in some obscure Latin American dictatorship. He did not even speak a word of German.

As if the ambassador had been reading Murray's thoughts, he continued, 'You're a linguist?'

'Sir.'

'Speak good German?'

'I'm told, sir,' said Murray modestly.

'At my level . . .' began the ambassador loftily, '. . . at my level,' he repeated, 'I find that everyone I need to speak to, speaks perfect English. There's little call to speak German any more. Common European language and all that. In this part of the civilized world, linguistic abilities are largely becoming a thing of the past.'

'Useful from time to time, sir. Reading newspaper comment and so on,' Murray ventured.

'We've got professional press readers in the embassy, Alex. They're in here by six each morning. I have a digest of the day's news on my desk by the time I arrive. All I need to know, I know, Alex. Just remember that. But I don't like surprises, so keep me fully informed about anything and everything you're doing. If you need help, well, talk to Paul Fawcett. He is a most reliable young man. I've a great deal of confidence in him. He would have made a good deputy, you know. Sadly, personnel thought he was far too young. It's not a good way to keep bright people in the service, not promoting them. I tried, but . . .' He paused. 'Well, there you are. Nothing personal, you understand, Alex. I'm sure, none the less, that you and he will work very well together,' he added patronizingly. He stood up. Murray rose with him. The interview was at an end.

As he walked towards the door, the ambassador called after him. 'Oh, and don't forget that billet-doux to my wife, will you, Alex? She's most particular on matters of protocol, don't you know?'

Murray left the ambassador's study, shutting the door quietly behind him, though he felt more like slamming it. In the outer office Sylvia Watt looked up from her desk. Hard-faced, bespectacled, hyper-efficient and cold, she looked severe at first, then she smiled a surprisingly friendly smile at him. He guessed that underneath that somewhat forbidding exterior she had a sense of humour.

'Good news is that he was rather more welcoming than he might have been,' she said, in a matter-of-fact voice. 'Believe me.'

'You were listening?' asked Murray, smiling back.

33

'He forgets and leaves his intercom switched on. I couldn't help it.'

'He seriously tried to block me coming here, Sylvia?' Murray was genuinely curious.

'When we know each other better, Mr Murray, you may find me a useful source of information. Until then, you'll find me the soul of discretion. On this, as on many things, my lips are sealed. But there's one piece of advance advice I do offer.'

'Yes?' asked Murray. 'Call me Alex, by the way.'

'He has this thing about Paul Fawcett. He thinks the light shines out of his whatsit. So does Lady Cornwall. His master's ears and eyes, if you see what I mean. Tell that puppy anything and you tell *them*. He's more than a little aggrieved at not getting your job. And, as Alan Clark used to say, he tends to be economical with *la vérité* if and when it suits him.'

'Points noted, Sylvia. Thank you – and for the coffee, by the way.' Murray beamed warmly at her, turned, and left the room. There at least, was one potential ally.

On his way back to his office Murray found Samantha in her room and asked her to get hold of Fawcett. 'Remember what you promised.' She looked at him nervously. 'He's very upset for some reason.' His assistant had lost much of her earlier bounce.

'Trust me.' Murray winked at her.

A few minutes later the young diplomat came in, closed the door behind him, and sat down uneasily opposite Murray. Fawcett, an over-plump man in his mid to late thirties, was supercilious at one level and gushing and over-eager to please at another. It was not a happy combination of characteristics. Murray had also heard that he was reputed to drink too much: a serious weakness in a service where duty-free alcohol was readily available. Right now, Fawcett was perspiring and looked particularly unhappy.

'Thank you for looking after me so well last night.' Murray could hardly be being sincere, and Fawcett got the message, knowing he had done the bare minimum. Dropping his new counsellor off at his hotel, and abandoning him as soon as he had checked in, had not been particularly clever. He now regretted that he had not even volunteered to pick him up that morning.

'Your duties are mainly internal political reporting, right?' Murray asked, unnecessarily. He knew the answer only too well.

'Largely, though the ambassador has me doing quite a lot of personal stuff for him too,' Fawcett volunteered, with a feeble attempt at a smile.

'I gather.' Murray looked unseeingly towards the window.

'Which is why I thought . . . he thought . . . we thought that it might be more useful if I swapped offices with you, to be closer . . . to his . . . er . . .'

'Which is why I thought . . .' echoed Murray, '. . . I'd have a quick look at that other office too. Before either of us settles in, if you see what I mean. I gather it's meant to be the counsellor's office.'

'Yes, well . . .' said Fawcett, looking ever more miserable.

'Doubtless the fire damage was a factor in your concern for me,' Murray added helpfully, in a tone that continued to belie his words.

'Oh, you heard. A little incident. Nothing to speak of,' said Fawcett quickly.

'So it didn't damage the desk then? I thought perhaps that was why that one . . . ?' Murray waved in the direction of the shabby furniture, and continued to smile coldly at Fawcett, who averted his gaze and stared uneasily down at his hands. Murray suddenly made up his mind. 'Look, I've decided, if you don't mind, even without seeing the other room, that we'll move everything back again. Is that OK with you?' he added sweetly. 'I'll clear it all with the ambassador, tell him you agree – if you don't mind. I know he is a stickler for the conventions: larger room for the more senior man and all that. And, Paul,' he added, as Fawcett stood up and made to leave, 'let's discuss problems *before* you act on them in future, shall we? I know how closely you work with Sir Edward, but you and I are going to have to play it honest with each other as well.'

'Of course, Alex. Anything you say, Alex,' stammered Fawcett, then he rushed from the room.

Murray picked up his telephone, pressed a button and summoned his PA. By the time she appeared he was waiting for her by the door. He smiled mischievously at her. 'Paul and I have changed our minds, Samantha. We're moving the offices back again. Will you put that all in hand? I'm going out for an hour or so – to let things settle. Make sure that Paul has everything in order by the time I get back, will you?'

Samantha beamed back. 'Oh, goody,' she said, giggling happily.

'And,' he added, 'could I see Security's report on that fire, please? There must be one, mustn't there? I take it you reported the details to London?'

Samantha paused. 'I wouldn't know about that,' she said uncertainly.

Murray turned and left her to follow up a message he'd received from administration that, while his apartment was not quite ready, he could go and see it, and talk to the decorators about what work he wanted done. It came with an apology: the administration officer was away on a few days' leave, but Karen Deighton, the consul, would be happy to show him round.

The consul, a determined, unmarried woman in her early fifties who came with the reputation of being something of a workaholic, met up with him at the front door of the chancery. 'Car's round the side,' she volunteered efficiently. 'Thought it would be better if I drove you.'

Murray took to her immediately. She was large, with close-cropped grizzled hair, heavy horn-rimmed spectacles over a rugged face, and the sort of gravelly voice that went with her one fashion accessory: a cigarette dangled permanently from lips that showed traces of an incipient moustache. She was said to have a back problem which could, at times, make her a bit irritable, but behind her pebble lenses her eyes had a sparkle about them which emphasized her other reputation – that of having a heart of gold. She was also very good at her job.

'Kind of you to spare the time,' Murray began.

'Couldn't leave it to Paul. Not the most considerate of people. Besides he's terribly, terribly important, and the ambassador might just need him.' She smiled conspiratorially. Murray did not respond directly: she would have picked up something of what had been going on, but it was early days for him to be taking sides. He'd take his time before jumping to conclusions about the web of tensions he had already detected within the embassy.

The apartment was large and, if somewhat characterless, had a pleasant outlook over the Tiergarten. 'I'm told they'll redecorate it any way you like,' she explained helpfully. 'Within Treasury budget guidelines, that is.'

'Looks pretty spotless. Douglas Young wasn't here long. I'm not sure it needs much attention.'

'Take the offer while you've got it,' she prompted.

'I'd rather move in.'

'Any way you like,' said Karen Deighton persistently, 'but you know the diplomatic service. If you turn the decorating down now, you'll have to wait three years before you get another chance. If I were you I'd live in your hotel for a bit longer.'

'I'll think about it,' said Murray as they left the flat together. 'By the way, why did Douglas Young leave so rapidly?'

She shrugged. 'Nobody told me. I'm just the consul. If he'd been a British subject and got himself into trouble here, I'd have known all the spicy details. As it was, one day he was at his desk, the next he wasn't. Lots of gossip. Nothing concrete.'

'Personnel department said "personal reasons". Married, wasn't he?' asked Murray.

'Yep. Nice wife. Children away at public school. Everything seemed fine. As I say, there was a lot of gossip.'

'What sort?'

'Pick and choose. Everyone seemed to know he was in deep

37

financial difficulties. Lloyd's and all that. My guess . . .' she paused and wheezed slightly.

'Yes?' Murray waited.

'Gambling debts. Started with just a flutter. Then it got to him. He became hooked. Even tried to borrow money from me, only a week or so before he left, as if I would have any spare cash!' She laughed mirthlessly, then broke into an unhealthy smoker's cough.

'He wouldn't have been pulled out overnight for something as minor as that. Not these days.' Murray was thoughtful.

The consul shrugged her broad shoulders. 'You'll doubtless dig out the truth in due course,' she said, then hesitated. 'By the way, if you're not doing anything for supper tonight . . .'

'Sorry, already booked,' he lied quickly. She was being kind but he wanted to find his feet before being drawn further into her confidences.

'Saturday, then?' She sounded only marginally disappointed.

'Why not? How very kind,' said Murray, unable, in the time available, to think up a further plausible excuse.

Back at the office, it took several more ill-tempered hours for the two embassy workmen to reposition all the furniture in its rightful place, but by late afternoon on that first day, Murray was more or less settled in an office with long windows looking out on to trees and pleasant gardens beyond. A spacious, highly polished desk had been restored to him, and a fuming Fawcett, doubly embarrassed at having been caught out, was relegated to the gloomy office which he had tried to foist on his superior. Murray briefly wondered whether the ambassador would attempt a last-minute scuppering of his plans, but Sir Edward, when he did appear, looked rather shifty, then quickly moved to other things, blandly saying that he left such detailed running of the embassy to his new counsellor.

Later, while Murray was sorting out his few possessions into the drawers of his desk, he felt like a minor detective when he found his hands covered with sticky, badly applied shellac – they had obviously had the desk repolished – and then, in the second drawer from the bottom, he discovered a fine black residue of burnt paper that had been carelessly left from the fire. So that part of the story at least was true.

It was late afternoon, and he was halfway through a pile of recent press cuttings and telegrams, when Curran, the close-cropped ex-regimental sergeant-major who was in charge of embassy security, the man who had been so unhelpful to him on his arrival the previous night, marched in, full of apologies.

'Didn't know nothing about you coming, sir. Nobody told me, sir. You could have been anyone. You do understand, don't you, sir?'

'Of course I do, Mr Curran.' He stood and the two men shook hands politely. 'Think nothing of it. I'd have done exactly the same in your position. Besides, I must have looked pretty scruffy after the journey.'

'You did, sir, if you don't mind me saying so, sir.' Curran was meticulously turned out, with regimental tie, stiff white shirt, knife-edge creases in his trousers, and shoes that were buffed and sparkling. Even now he looked somewhat disapprovingly at the less formally dressed counsellor who had retaken his seat behind his new-found desk.

'You have other things on your mind, Mr Curran?'

'Sir. You're ultimately responsible for embassy security, sir. I report directly to you on that, as you know, sir.' His conversation was becoming tediously spiced with 'sirs'. 'Well, my repeated requests for security shutters for the ground-floor windows, and some sort of barred gate for inside the front door, have been with Foreign Office supplies department for months. I've just heard it'll be another six months before we get them. I'm worried, sir.'

'Suppose they think the heat's off now there's little threat from the IRA and all that?' Murray volunteered.

'Yes, sir. That's only one aspect of security, sir. It's those other blighters who'd like to get their hands on our secrets.'

'If we have any more secrets left to steal,' said Murray lightly. His mind was already on other things. This was one issue that

39

could wait. 'You're right, Mr Curran. I'll send a telegram pushing for an earlier delivery.'

'Thank you, sir. Just that I'm responsible and – '

'I quite understand, Mr Curran. Leave it to me.' Murray made a mental note. The man still hesitated. 'And?' he added.

'Fire extinguishers, sir. We need a whole lot more. It was pure luck that one of the few we had was right outside this room.'

'Must have been,' said Murray casually. 'Tell me; what exactly happened?'

'Thought you'd have heard, sir,' said Curran, momentarily puzzled. 'Very shortly after Mr Young . . . er . . . left, late that same afternoon like, I was on duty. Locking up downstairs when I smelled smoke. I rushed upstairs and found a pile of paper and files burning on your desk.' He pointed. 'They've made a good job of restoring it. The wastebasket was also alight.'

'Two fires, eh?'

'Quite, sir. Very odd, I thought, but Mr Fawcett and the ambassador said it was obviously an accident.'

'Can I see your report on the fire, Mr Curran?'

'Mine, sir? Didn't do one. They said they'd do all that was required.'

'Thank you, Mr Curran,' said Murray quietly. 'You leave these points with me. I'll get you the bars, and more extinguishers.'

A morning meeting in chancery, the political section of any embassy anywhere on the globe, is where the inherent conflicts in the somewhat cloistered lives of its diplomats tend to be first identified. Such gatherings provide a necessary focus for the work of the embassy, where a team spirit can build up, or where contingent problems, as they emerge, tend not always to be work-orientated but more social or personal. Like any taut, cohesive community in an alien world, the staff, Murray knew, would have to be harnessed to common objectives rather than allowed to spend time competing with or antagonizing each other. As number two in the embassy, he recognized that his job was to work out the necessary compromises between internal rivalries and external crises as they developed.

By ten o'clock the next morning, nine of his senior colleagues had filed in and taken what were obviously their accustomed seats around the walls of his office. One by one Fawcett introduced those whom Murray had not yet met. He quickly identified those with whom he felt he might empathize. One was a tall, spare, cavalry officer, Brigadier Dicks, the military attaché, who, he remembered from the files, had won an MC in Northern Ireland. Murray also liked the cut of Anthony Fox, the coldly urbane MI6 station chief, whose saturnine good looks were reputed to make many a female heart flutter. Next to him was Karen Deighton, with whom, to his slight trepidation, he was due to have dinner Saturday night. Fawcett, pink, podgy and flustered, sat beside him on his right. Murray looked round the room. Some of his new colleagues were alert, others slightly suspicious, as if waiting to get the measure of him. They would have picked up a certain amount of gossip about him from the diplomatic grapevine. It was always the same: they would be wary until they got to know his style and how approachable he was. He determined to make his mark from the outset.

'Delighted to meet you all,' he began. 'Perhaps we could begin by each of you talking for a couple of minutes about your present problems, job load and concerns. It'll help me get the feel before I start throwing my weight around. I'll try not to interrupt too much.' He smiled agreeably. Half his audience smiled with him, the others kept their feelings to themselves.

He listened with varying degrees of attention, analysing them as individuals more than taking in what they were saying. The military attaché described the increasingly heated debate within the German armed forces about how much they should get involved in future international peacekeeping operations. The consul reviewed her current case of a British pop star who was languishing in a Berlin jail for heroin possession, and the problems she was having with his many outraged fans. She also put down a marker about a forthcoming England–Germany soccer international that was scheduled for Berlin in the early spring. There would be the inevitable problems caused by the huge influx of English fans. Anthony Fox cautiously revealed new intelligence, gleaned from recently accessed Stasi files, about the heavily blemished backgrounds of certain prominent German politicians. It was, Fox suggested, all a little bit passé: did who had once spied for whom still have much relevance at the turn of the century? Fawcett followed him, giving, Murray had to admit, a brisk and wide-ranging assessment of the current German political scene: the battle between right and left over the integration into the community of other less developed, former eastern bloc states, and what to do about the vast numbers of illegal immigrants, coupled with reports of increasing tensions, in the refugee camps on Poland's eastern borders. The only person who appeared to be gaining from that particular controversy, Fawcett said, was Dieter Krauss, the ex-professor of mathematics from Munich, who was the increasingly talked-about leader of the radical right. His policy just avoided calling blatantly for 'Germany for the Germans'; that old familiar was dressed up in respectable new clothes, appealing as it did not just to the thugs in the streets, but to a growing intellectual community.

Fawcett explained the other danger about Krauss: he was a charmer, with a character and style that came across particularly well on television. Whatever his politics, he looked pleasant and approachable, unlike some of the stiff-necked figures who led the other major parties. It was that, Fawcett argued, that was bringing so many votes his way; his utter reasonableness.

At the end of his contribution, Murray found himself praising Fawcett for his assessment, and the young diplomat glowed with appreciation. The gesture was not lost on the others in the room. They would all have heard by now about the attempted room switch, and would have had their laugh at Fawcett's expense.

When they had all had their say, Murray spoke briefly. 'I want to reassure you that, while I have served in Berlin before – it was fifteen years ago now – I trust I don't carry any attitudinal baggage from that time. The ambassador's a bit worried about me.'

When he laughed, he noted that most of the others echoed his amusement. 'I'll try to prove him wrong. This united Germany requires a totally new handling, a new approach. On the other hand, I never used to believe in national characteristics. But anybody who has served in the diplomatic service soon realizes that there are such things. We in Britain have them in plenty too. So we have to be constantly alert to traditional German attitudes, be it from extreme left or extreme right. If we let things go unreported, they go unchecked. That's our function. We don't get involved in Germany's internal politics, but we must be damn sure that we know what's going on. That way it's good for Britain, good for Britain's position in Europe, good for British trade.' As he finished, he realized he had forgotten to give the commercial counsellor, Bobby Sofer, his turn. Sofer, a tubby, balding, effervescent little man in his mid-fifties, who had started off in the Department of Trade and Industry and who had gained a high reputation among the major British companies operating in Germany, was everybody's favourite new-style diplomat. He was always at the heart of the embassy's social life, a great party-giver who possessed an abundance of good humour. He was reputed to be able to solve disputes before they reached breaking-point, though, like Murray, he was also not quite top-drawer enough to suit the ambassador's tastes.

'Something I should warn you all about,' Sofer said, when Murray turned apologetically to him. 'A massive insider dealer scam is about to burst in the German courts. Big-name British banker's involved, I hear. My sources say it's going to blow the lid off a lot of institutions and particularly one major City bank. Watch this space.' Sofer turned and smiled mischievously at his audience, but when questioned, refused to give any further information or name names. 'Lot of gossip,' he said firmly. 'Wouldn't be fair. I'll tell you as soon as I know all the facts.'

The moment the meeting was over, the internal telephone on Murray's desk buzzed. It was Sylvia Watt with a summons from the ambassador.

'How are you settling in?' Sir Edward asked distantly as Murray entered. The latter knew he could not care less, nor would he listen to his reply.

'Fine, thanks, sir. Just met all my senior colleagues. Good team,' said Murray. 'I move into my new apartment in a week, once it's been smartened up. Not much needs to be done. Douglas Young left it in good shape.' Murray paused, thought, then risked his frequently repeated question. 'Why exactly did he leave so quickly, sir, if you don't mind me asking?'

'I do mind you asking, Alex. That's a closed book,' said the ambassador firmly. 'Let's get to grips with your agenda: what's your schedule?'

'As yours, sir. Monitoring the political scene, working with Bobby Sofer. You know about this insider dealer scandal he's following?'

'I've heard rumours,' said the ambassador vaguely.

'We'll have to take a hard look at the running of the embassy too, what with the inspection team coming out. Back in London, Pearson said – '

At that the ambassador turned abruptly and stared irritably at his deputy. 'Let me share my thinking with you on that, Alex,' he said sharply. 'I have strong views. The embassy stays exactly the same size, at least until we've fully settled here in Berlin. No cuts; not one; that's my objective.'

'A certain amount of fat could possibly –' Murray unwisely continued.

'No, no, and no,' the ambassador interrupted. 'The embassy stays at its current size. That is my goal. That's yours too.'

'I hear what you say, sir. We've still some time before they arrive.'

'Now, your reading of the current political scene? Give me a run-down: new man with new opinions. Be frank.'

'You'll have to correct me, sir, but there's rather too much made in the British press of the right-wing threat – for all the old reasons. Even so, Professor Dieter Krauss needs watching.'

'I met him. He's surprisingly sound. Charming too. Not nearly

44

as neo-fascist as people paint him. In any case I've got some sympathy with his views,' said the ambassador, then checked himself. 'I've no such right-wing leanings myself, you understand, Alex? None. But if you've got a hell of an illegal immigrant problem and a powder keg on your eastern doorstep, there's a lot to be said for the tightest border controls. If I were a German I might just vote the same way.'

'Agreed as to the problem, sir,' said Murray and meant it. 'NATO's got to help them keep a firm grip on the border situation, but internally, there are some pretty ugly bedfellows in the Krauss camp. A disturbing amount of intellectual respectability's being given to some of his views, not just here, but in France, Italy, even Britain. I read in one of your telegrams about Europe's right-wing parties organizing some sort of international conference some time soon.'

'We'll have to monitor that closely,' the ambassador replied, his reluctance showing clearly. 'If only because our damn tabloid press could make such a fuss about it. In my view, too much of our foreign policy is driven by reacting to ignorant media opinion.'

'Yes, sir,' said Murray, standing as Sir Edward got up and walked in front of his desk.

'One last thing before I let you get back on with your work,' he said. 'Paul's nose is a bit out of joint over the swap of offices, but no harm done. I leave that to you both to sort out. On the political front, however, keep close to him. He's good: he knows his subject. I want no surprises. Keep me fully informed. No surprises, do you hear, Alex?'

3

Corporal Tate, who was nothing if not introspective, lay stretched out flat on his bunk in his spartan living quarters. The door was firmly shut. Off duty for the next eight hours, he would have time to think. He was only partially dressed; his combat uniform hung neatly on a hook behind the door of the tiny room. Locking his hands together on the pillows behind his head, he stared up at the ceiling.

All things considered, he felt reasonably content with life at the moment. He had just finished a long telephone conversation with his wife Betty back in Colchester. She was also fairly happy, the baby was doing well, and her mother was staying with her at the moment which meant that she was much less stressed than she sometimes was by having to leave the little one in the school crèche. Betty was an attentive mother and a devoted wife. The only jarring note had been her asking, for the hundredth time, if he had decided when to leave the army. He knew he had promised to give her a final answer by Christmas and that was almost a month ago now. What he did not tell her was that promotion was in the air, and that meant more money, more authority, more status. He liked the thought of an extra stripe on his arm. Having had all ambition crushed out of him in his youth except an unquenchable desire to escape, he was now letting it flourish. He wanted to be successful, if only in his own eyes. He wanted a life; that was his motivation and his goal, though he was astute enough to realize that his ambition would always keep a bit ahead of him, changing and growing, like a beacon or a grail. Which is why Corporal Tate told his wife he needed more time. There had been a long silence at the other end of the telephone and then the 'Oh, well, I suppose . . .' of Betty's usual calm acceptance of the situation. That was why they had always got on so well together despite the long separations that service life dictated. What would be would be in both their lives.

Tate flexed his arm muscles, then his legs, then his pelvis, then his shoulders, holding each taut, then relaxing them in turn. It felt good. That was the other reason for staying in uniform: he kept his gangly body fit. He saw what people of his age in civilian life let happen to their figures. He was proud of his; he liked being able to run and climb and swim and shoot straight. He wanted to defend the realm from its enemies. That was why he had joined the army, yet that was his sole area of discontent right now. Where was that strange creature? Where was the enemy?

He switched on the radio to listen to the BBC World Service news. An earthquake in Latin America, a typhoon in the Philippines, an aircrash outside Amsterdam. Everything seemed so remote even when the programme turned to broadcasting news about Britain: a by-election, a government minister and a call-girl, union members striking for more pay at some car plant. All equally far away from his life over here on NATO's eastern front.

There was a sharp knock on the door.

'In,' he called, and Sergeant Brace marched in noisily. He was carrying a bundle of civilian clothes over his arm.

'OK, Corporal. We're going for a drive,' said the sergeant, throwing the clothes at him.

'Hey, what's all this, Sarge? I'm off duty until eight.'

'So you are, Corporal Tate. From now till then we're going to play tourists.' Sergeant Brace held up his hand to forestall further complaint. 'Colonel's orders, Corporal,' he said.

Another life, another world again. Ivan Katerski touched his face gently to feel the raw skin where he had just shaved off his beard. He deserved better after his testing mission arousing the masses. Even by Moscow standards it was a desperately drab and dismal apartment they had allocated him. The man scowled inwardly at his use of the noun as a proper description. This was no apartment; this was two bare, cement-floored rooms, with a scrap of linoleum, a dirty mattress on a trestle bed, a wooden table and broken chair, and a shared toilet somewhere far along the corridor and down a flight of dank stairs. Cockroaches scuttled everywhere; there was a permanent smell of rotten food in the air. This was what he had been offered as accommodation in return for all he had done for them recently. Again he asked himself, as he had done in the ruins of that church over on the border, what was he trying to achieve? Trying to keep warm, trying to find something reasonable to eat in the market, trying not to pick up lice or worse from those he met and worked with. Why hadn't he, even now, decided to move into one of the better western hotels like the Kempinski? He could afford it. He could afford to pay his own way to serve his ideals. But Vladimir himself had firmly insisted that he keep his head down, for the moment at least. What was he, formerly known in all the right places in City society as the mercurial merchant banker, Ian Carter of Knightsbridge, London, doing here? It was a long story.

From his earliest childhood Carter had realized that he was different. In those far-off days, his father, whom he worshipped but saw so infrequently, had spoken to him only in that strange language which was of no use when he mixed with his playmates at the little local school. Later, he had always spoken Russian to him at home, and because his gentle, fey, romantic mother only and always spoke to him and her husband in English, by a mixture of threats and habit he became more or less bilingual. As he grew into his early teens, Carter increasingly realized how different he was. At least that was how it had been at first, but, as his father was a man of passionate and rapidly changing whims, when eventually it was decided that Ian would be sent away to boarding school in the far north of Scotland, the old man suddenly refused to speak any Russian with him any more. One day he was instructed to speak only English in future. He was to grow up as a true British gentleman, through and through. At that same time, at the height of the Cold War, he was also summarily stopped from ever calling himself Ivan Katerski, even in the privacy of his own family. He became, from one day to the next, just Ian Carter with a 'C'. It took time to adjust to his father's latest whim, but in the end he was glad: it meant he was immediately accepted by the other boys at his new school. He discovered that conformity led to an easier life, so he scrupulously followed his father's other wishes and made every effort to appear just like the other pupils, totally British, never revealing that he was anything other than his Scottish mother's son.

But when he became seventeen and reached the dizzy heights of the Upper Sixth, he started to take a deeper interest in politics and began to follow the vicissitudes and problems of the old Soviet Union. Only then did he begin to think of revealing his distinct and separate roots to others. A natural if repressed romantic, he secretly began to nurture his hidden inheritance, that he had one parent who was different, that his true name was a strange one, that he was linked by blood if not by birth, to a country of which he knew next to nothing. The exotic began to exert a stronger pull than the familiar. His percipient housemaster noticed that he had begun reading Russian literature in translation. Within himself he started dreaming of his forgotten forefathers, though at the same time he remained conveniently comforted by the privileges and security of his Britishness.

Motivation, like truth, is difficult to unravel, but gradually, for a range of reasons, he revealed to one or two of his closest schoolfriends that he was of half-Russian origin, and when he saw that they were fascinated by this hidden facet, he began to cater to it and embellish it. Bit by bit he built a character for himself that was, once again, different. Rather than aping the British youths around him, when the rumour somehow took hold that he was of aristocratic stock and in some way related to the last of the Tsars, he did not go out of his way to deny it. Because he was handsome and good both at sports and in the classroom, he became something of a hero to the younger boys. He revelled in his new-found image. But, unlike many of the other young descendants of Russian émigrés whom he increasingly sought out and met up with when he returned to London on holiday, he did not hanker after a past forgone. He did not see any prospect of gaining access to the Russia that his father, his grandfather and all his forefathers had known. He was different but, compared to some of these nationalistic new acquaintances, he was just as his father wished him to be, a typical British public school boy. He was Ian Carter. No one, not even his father, called him Ivan any more, nor did any piece of paper or document anywhere, including his passport, refer to him as Katerski.

And so it remained until the coincidental death both of his father and of the Soviet Union. Some time after that, his call came. Whatever the harbinger said, that summons largely came from within himself. Which was why he sat now in that cold, cockroach-infested room, with only a greasy palliasse of straw on which to sleep.

Murray had spent the previous evening quietly in his hotel room, re-attuning his ear to the language by watching German television non-stop, and otherwise unwinding and relaxing for the first time since his arrival. Then, that Saturday morning, he rose early; avoiding the temptation to go into the embassy and catch up with his huge backlog of action files, he spent most of the day wandering the restless streets of Berlin, along the Kurfürstendamm, past the Gedächtnis Kirche, injecting the mood of the city under his skin once again. Everywhere he felt a vibrant sense of life and movement. He tried to build a picture, as any visitor does, of how it once had been, recalling old newsreel films and photographs, but also stirring up his own more recent memories that stretched back to his first trip there as a student in the late sixties. To him Berlin had always been a place of images; a shell of a city after the war; the Airlift; the divided capital; the blood-soaked, graffiti-covered Wall; the sinister spies secretly exchanged over the cross-border Glienicke bridge. Some things remained constant throughout, like those two architectural symbols, the Reichstag, no longer the roofless ruin that he remembered, and the mighty Brandenburg Gate. Round each corner were more snapshots of past and present: the once-romantic Unter den Linden, the U-Bahn, the Kafé Kranzler where he found *Hausfrauen* in hats still sat eating huge portions of *Kuchen mit Sahne* as if nothing else had changed. Later he came to the former Checkpoint Charlie, where tacky souvenir sellers displayed their wares: discarded East German and Soviet uniforms and cap-badges, and the 'art forms' that were pieces of a once-bedaubed concrete wall.

Offices and banks now stood proud and distinguished on ground that had been a strip of death. Much else about the Berlin Murray saw – east and west – was new-built, bright and sparkling, where handsome young men and women paused to stare in the windows of elegant shops, visited modern art galleries and strolled through magnificent museums. He unashamedly followed the tourist trail, spotting the daytime signs of Berlin's nightlife, the cabarets and clubs with their faint echoes of Brecht, Weill and Dietrich, and things much more sinful. But all that would have to wait until another time.

That evening he had his promised dinner date with the redoubt-able Karen Deighton. He remembered what he had read about her in the files; devoted to her job, particularly since, some years previously, she had lost a long-term companion in a car accident. The death of his own young wife all those years ago would allow him to sympathize with her. After the crying was over, there was always an emptiness, an aftermath of unfulfilled longing for someone who was no more.

She picked him up from his hotel just after seven, and drove him back to her surprisingly tastefully decorated flat. She had made a decided effort: a rather good dinner, some excellent Mosel, and, as the meal progressed, an agreeable amount of intelligent talk.

They gossiped lightly about the embassy and its personalities, then, to his surprise, she started talking politics with an under-tone of unexpected vehemence. 'This swing to the right here is frightening and frightful,' she said forcefully. 'I've seen H.E.'s glib reports to London that it's all blown up out of all proportion by the press. I've also seen the hard contrary evidence. Cruel, ugly facts. You won't ever have driven around some of the backstreets of east Berlin on a Saturday night?'

'Obviously I haven't . . .' he began. He looked at her with disguised amazement. This conventional fifty-something-year-old, in her horn-rimmed glasses and billowing frocks, hardly seemed the type to cruise the night away.

'You should,' she said, turning away with a remote look on her face.

'Let's,' said Murray seizing the moment. With no indication of his having interrupted a good social evening, Karen excitedly agreed. 'OK, I'll take you now,' she said bluntly. 'Over east, where the skinheads hang out. You'll see it how it really is.'

'How d'you know all this?' Murray was intrigued.

'A consul gets involved with real people. Dirt under the fingernails stuff.' She smiled briefly. 'None of your gilded diplomatic theorizing and political game-playing. Last time Arsenal played here, a lot of their so-called British fans ended up in jail. My German police friends – I've a lot of time for them – showed me where they'd go hang out. A lot of "blood-brothering" goes on between thugs from whatever nation. I've seen the whole show. They even dress alike: shaven heads, tattoos, gestures and their steel-toed bovver boots. Only their national flags are different.'

She drove resolutely rather than well, taking him from her apartment block through the brightly-lit streets around the city centre. The nightlife that spilled on to the streets despite the cold seemed to be mainly young people re-creating a world unknown since the inter-war years. The throb of techno and jungle music echoed from the doors of countless nightclubs. Soon, however, she turned off into the former East Sector. There he caught only occasional glimpses of the neon lights of seedy nightclubs and bars, while, at each street corner, little clusters of painted prostitutes awaited their catch. Karen gave him a running commentary as she went. She knew exactly where she was going, what everything meant, and soon they were passing through dark, dismal canyons between Stalinist apartment blocks, only occasionally enlivened by the garish windows of some *Bierstube*.

As they drove on, they passed gangs of youths hanging around aimlessly, noisily revving up their motorcycles outside other seedy nightspots.

'Not a pleasant sight,' said Murray as they drove rapidly past one group of leather-jacketed bikers. 'Black seems to be the only colour.'

'London can be like this too,' muttered Karen, looking to left and right as if, for a moment, uncertain of her way. 'Now . . . where are my special hooligans?' she muttered to herself. 'Ah, yes. Down here, I think. There's a place . . . somewhere around here . . . a big bar with a garden or yard where the hardcore skinheads tend to gather.'

'On a bitter night like this?' Murray queried, looking across at her, noting the intense, single-minded expression on her face. She seemed to be enjoying herself.

As he spoke, they turned a corner, and there in front of them stood a crowd of two or three hundred mainly shaven-headed young men, most of them with beer mugs or bottles in their hands, huddled together against the chill Berlin winter. One of their number was standing swaying on the top of a trestle-table, haranguing the rest.

'Let's park,' suggested Murray. 'Go and eavesdrop. Could be interesting.'

'You've got to be joking,' said Karen Deighton, forcefully. 'They don't like strangers and I'm no hero.'

'Anything you say,' responded Murray, disappointment in his voice. As they drove past they heard a cheer go up from the crowd, while from around another corner immediately in front of them, half a dozen other youths suddenly appeared at a run.

'What've they been up to?' Karen muttered suspiciously as she sped rapidly past them, foot firmly on the accelerator. The young men paid no attention to the car, intent as they were on reaching the safety of the mob.

Ahead of them the two diplomats saw, almost at once, the cruel answer: a drab four-storey building already had flames licking their way upwards from the broken windows on the ground floor. As Karen slowed down briefly, there was a dull explosion, and the whole front of the house was suddenly engulfed in a wall of flames. Was that a scream above the roar of the fire? Was that a figure at a top-floor window desperately trying to get out? From behind them they heard the sinister howl of a police siren, then numerous ambulances and fire engines appeared from nowhere. Murray turned in the passenger seat to look back down the street towards where the crowd had stood outside the beer hall. Even from that distance he could see that the skinheads had all vanished into the shadows.

'And that was?' he asked, deeply shocked. They had pulled to a halt a hundred metres or so from the fire. He had never been so close to a burning building.

'Want an educated guess?' Karen responded, resolutely slipping the car into gear. As she did so, Alex noticed what she had already, a uniformed policeman waving at them to move on.

'Yes?'

'A dosshouse for Turkish or east European refugees.'

'You serious? We'd better stay and tell the police what we saw.'

'Serious? Stay? What good'll that do?' Karen muttered. 'Except raise a lot of questions as to why the two of us should be cruising around in this insalubrious part of the city. No, Alex. Let's get the hell out of here. Sorry to spoil your evening,' she added apologetically. 'But after this, if you don't mind, I think I'll drop you back at your hotel.'

To the counsellor, sometimes known as the head of chancery in an embassy, fall all the functions which, in a regiment, would be the responsibility of the adjutant. Murray was the man who coordinated the work of all the departments, in particular heading up the political section, the chancery, but his daily tasks also included overseeing the administration, the finances, and ensuring a good flow of communications to and from the Foreign Office in London. Every detail, from the highest political negotiating with the German government on major issues of international relations, down to the provisioning of the embassy canteen, even supervising the employment conditions of the embassy gardener at the ambassador's residence, were constituent parts of his all-embracing duty. Murray's skill was to delegate the detail and get those with specialist functions to work together as a team.

When the news of his arrival spread around the international diplomatic community in Berlin, because of that key position within the embassy, Murray soon started receiving numerous invitations to attend diplomatic lunches, receptions and dinners. On a busy evening he might eventually expect to have to attend up to two or three receptions, including the endless round of national days of the various countries represented in Berlin, followed perhaps by a black-tie dinner, having already fitted in a working lunch earlier in the day. He knew that in 'dining for Britain', as he called it, he would have to watch what he ate and drank; those twin dangers of diplomacy, overweight and alcoholism, were ever-lurking enemies. Wherever he had been posted in the past, west Africa, east Europe, and in New York, he had always been highly selective about which invitations he accepted. It was the ambassador's function to attend most of the key national days; Murray would only go if he had to deputize for his superior or if he felt there was something specific to be achieved by so doing. Entertaining was the grease which kept the machinery of international relations running smoothly. It could also be a distinct pain.

An invitation from the American Ambassador to Germany was not one such occasion, particularly because the Present incumbent, Vernon Cranston, was an old colleague of Alex's from away back in the days when they had both been sent on the same year's sabbatical to the Harvard Business School. He and Cranston had always got on well. Cranston had been a regular US diplomatic service grade then, but had later left to go into politics and had, for a while, risen to be an assistant secretary to the President of the United States at the White House. In the American scheme of things, when that president was re-elected, Cranston found himself nominated, then approved by the senate foreign relations committee, as their new ambassador to Berlin. Cranston was now much senior to Murray, but that did not mean that they had not remained close friends, particularly after the death of Murray's wife to whom Cranston had briefly been close. Indeed almost the first telephone call of greeting after his arrival at the embassy had been a genuinely warm one from his old diplomatic friend.

When Sir Edward Cornwall arrived in his usual formal style at the American Residence, he was, consequently, more than a little surprised to see that Murray was already there. His deputy had just arrived *en poste*; how could he have made his mark so rapidly? But the British Ambassador had other things on his mind such as talking to his colleague the French Ambassador about the latest outbreak of neo-fascist hooliganism, and thought little of Murray until later, when he came upon him and his other *cher collègue*, Vernon Cranston, chatting rather too intimately together in a corner. It was most irregular. He would have to have a severe word with Murray to ensure that he observed the necessary *étiquette diplomatique*, and warn him not to push himself beyond his rank. Sir Edward thought the same way as he spoke, loading his conversation with contrived French phrases, ones which were once in common diplomatic usage when he had first joined the service. Whatever words he used, it was certainly not *protocolaire* for a mere *conseiller* to hobnob so familiarly with such a senior ambassador.

To his distinct irritation Sir Edward almost felt like an intruder when he moved in on their well-advanced conversation.

'I know what your government's attitude will be; massive destabilizing forces battering at Europe's front door from all over the place . . .' Cranston was saying, an over-friendly hand clasped on the other man's shoulder.

Murray had his back to Sir Edward but the latter heard his reply.

'Come off it, Vernon. Only the threat of illegal immigration from Russia, the Ukraine and Belorussia really affects us. The

French, Spanish and the Italians have to take the lead in combating the Muslim fundamentalism that drives the inflow from north Africa.'

'Wrong again, Alex. As always,' said the US Ambassador robustly as Sir Edward Cornwall listened in chilly astonishment. It was quite intolerable that Murray and Cranston should already be on first-name terms. A few home truths were needed. Murray would have to learn to know his place.

'Well, good evening, my dear Vernon,' he said, with an icy smile, 'I hope my Mr Murray here isn't taking up too much of your time?'

'Absolutely is,' boomed Cranston with a vast grin. 'Alex's a terrible social climber. No tact . . . and too quick with his judgements, particularly when dealing with his elders and betters.'

For a brief moment the British Ambassador thought that he had Murray where he wanted him, but then the American let out a huge bellow of laughter. Sir Edward waited for an explanation; with growing irritation, he noted that Murray was also grinning widely.

'Sorry to set you up like that, Edward,' said Cranston turning and slapping his colleague's stiff and unwelcoming back. 'Alex and I have known each other for years. On the same Harvard course in the seventies. I tell you, he's difficult. I mean difficult. Was then, and I bet still is. Glad he's not on my staff, I can tell you,' he added, turning to slap Murray equally heartily on his shoulders in turn. The latter's smile had become a trifle wan and forced, recognizing that the joke had gone too far. He guessed correctly that his superior would be far from amused.

'I see,' said Sir Edward, both embarrassed and annoyed.

''Fraid I left in such a rush this evening,' began Murray, stiffly, 'I didn't have time to . . .'

'. . . To keep me informed as to whom you know,' said Sir Edward with a thin smile. 'Anyway, Vernon, if you have a moment perhaps we could . . .' Sir Edward rudely and deliberately steered the American away, leaving Murray standing fuming in the corner of the room. Cranston turned, and for a moment Murray was petrified that he was about to wink conspiratorially at him. That would really have done it. Instead his friend forced an equally severe look and walked off purposefully, his British counterpart by his side.

Murray glanced at his watch. It was time to leave both the party and, maybe, if things didn't start improving soon, Berlin. He had hardly arrived, yet at each step he seemed to have further screwed up his relationship with his boss. He knew Sir Edward well enough already to realize that the American Ambassador's tease would have gone down very badly indeed.

As he was making for the door, a tall, fair-haired woman came up and introduced herself. 'Not leaving already are you? You must be Alex Murray,' she began. 'Carol-Anne Capaldi, political counsellor, US Embassy.'

Murray suppressed an instant judgement that here was a typically brittle, professional American woman. One of a type. Then he made a rapid second appraisal. Attractive, indeed rather more than just attractive, particularly when she smiled, as she was doing now.

'Know the chief, I gather,' she said by way of introduction.

'For decades. Much good it will do me with mine. Sir Edward prefers to be the only link with his equals.' Murray grinned briefly but looked far from happy.

'I wouldn't worry about your Sir Edward. I'll go chat him up,' said Carol-Anne. 'He's just shy.'

'Chilly to frigid in my book.'

'Maybe he warms to the female of the species. How're you settling in?' she asked, rapidly changing the subject.

'So-so,' he replied. 'Too much work on my plate to find time to get my living quarters into order.'

'Took over Douglas Young's apartment, did you?' She did not wait for a reply but went on, 'He left in a hell of a hurry. Lots of gossip in the dip corps about that.'

Murray kept to safer ground. He remembered noting her name on his appointments list. 'I've got a diary note: we're meeting soon, at your embassy; brain-storming session on what we all think of Germany's policies towards eastern Europe. That right?'

'Correct. In a couple of days' time,' she responded efficiently.

'Trouble is, the Germans can't disassociate their present actions from their past experiences.' Murray shrugged.

'Like the rest of us. You blame them?' She smiled at him, noting how uptight he seemed.

'Suppose not. At long last they finish with post-Nazi recriminations, war-crimes trials and so on, then they have to disinter their history all over again with revelations and soul-searching over who spied for whom.'

'Stasi files? That's all old hat by now too.'

Murray nodded in agreement. 'Should be, but . . . What would you do if you were German? Their national guilty conscience. Call a halt as the liberals want, or opt for retribution?'

'Not sure. Much to be said for the "amnesty not amnesia" argument. Forgive but don't forget.' Carol-Anne sipped thoughtfully at her drink. It was a problem that never went away.

'Not just a government decision, either,' Murray speculated. 'Every national has a right to scrutinize their own files. Then take legal action against those who spied on them. It's freedom of information gone mad,' he added.

As Murray and Carol-Anne Capaldi stood talking, Fred Cree, a British journalist working for the *Guardian*, sauntered up and joined them. Cree saw himself as one of life's victims, a man with a complexion of unappealing texture, a mix of childhood impetigo and heavy beard growth that gave him a permanently unwashed appearance. He looked at life through a pair of red-ringed, watery eyes, which peered constantly around him with a mixture of curiosity, suspicion and, above all, envy. But as Murray would discover to his cost, his off-putting personal appearance camouflaged a rarefied news sense. He was disliked but feared because when he started work on a story, he was seldom shaken from his quest, particularly when it came to dethroning the great and the good. He was a born leveller. His critics said that it fed his grudge against the world.

Carol-Anne turned to greet him. 'Have you two met?' she asked cautiously. The two men shook hands. Murray had always been particularly suspicious of journalists but he was caught in mid-argument. Cree picked up the tail-end of their conversation.

'You think the German government should halt the release of Stasi files?' Cree asked innocently.

'Off the record?' Murray suggested.

'Course,' said Cree impassively.

'They're indecisive. Open the lot or burn them and let bygones be bygones.'

'They've got every excuse for delay,' broke in Carol-Anne defensively. She didn't like the way the conversation was going.

'I know that,' said Murray. 'But they're indecisive on a whole range of fronts. They couldn't decide what to do with Nazi war criminals until they grew so old as to no longer matter. Then they couldn't make up their minds what to do with all the former East German leaders: an amnesty or bring charges right across the board. After all,' Murray continued with unusual lack of caution, 'while the police and foot soldiers have been punished for shooting people dead on the Berlin wall, a lot of the string-pullers have still to be brought to trial.'

'Bit unfair,' interrupted Carol-Anne, trying to bring the conversation to a close.

'Maybe, but then look at their attitude to east Europe.' Murray had now warmed to his argument. 'They don't know whether to be hard or soft with the Russians. They try to be liberal on immigration. Then, if the neo-Nazis don't get punished for burning down refugee hostels, the world points an accusing finger at them. And yet . . .'

Knowing something of Cree's reputation, Carol-Anne decided to save Murray from himself; he had said enough. She pulled him away to meet some other guests. 'Indecisiveness it is,' thought Cree, left to his own company. With skilful editing he had just picked himself a winning headline.

Later that evening Murray again went walkabout through the dark streets, picking up other fragments of his memories. For forty-five years after the war, Berlin had been more a metaphor than a city. Enough of the smells of old Nazism had remained to nag at the conscience of a liberal, even left-leaning town. The Russians growled angrily around the walls of Europe's capitalist showcase, while through the middle ran that great scar, that Mecca for tourists, which made them shudder with its sense of history. Berlin had, above all, always watched Russia. Today, to quote one cynic, 'It has more Russians living in it than there were in 1945, and they're doing more damage'. Around the spot where Hitler shot himself in his bunker, still unmarked for fear of some disgraceful pilgrimage, Murray paused briefly in front of one of a thousand building sites. Later, where Checkpoint Charlie once stood, he heard a passing American voice asking 'Is this where it was?'

Murray had first come here when the four great powers still ruled their separate zones. That was the island city which President Kennedy made one with the civilized world. Everywhere he wandered that night, Murray sensed the real or imagined shadows of a sparkling yet decadent past. Like so many, he could not escape the echoes of jackboots, *Kristallnacht*, the burning of synagogues and of the Reichstag, political cabarets, weak Weimar conciliators, Brownshirts and a decadent café society that gorged itself, whilst swastikas and red flags fought for position on the rooftops. It reminded him in a strange way of his last posting in New York, another city that never slept, with its mix of great restaurants and garish, seedy nightclubs that catered to every sexual taste. He suddenly realized that he loved being there. Whatever the problems he had with his ambassador, Murray was suddenly resolute, determined to stay. He was excited and glad to be there. He walked on and on until he was tired enough to sleep.

A couple of days later, Murray arrived at his office in cheerful mood, whistling to himself under his breath. His spirits were high. His life was beginning to take shape. His euphoria was cut brutally short. At the door of his office stood Paul Fawcett, a well-manufactured look of concern on his chubby face. In his hand was a fax from the Foreign Office news department reporting an article from that morning's *Guardian* under the heading: 'British concern at German indecision'. The byline was that of the journalist, Fred Cree, and it quoted an unnamed but highly-placed British source in Berlin who had forcefully expressed his worries about German weaknesses in dealing both with their internal problems, and those facing them on their eastern front. Murray read the article with increasing fury. He was not quoted by name but he would not be able to deny that he was the source of the remarks. That bastard Cree had, strictly speaking, not attributed them, but . . . Seething with rage he was about to summon Samantha and dictate an explanation to the ambassador when his internal phone rang. It was a pre-emptive summons from Sir Edward.

'That, I presume, was you?' A copy of the fax was waved in Murray's face as he entered the ambassador's office. 'I saw you talking to Cree at the American Residence two nights ago. Surely to God, Murray, you know never to say anything serious in front of bloody journalists?'

'Sir.' Murray was furious both with himself and with the way the ambassador was ticking him off like a child.

'We, in this embassy, take the greatest care not to offend the Germans. Yet within days of arriving, you dare to antagonize them with ill-thought-out accusations of indecisiveness. Call yourself a diplomat?'

'I hadn't realized,' Murray began.

'You hadn't realized . . . God, haven't you experience of dealing with the media? They're never, never, to be trusted.' The ambassador waved the fax again. 'Did you actually say all of this? Did you?' he repeated. Murray could see furious flecks of colour building up in his cheeks.

'I was talking to the political counsellor at the US Embassy at the time. Cree came up. He overheard,' said Murray lamely. He tried to explain rather than to apologize.

'Overheard? Cree appeared and you didn't stop talking? So the US Embassy also knows you were the source? I do not believe it. It'll be round the diplomatic circuit and reach the German

Foreign Ministry by lunchtime. Look, Murray, I will not stand for this slipshod behaviour. Any more of it and I'll demand your replacement. I will not have our bilateral relationships jeopardized by your sloppy talk.' The ambassador was almost choking with indignant fury.

'Sir.' Murray knew that to say anything further would inflame the situation. He turned to leave. As he reached the door, Sir Edward bellowed after him, 'And you haven't even had the courtesy to write to my wife to apologize for your behaviour when you first arrived. She doesn't relish being treated like a cloakroom lady, you know.'

Back in his office, Murray, in renewed heavy gloom, worked his way through a pile of letters and telegrams that had arrived from the Foreign Office in London and needed his attention. Most important political and administrative correspondence came first to him, to be submitted up to the ambassador if it was important enough, or passed down the line to other members of staff for action.

One letter, on black-crested paper, was sitting at the top of the pile. It was from the chief clerk – the principal administration officer in the Foreign Office – confirming that they were sending out a team of inspectors to evaluate staffing levels at the embassy. There was the usual preamble about Treasury constraints and the need for economies. As he was reading through the letter, Fawcett ambled in, ostensibly to sympathize over the *Guardian* article. Murray handed the letter to him.

'Your view, Paul?' he asked softly.

'Mine doesn't matter. The old man has a firm one: no cuts at any price. He'll be extremely anti any suggestion that we are not the right size.' Fawcett had his answer ready.

'Then I see more problems coming, Paul.' On a sudden impulse Murray added: 'Looking at our overall numbers, maybe a ten per cent cut here?' He smiled to himself as Fawcett turned and rapidly left the room.

It took less than ten minutes before the ambassador was on the line again. 'Let me see the letter about the inspectors, Alex.

Straightaway, will you. I've had quite enough trouble today already. I want no arguments from here suggesting that we are other than perfectly staffed.'

'Sir,' said Murray, putting the phone down. He now had all the confirmation he needed as to where anything he said to Fawcett went.

Early on in life, Alex Murray had found a defence mechanism that had often stood him in good stead. He could isolate problems, pigeonholing them until he was ready to deal with them or they had sorted themselves out. He worked non-stop, eating sandwiches at his desk for lunch. Around seven that evening he decided to call it a day. As he was leaving, Sylvia Watt, the ambassador's PA, put her head around the door.

'How're things?' she asked kindly.

'Bloody to horrible,' growled Murray. 'Not top of the pops with himself, as you must know only too well.'

'Few are,' she responded. 'It'll blow over.'

'With young Paul stirring it?'

'You've gathered?' She maintained her smile.

'I should have listened to you,' Murray grunted.

'How's the apartment?' she asked, sounding as if her interest was genuine.

'Slow too. Haven't had time to sort myself out.'

'Have you a housekeeper?'

'I thought I'd wait and . . .' Murray looked up, indecisive.

'I've just the woman for you,' said Sylvia Watt emphatically. 'She's called Frau Müller. I'll arrange for you to see her tomorrow.'

'I'm not sure I want . . .' he hesitated. Sylvia was in danger of bullying him into a hasty decision. He wasn't in the mood for decisions.

'You want Frau Müller. I assure you,' said Sylvia firmly. 'It's the best news you've had all day.'

4

Corporal Tate had never seen anything quite like it. He had been to refugee camps before, evil-smelling squatter settlements on a bone-dry African plain where sanitation had been non-existent and where water had been the most treasured of all commodities; small, mean ones in Bosnia, where the women were as hard as the men as they had to be to keep themselves safe from attacks from other marauding groups. But in both scale and in deprivation, this was totally beyond his comprehension. It was not just people that populated that bleak area. Black rats, brown rats and other rodents infested the camp in a way that reminded this literate soldier of a long-forgotten reading of the Pied Piper of Hamelin. The rats were fatter than the people. They had lost their fear, running in threes and fours as if they were themselves on patrol. No one had the energy to do anything about them, though they marked out another potential enemy for the squatters; cholera and typhoid had reappeared to haunt this grim mass of humanity. There were no other animals to be seen; even domestic pets were soon devoured.

Sergeant Brace, hard man and disciplined though he was, was deeply shocked. 'Christ almighty. Like frigging maggots,' he muttered as they drove past in their anonymous, mud-spattered, four-wheel-drive truck with its Polish number plates.

They were dressed in civilian clothes, carried their British passports, and had expensive cameras with them. They might just pass for journalists. They were not spies; if they had been picked up, then they would have admitted that they were NATO soldiers who had somehow strayed across the border. It was easy enough to do. NATO, after all, knew where the weak links were;

at one of those crossings they had openly driven across. And, in reality, they were not spies in the accepted frame of things. They weren't trying to find out about Russian or Belorussian military dispositions since, at a higher level of espionage coupled with what was known from communications intelligence, all that was probably better understood back in Brussels than it was in Moscow itself. No. The two NCOs were fact-finding, looking for a bit of local colour on the ground.

Colour was what was lacking. Everything was black, grey, or grey-white. Bundles of humanity tucked themselves away in any rude shelter they could find, or under the plastic and tarpaulin tents provided by western aid agencies. Bundles of living beings, sleeping, existing, standing in queues, long straggling lines of people, muffled to the eyes with blankets and occasional anoraks, waiting patiently for their daily access to what meagre fare the food kitchens offered. The latter, mobile caravans or converted buses, were pulled together in a circle with awnings strung between them, rather like some hideous snowbound version of the defensive huddle of covered wagons seen in ancient black-and-white cowboy movies. These little encampments, easily picked out by the red crosses on the sides of the wagons and by the billowing smoke and steam that rose above them, were basic oases of salvation amid an all-pervading, icy wasteland.

Sergeant Brace drove slowly along a rutted track, glad of the permafrost which stopped everything beneath the wheels turning into impassable, slushy mud. Their slow progress was brought almost to a halt from time to time, as the milling refugees nearest their vehicle turned curiously or to beg. The little children were the most difficult to ignore; pinched white faces turned upwards, hoping against hope for something; a coin, bread, anything. Still more strangely shocking, a young woman suddenly pulled open her heavy greatcoat as they passed, revealing naked flesh covered only partly in a garish red satin basque, as she offered them her only worthwhile possession. As lecherous as any in the army where sex could be bought, even Sergeant Brace was horrified.

'Let's get the bloody hell outa here, Corporal. Put your foot down. I need a long hot shower.'

That early February day, when eventually he reached Moscow party headquarters, Ivan Katerski kept his fur-lined coat wrapped firmly around him. He knew instinctively that there would be no heating down there in the cellars. Theirs was a triumphalist movement on the extreme patriotic wing, yet, somehow, Ivan always felt that the drab settings in which they met, the ideological banners on the walls, the nauseating cocktail of cabbage and carbolic smells, were more appropriate to some underground communist party cell. Yet why should this really be so strange? There had been so little time for Russians to change many of their deep-rooted attitudes; these very cellars had, after all, been part of the Soviet Ministry of Information until a few years ago, when some minor official had been bribed to allocate them to their new political use.

He was waiting for Vladimir. He always seemed to be waiting for Vladimir. Vladimir was almost certainly in bed with some whore at the moment, or drunk out of his mind, or sleeping one or the other off. But Vladimir was always forgiven, because, when sober, when not indulging in some frenzied sexual or alcoholic orgy, he was the great orator, the charismatic Russian leader, the inspiration to so many hundreds of thousands of ordinary men and women, with his stirring rhetoric and his echoing calls of patriotism.

Ivan Katerski sat slouched in a broken-springed chair, nursing a polystyrene cup of weak coffee someone had reluctantly produced for him. Once again he fought back a longing to throw in his hand and return to the comforts of his Knightsbridge house, the laughing companionship of his friends, and the delicious body of some young girlfriend. Here, here in this cellar, he was a nobody, just someone else waiting patiently to do something for the great Vladimir. Waiting, always waiting. He pushed temptation firmly to the back of his mind, since deep down he knew that throughout his recent life he had been preparing for such a time, such an opportunity to be of service to something other than himself.

If he had begun dreaming about a new, free Russia in his last years at public school, those feelings flowered and prospered when he went on to New College, Oxford, to read PPE. There he attended private lessons in advanced Russian, and joined the Conservative Bow Group, taking a vigorous part in debates, and eventually rising to become their vice-president. But right-wing British Conservatism and British politics generally failed to excite him. By contrast, throughout the late eighties and early nineties, he had watched with ever-keener interest the rapidly changing political climate of the land of the most telling half of his blood.

After graduating, he thought at first of going straight into some City finance house, but instead he returned to Scotland, to Edinburgh, to work on a PhD in Russian political studies. He loved that cold, stone-grey city, making more friends there than he had ever made at school or at Oxford. That much, that love of Scotland, he had inherited from his neglected, but always caring mother. Among those new friends, he included a number of older east European refugees, some of whom had escaped from Hungary or Poland as long ago as the sixties and seventies. There were a few Russians among them, but though they had suffered too, they were seldom popular. They had always been, with the Germans, the other oppressor race. So he still opted for caution, still opportunistically called himself Ian Carter, as he listened to their expatriate dreams. A few of them questioned his ability to speak such perfect Russian. He tended to shrug and said that he was lucky: he had a natural aptitude and ear for languages; he had, he claimed, perfected it at Oxford, which was true. Later, as his friendships became more intimate, he let a few of them into the secret of his half-Russian parentage and the story gradually got round. Why not? From then on he was seen by some, particularly his transient British girlfriends, as a mysterious, almost romantic figure, and when the rumour that he might have some princely blood in him travelled to Edinburgh via former pupils from his old school, this added polish to his unconventional image. In his rented flat in Edinburgh's New Town, visitors spotted more and more hints and artefacts that betrayed his Russian origins. There were shelves of books in Russian; there were rugs and sculpture and paintings and even a handsome silver-mounted icon, for he appeared to be quite rich. Of his family they knew, and he spoke, little: by this time his father was dead, and his mother, his remote mother, his burden of guilt whom he visited but seldom, had returned to Scotland to be sheltered, with her vanishing memories, in an old people's home by the wild North Sea.

He was still waiting, waiting for Vladimir. They all were waiting. Vladimir had sent a curt message. He was running late. He would meet them at the rally. They moved on from the cellar in a fleet of battered Zil cars. Now he sat waiting for Vladimir on a hard chair, at the end of a trestle-table, on a platform in a packed hall, somewhere in the highrise, desolate outskirts of Moscow. The people at the political rally, most of them fur-hatted men with a scattering of women in headscarves, were increasingly fretful and impatient. They had come to greet their leader, their hero, their Vladimir. He was the only one who had the charisma to lead this new, decadent, Jew-ridden Russia, dear Mother Russia, to its true destiny and salvation. Vladimir would, single-handed, wipe away the Mafia corruption, solve the food shortages, the lack of heating, the dearth of everything and anything that had been promised by idiots like Gorbachev, Yeltsin and those other damned pseudo-liberals. And he, Ivan Katerski, was there waiting in the wings, ready to handle any western, English-speaking press that might turn up. Since his return from the 'Front' as they called it, his job had been made very clear to him: he was to interpret Vladimir's more extreme views in a positive way to a wider world.

Where the hell was Vladimir? Were his closest aides trying, as so often, to get him sober enough to stay upright on the platform? Perhaps they were making him vomit. Ivan had once seen them forcing his comatose hero to swallow a mix of salt and yoghurt, getting him to throw up, to bring him to a state where he could rally the faithful in the way only he could do so brilliantly.

As he sat watching the audience grow ever more restless, Ivan Katerski thought again of his earlier life. It was really only after his father's death that he had missed him; after that, his relationship with his half-brother and his mother became increasingly distant. He abandoned all his pasts for a while and even his political drive became blunted as, armed with his PhD, he moved back to London as economic adviser to one of the big merchant banks. To them he was as British as they came in his tailored suits and his handmade shirts. True, he had not been to a traditional English public school – Scotland had seen to that – but New College gave him impeccable credentials for a job that he did exceptionally well. He had a natural nose for high finance, worked diligently, was extremely well-paid and invested his huge bonuses wisely, gradually acquiring a substantial stock of capital. He had quickly arranged with his half-brother to sell his parents' big house in Swiss Cottage when his mother had moved back north, and, with his share of the proceeds, bought a flat for himself in Knightsbridge which he furnished with the best of his inherited antiques and paintings, supplemented by many more recent purchases of his own.

It was about then that he began, almost without realizing it, to construct something of a double life for himself, perfectly reasonably, perfectly honestly. One half of that life was Ian Carter of the City and his fashionable club in St James's; the other was Ivan Katerski who increasingly frequented another, seedier club just off the Gloucester Road, which catered solely to Russian *émigré* society. It was there, in those faded rooms, that he listened to old men talking of how it had been in the Tsar's days, and there that he began to long to see modern Russia for himself. But his daytime life was a busy one. Instead, he went skiing to Gstaad in winter, to Barbados or Monaco in the season, and a long succession of glamorous girlfriends meant that his other leisure time was more than fully accounted for.

He had started going to the Russian Club largely to ensure that he kept his language in good working order after his father's death. He felt driven to keep at least this one inherited gift in highly polished condition. Thus, late one evening, after a formal City dinner, still in dinner jacket and black tie, he dropped in for a nightcap and, in the bar, he found himself talking with a grey-haired, elderly man, to whom he had never previously been introduced, but whom he had seen at various social gatherings in the past. The man, Dimitri Platov, explained that he was a retired professor of Russian from some northern English university. His name was vaguely familiar to Ivan as someone who had translated a number of Russian writers into English. Platov, who emerged as an erudite figure with considerable personal magnetism, soon captivated the young man with his compelling theories of what he saw developing within Russia. Ivan, highly impressed by the old man's depth of understanding, readily agreed to have dinner with him the following week.

'Not at the club,' Professor Platov said. 'Too many memories lurk here. I know a good little restaurant just round the corner. We'll meet there? Shall we say eight o'clock?'

It was out of his normal habit and he had to cancel an evening with a highly nubile and available girl, but he had gone to the restaurant the following week, and the two men talked on late into the night. Towards the end, once he had the measure of the young man, Professor Platov began cautiously to suggest that it was wrong for someone in his privileged position merely to wring his hands and accept the Russian status quo. Something must be done. Something could be done. The Russian people were downtrodden, buried under the ruins of a vile communist past. The old evil empire and the new corrupt one that was taking its place, must and could be overthrown. Ivan Katerski was greatly moved by the old man's authoritative rhetoric.

'How can any one person make any impression on such a

71

monolithic, or,' he hesitated, 'such an anarchic state?' It was the simplest and most confounding of questions.

'Work from within the system.' The answer, from anyone else, would have sounded absurd.

'How?' Ivan hardly dared breathe the word.

'I have contacts. I would like you to meet them. I know they would value meeting you.'

It was thus that Ian Carter, otherwise known as Ivan Katerski, first came face to face with something novel and exciting. Professor Platov inspired him and showed him how he could become involved in the greatest struggle of all, to save the country of his blood.

That was then. This was here and now in Moscow. The crowd was very restless now. Where the hell was Vladimir? He half-turned as, suddenly, from the back of the hall, there came an expectant hush, then the cheering as their hero arrived, at long last, to meet his people.

Frau Müller was an inspired choice. Within the week she had taken over, and injected immediate order into his domestic life. She came for the interview on Tuesday and by that same afternoon she was already in full possession of his apartment, apron on, vacuum cleaner and dusters flying. A woman in her late fifties, dark, severe, unsmiling but, as Sylvia Watt had patiently explained, and as Alex Murray was soon to verify, she had a dedicated spirit. When he returned that first night, his apartment was totally transformed, clean and fresh-smelling. For the first time he felt at ease and at home in Berlin. Frau Müller had prepared something delicious for him to eat, complete with strict instructions in German that even an idiot could understand, on how to heat the dish to perfection in the microwave.

Consequently Murray was in a reasonable humour that Wednesday morning as he set off for the US Embassy to attend what had been named 'The NATO Working Group on the Eastern Border Problem'. The title camouflaged a wide range of subjects and a vast geographical spread. 'The Border' was everything from the 'New NATO' eastwards, with the frontiers with Russia, Belorussia, the Ukraine and Moldova the main problem areas. Murray was the senior British delegate on this standing committee of middle-ranking diplomats; they met once a week to coordinate and monitor events and report back to NATO headquarters in Brussels. Two people came from each of the western embassies, a diplomat – in the British case, Murray, plus the military attaché, Brigadier Dicks. The meetings, which alternated between the various embassies and the German Foreign Ministry, were usually chaired by Otto Klingenfeldt, the head of the European department at the ministry, an amusing, articulate man with a domed, bald head and an incongruous pencil moustache, who spoke in an English so perfect as to put most native speakers to shame. Despite muted protests from the French who, as usual, tried to insist that the talks should be bilingual, English was the common language. That day, America was represented by Carol-Anne Capaldi and, accompanying her, the US military attaché.

Murray arrived to discover her already seated at the conference table, in the chair next to the one he himself had been allocated. The first item on the agenda was how to convince European public opinion, via a fickle media, that there was an urgent need for the eastern border defences to be further upgraded and reinforced in order to stop any more economic migrants flooding west. Official NATO and European Community policy had long been to contain them firmly within their country of origin by providing emergency food aid where necessary. There was naturally a high degree of political and military sensitivity over any images of new barbed wire, reconditioned watchtowers, armed border patrols, and floodlights, all of which brought back such dire memories of the Cold War. Liberal papers in Britain did not like the containment policy nor the way it was being implemented, and were openly critical; many American Democratic politicians equally condemned what was going on. Few offered realistic alternative policies.

'I'm just back from a three-day fact-finding tour of eastern Poland. We've been using carefully selected military personnel to check on what's going on on the other side, and it all adds up to a pretty horrific picture. I have to say that I was deeply shocked by some of the reports: it would be difficult to exaggerate the scale of the problem,' Brigadier Dicks opened the discussion. 'We're talking of literally hundreds of thousands of people. Men, women, children. Their living conditions are appalling. There are no attempts by Moscow or Kiev to persuade them to return to their homes – quite the reverse in fact. Food supplies are, at best, erratic and the weather, as we know, continues to be horrific.' Dicks gestured towards the windows of the room; outside a snowstorm had blown up while they had been talking.

'The State Department believes that the UN High Commissioner for Refugees is getting his act together at long last,' Carol-Anne Capaldi interjected. 'A major famine relief effort.'

'Few hard signs of that on the ground,' Klingenfeldt added. 'We've got NATO military observation posts every two or three kilometres along the Polish border.' He pointed to a large-scale map mounted on one wall of the room. 'They, with our own intelligence reports, indicate that food deliveries are sporadic, due, as usual, to the Russian Mafia creaming off their percentage on the way.'

'A critical situation, agreed. But it would be very much worse if . . .' Murray paused as the others looked at him enquiringly, sizing up the newest member of the committee, '. . . if a right-wing leadership was to come to power in the Russian presidential election ready to . . .' He paused again.

'Ready to what?' asked Carol-Anne.

'Ready to make maximum capital out of the situation. Do something drastic, trying to blackmail the West, threatening us by saying that either we give them much more aid, or they'll stand back and let the masses overrun the border. Think of it. What would we, NATO, the Poles, the Hungarians do? What if they simply pushed down the wire fences and marched westwards? Do any of you remember the so-called *Marcha Verde*? Around the time that Franco was dying and Spain was in political confusion, the Moroccans simply organized unarmed men, women and children to march over the border into Spanish Sahara. In a few days they annexed permanently what decades of strife with Spain had failed to do, all without a single shot being fired.' Murray paused. He had their attention. 'Would NATO troops, in the last resort, be willing to shoot starving men, women and children?'

'We haven't reached anything quite so drastic as yet,' Klingenfeldt muttered, with a decided lack of conviction. Murray was very new in town. He hoped this abrasive British diplomat wasn't going to start rocking the boat by pushing his apocalyptic theories. 'We would act long before – '

'Our government's quite clear what must be done. You all know our views. We must increase food aid urgently. Better distribution . . .' the French political counsellor interrupted, breaking the tension.

'What evidence d'you British have, Alex, that Russian political leaders might stir things up in that direction?' asked Carol-Anne.

'I have to admit,' Klingenfeldt volunteered before Murray had time to respond, 'we have it from our Moscow embassy that nationalists, like that fanatic Vladimir, have already moved in on the act. They've had party activists out and about, stirring things up. They see their opportunity, not to help their people, but to further their own political cause.'

The meeting broke up after two hours with few decisions reached beyond everyone agreeing the terms of an interim report back to NATO HQ. It was as bland and anodyne as such multilateral statements always are.

As they were leaving the embassy, Carol-Anne delayed Murray, observing, 'One thing we didn't even begin to discuss. How much is all this playing into the hands of right-wing groups here in Germany? And, for good measure, in France, the UK and elsewhere?'

'Not our brief – for that meeting at least. Not in front of Klingenfeldt, at any rate,' Murray responded.

'I'm not just speculating. The CIA have shared with your intelligence community in London pretty convincing evidence of a deliberate policy in some quarters in Moscow to encourage ever more starving people to move right up to the border, to get the West to act. We feel they're deliberately seeking to infuriate right-wing groups here. It'll end up with everyone forcing through much tougher immigration laws.'

'You're not suggesting that extreme western politicians are in cahoots with people like Vladimir?' asked Murray with growing interest.

'Not directly. No firm evidence anyway. But it would suit them, wouldn't it?' she speculated.

'I hate conspiracy theories,' said Murray dismissively. 'As you've just heard, the great march west is my nightmare scenario. Extremists like Vladimir don't need much international plotting to get that sort of agenda going.'

'As to how this impinges on the German political situation, are you monitoring the right-wing rally here in Berlin this Friday?' asked Carol-Anne curiously.

'Low key, I think. I'm far too new here. I expect one of our people, Fawcett perhaps, will go.' Murray hesitated.

'Not yourself?' she insisted.

'Wasn't thinking of it.' Murray shrugged.

'I am. Why don't you come along?'

'Bit obvious, wouldn't it be, you and me watching?' He was cautious, given his experience with Cree's recent headline.

'Don't see why. They'll be too busy cheering, shouting and waving their banners to notice us. Why don't you join me?' she repeated. 'We might have a bite to eat afterwards if you're free.'

For reasons not at all to do with his political brief, Murray carelessly accepted.

There were flags, there were banners, there were burly young men in armbands standing at every doorway, but otherwise that Friday evening there was a remarkable sense of order about the meeting. Well-dressed, respectable-looking men and women of a variety of age groups sat in orderly rows facing

76

the flower-bedecked platform. No one questioned or appeared to notice the two diplomats as they entered the great hall and went and found a discreet corner of a balcony overlooking the main auditorium. On the platform, behind the speakers' table, a range of flags included the French tricolour and the Union Jack alongside the flags of Germany, Austria, Italy, and what looked like Holland. As the conference chairman, Professor Dieter Krauss, a neat little man with rimless glasses and a well-trimmed goatee beard, stood and came to the lectern, a burst of well-disciplined applause came from the six or seven hundred enthusiastic people in the audience.

At one level the professor's speech was a masterpiece of understatement. There was little polemic; there was no racism, no calls for ethnic purity; it was, on the face of it, a moderate plea for sanity in dealing with the so-called *Gästarbeiter*, the foreign 'guest workers', and the threat of further uncontrolled foreign immigration. Germany had enough issues of its own to deal with: rising unemployment, trying to continue to weld together two disparate parts that had been so viciously separated for over fifty years. Germany's western neighbours, equally, had sufficient domestic problems without importing more from other less developed countries. It was incumbent on the international community to work together, via the United Nations, to deliver food supplies in sufficient quantities to defuse the crisis that was looming on NATO's eastern borders. Krauss's speech was one that any moderate politician from any of the European democracies might have made. Yet, behind it all, behind the routine logic, Murray sensed a hint of menace, a 'but if they do not listen' threat. How logical it all seemed. There were no triumphal calls for one northern nation, one people, one *Volk*, but the audience knew their man and his hidden agenda, and they applauded him to the rafters.

Krauss was followed by other speakers from France and Britain. Murray had heard a bit about Matt Huggins, who had emerged from the East End of London school of political thought. He was a great shaven-headed bruiser of a figure, with a powerful rhetoric to match. Much to Murray's amazement Huggins spoke good German, which in itself was greeted with great acclaim by his audience. Huggins played the demagogue, making much of the great historical misunderstandings between Britain and Germany. As countries with shared aspirations, they had too often been forced into war by their misguided leaders. They were two peoples with a common cause and a unique sense of history. He was much less cautious than Professor Krauss: without any politically correct qualms, he called for a Britain for the British, a France for the French, a Germany for the Germans. Again the house rang, this time with even more prolonged applause. Murray fantasized that Huggins would finish his oration by raising his arm in the fascist salute. In fact his gesture of gratitude for the warm reception he was given was a modest, friendly wave.

After the speeches a choir of young boys and girls, all dressed in white, appeared and sang stirring, patriotic songs. But while the words were moderate, Murray recalled something of the scene of the young blue-eyed, blond Nazi, singing the Fatherland song in the *Biergarten* in the film *Cabaret*. Yes, he had expected to see hundreds of banners, chanting and calls for racial purity. But this peaceful, well-behaved rally was no less menacing for being short of all that.

Murray and Carol-Anne slipped away well before the end. Over dinner they fully intended to discuss Professor Krauss, his ideals, and his bedfellows. For both of them, however, work and play went hand in hand from the beginning, and bedfellows became the operative word.

The unseen shadow over their evening was that the ubiquitous Fred Cree had also been present at the rally. From an equally discreet vantage point in a side gallery, he quickly spotted Carol-Anne Capaldi and Alex Murray sitting close together watching events from the balcony below. As was his habit, he began mentally composing his next headline: 'Western Embassies anxiously monitor right-wing fascist groups'. When, at the end of their evening, Murray and Carol-Anne went to bed together, Fred

Cree, always delighted to add spice to his otherwise stunted life, rang his buddy, Paul Fawcett, and told him all he had seen, and the line he intended to take in his forthcoming article. Fawcett, equally ready to bear with equanimity the indiscretions of others, suppressed the desire to ring his boss that same evening. Such a delicious tit-bit would easily wait till the following day.

Murray pulled himself from Carol-Anne's bed some time late on the Saturday morning and, once dressed, they went for a drive together, out of the city, stopping at a picturesque little village guesthouse to the east of Berlin where they had a flirtatious lunch, washed down with quantities of passable local wine. Then, to clear their heads, they walked for a while amid snow-covered fields and woods behind the village, and so it was late in the evening by the time they arrived back in the city.

There were four separate messages waiting on the answering machine at Murray's flat, each one telling him to ring Fawcett urgently. When he eventually got hold of him, he was told to look under his doormat where he found a brown envelope containing a fax with a story run in that morning's *Guardian*. Again it was under Fred Cree's byline; it was about western embassy personnel monitoring right-wing German political movements. This time Murray was mentioned by name.

'The ambassador's shouting for you something crazy. He's been searching for you all day,' Fawcett yelled down the telephone with ill-disguised glee. 'I gather that there are to be questions in the House of Commons next week about what's been going on. By the way, did you and Carol-Anne have a good day?' he added.

Murray slammed the phone down on him without replying, then telephoned a less perturbed Carol-Anne. 'If I were you,' she suggested, 'I'd sleep on it. Things are always better in the cold light of day.'

They were not. 'Far be it from me to comment on your private life,' snarled Sir Edward in pent-up fury, as he took his subordinate to task first thing on Monday morning. The ambassador had gone off shooting on Sunday, but forty-eight hours had not moderated his temper.

'I'll ignore that remark, sir,' said Murray, equally livid. 'If you want me to apologize for doing my duty, which is, as you instructed me, to put my fingers on the pulse of what's going on here in Germany, you can have my resignation now. You appointed me the UK member of the NATO working group. Carol-Anne Capaldi from the US Embassy suggested I join her at that rally. I went. It's my job.'

'Why the hell didn't you tell me you were going?' Sir Edward was decidedly unimpressed, but was wary of Murray's link with his American counterpart.

'With respect, sir, d'you expect me to let you know every single thing I do? If I did that you wouldn't have time to do anything else.' Murray had to control his desire to shout.

'Don't be bloody impertinent, Murray.' The ambassador was deeply riled.

'Sir, I don't see much future in this conversation.'

'Nor do I, Murray. I tell you, this is your final warning.'

Murray turned, stalked out of the room and stormed along the chancery corridor, noticing with additional fury that Fawcett seemed surprisingly intent on the papers on his desk as he went past his room. In the background he glimpsed the resolute figure of Karen Deighton, who, brought fully up to date with the details of the current crisis, was doubtless wondering whether to turn up with the offer of a supporting shoulder to lean on.

Back in his office, Murray's anger festered unabated. How dare that old stuffed shirt start preaching about his relationship with Carol-Anne Capaldi. He knew where that bit of gossip must have come from. Fawcett had earlier admitted that he had checked up on Carol-Anne's movements via a chum at the US Embassy; 'To see if I could find you,' he had added uncertainly. That inflated young man was skating on the wrong side of very thin ice.

Private and public events have a habit of impinging strangely on each other, and the ways of politicians on the make are hard to fathom. Just as he was considering how to draft his letter of resignation, he took an unexpected phone call from London. Dr Mark Ivor, an old friend from university days and one of the British Prime Minister's unofficial strategic advisers, was on the telephone – to congratulate him, he said.

'Sorry?' Murray began hesitantly. 'Don't follow, Mark.'

'I've just come from Number Ten. They're delighted by the story in Saturday's *Guardian*,' said Ivor. 'Well done, Alex. As it happens, the Prime Minister was looking for a peg for a rather tricky speech to party workers on British foreign policy; he particularly wanted to deal with some flak he's been getting on UK immigration controls and how the lack of them inflames right-wing sentiment. It impacts on our strategy towards the trade unions who are always worried about the threat to their members from cheap foreign labour. You know what a hot issue that is here just now. That report was splendidly opportune. He's using the fact that you've been monitoring right-wing attitudes to the problems in Germany as a keynote part of his address. He's taking full credit for initiating it. Hope you don't mind.'

'Mind what? He's doing what?' said Murray, totally confused.

'You're being slow, Alex. Let me restate it: the PM's taking full credit for the fact that British embassies throughout western Europe, i.e. you, are closely watching the resurgence of extreme nationalism, coupled with monitoring the illegal immigrant problem. He's quoting directly from Cree's report as ammunition.'

'He's doing what?' Murray repeated, sitting back in his chair, a smile of unbelieving satisfaction slowly spreading across his face. He felt the tension that had been building up across his shoulders gradually melt away. He knew how the pre-eminent spin doctor, Mark Ivor, the man whom the press had so frequently labelled the modern Machiavelli, usually worked. They had occasionally conspired together in the past. This time there had been no need: it had just happened that way.

'Is something the matter, Alex?' Ivor asked anxiously. 'You don't seem with it this morning. Don't you understand? You ought to be flattered. It suits Number Ten that you've been seen to be watching. Our highly alert diplomatic service is perceived to be at its most professional – all that stuff. A telegram's coming, congratulating the ambassador.'

'Congratulating the . . .' Murray almost choked as he tried to suppress a laugh.

'I've seen the text. It should be with him about now,' Ivor continued, blissfully unaware of the effect he was having on his friend in Berlin.

As he slowly replaced the receiver, a beaming Sylvia Watt marched into his office. 'H.E. wants to see you. He's in a deeply reflective frame of mind.'

'Wonder why?' said Murray, anticipating a healthy dose of *Schadenfreude*. He walked to a side table, poured himself a cup of lukewarm coffee, sipped it and then walked slowly and deliberately to the ambassador's office.

The rest of the day went very well indeed. After relishing the ambassador's embarrassed climb-down, Murray went off and, without explaining the circumstances, began by setting Fawcett the time-consuming and enormously tedious task of summarizing all the telegrams and internal embassy memoranda about German immigration policy over the last six months, to send to the Foreign Office to back up the Prime Minister's request for more information. He instructed Fawcett not to go home until he had finished. With that out of the way, Murray turned his attention to more mundane matters; the administration officer wanted to see him urgently about a variety of problems to do with accommodation and the re-roofing of an annexe, for which the German contractors were quoting exorbitant rates. Karen Deighton arrived to consult him on a tricky consular problem she was having, and a triumphant head of security, Mr Curran, came in to announce that at long last a supply of shiny new fire extinguishers had arrived. That latter fact briefly reminded Murray that he still had some research to do about his predecessor's sudden departure, coupled with the unexplained business of the office fire.

*   *   *

Weeks went by and Murray settled in well, eased on the home front by the excellent service he received from Frau Müller. He and Carol-Anne saw an increasing amount of each other, while taking considerable care to avoid flaunting their relationship. It was not that either of them had anything to hide, but they did not want to be considered an item, a partnership set in cement. From the moment he first met her, Murray realized that she was something of a coiled spring, camouflaged by an indefatigable American cheerfulness. She had opinions about everything and tried to elicit the same from him which he sometimes found somewhat exhausting, particularly since he had long become used to spending much of his private time with his mind in neutral. Those few who saw them together recognized, however, that the negatives of her spinsterhood were easily balanced by those of Murray's long-term bachelor state.

At the embassy, following the telegram from the Prime Minister and Murray's belated dispatch of an enormous bunch of flowers to Lady Cornwall, relations with Sir Edward were, if not in perfect harmony, at least reasonably smooth on the surface. The entire staff were also increasingly preoccupied with preparations for the forthcoming visit to Berlin by the British Foreign Secretary. He was due to arrive in mid-March to attend a NATO meeting, but because it was a major ministerial visit to the new seat of the German government there would be many bilateral implications as well. Murray set up a working party under the chairmanship of Fawcett to coordinate the detailed administrative arrangements. He expected that, as with all such complex visits, somewhere down the line something would be bound to go wrong, and Fawcett could swallow some of his own medicine.

That particular Tuesday morning Murray came in early to finish drafting a telegram to the Foreign Office reporting on the latest meeting of the NATO working group. The Germans and the Poles had come up with disturbing intelligence out of Moscow about political activists again fomenting trouble along the border. The NATO group decided to request Brussels for further military reinforcements to be placed on standby pending further monitoring of the situation as it developed.

It was just after eight-thirty when Sylvia Watt, followed closely by Curran, came bursting into his office.

'There's been some sort of break-in, Alex. The ambassador's office is in a bit of a mess. Somebody's been through all his papers and even forced open the steel drawers of his personal filing cabinet. He'll go stratospheric when he arrives,' said Sylvia grimly.

'Those bars and steel shutters – I warned London, sir, I did,' said Curran.

'Calm down, Mr Curran. How did they get in?' Murray started moving in the direction of the ambassador's office, intent on inspecting the damage for himself.

'Window's been forced on the ground floor at the back of the building. One of them what that I asked for bars for, sir.' Curran bristled with a mixture of bad grammar and righteous indignation.

'What action have you taken?' Murray demanded.

'Nothing so far, sir,' said Curran. He was almost standing at attention.

'The German police?' Murray asked. He realized what the response would be as soon as he had spoken.

'No way, sir. Diplomatic immunity and all that.'

'Quite right. And it's only the ambassador's office that's been touched?' Murray was more than a little curious. They reached the office as he spoke.

'As far as we can discover . . .' Sylvia Watt began.

'Identify anything missing?' Murray asked her.

'Can't see anything so far,' she responded cautiously. 'More a mess than anything else. All the *Secret* or *Confidential* files are locked away in the secure archives in the strongroom of course, so they're OK. The ambassador's mementos, silver-framed photographs and so on, seem all to be still here. I'll have to check with him, of course. I rang him first thing. He's on his way in now.'

84

'Silver frames, eh? What else would an intruder be looking for? Are you quite sure no other part of the building has been disturbed?' Murray pursued his point.

'Turned up nothing else, sir,' said Curran precisely. 'Dave, my deputy, is with Miss Deighton, checking the whole building right now.'

'One office? That strike you as odd, Mr Curran?' Murray asked. He was staring thoughtfully at the paper-strewn mess that faced him.

'Now that you mention it, sir,' replied the security officer.

At that moment the ambassador himself appeared. 'What the hell's going on?' he demanded. Sir Edward had obviously left home in a rush and was uncharacteristically dishevelled.

'Appear to have had a break-in, sir,' said Murray.

'I am aware of that, Alex.'

'I asked London for bars –' Curran began.

'I want a complete inventory of everything that's been disturbed. You coordinate that, Sylvia.' Sir Edward's eyes darted round the room. 'Strange. So far, I can't see a thing . . . God, look at that damned mess.' He stared down at the piles of paper and files strewn at random across the carpet in front of his filing cabinet.

Murray grabbed Curran by the shoulder and pulled him to one side. 'Keep everyone else out of this room, Mr Curran, and away from the window where the break-in was,' he hissed.

'Sir,' Curran nodded.

That afternoon, having overcome the ambassador's initial objections, the German police were notified, and a superintendent arrived at the embassy accompanied by a forensic expert, to test for fingerprints and take photographs of the window that had been forced on the ground floor. Sir Edward was adamant about preserving their embassy's diplomatic immunity; no German was to be allowed access to the ambassador's office, though he accepted that might have to come later.

'I don't like them being involved at all,' Sir Edward had protested. 'Diplomatic premises have very special privileges.

We don't want the Berlin authorities to think we're lax on security.'

'No, sir. But we have a duty to involve them in looking at *how* the culprit got in,' Murray argued. 'I've prepared a draft report for the Office and will add on anything that the police discover.'

Murray stayed with the German police until they had finished their investigations. They were as methodical and precise as he had expected; the superintendent was politely philosophical about not being allowed to investigate the scene in the ambassador's office. They took away the broken glass for their tests; they dusted the windowframe for fingerprints and took many photographs. When all the evidence had been scrutinized in the lab, the superintendent wasted no time and came to see Murray late that same day. They spoke German together.

'I have one part of your solution,' said the policeman, gravely.

'Yes?'

'There was no break-in.'

'Tell me,' said Murray quietly. He was not as surprised as he might have been.

'An inside job.' The German was clipped and precise. He had the photographs; he spoke rapidly, frequently referring to his notes. 'Conclusive evidence. An amateurish attempt has been made to make it appear as if somebody had come from outside. Everything else firmly indicates that whoever forced open that window – wearing domestic rubber gloves, we suspect – came at it from within the embassy building. For final confirmation of course we would have to make additional tests inside your building and in your ambassador's office. It is up to you . . .' The officer paused uncertainly, then shrugged. 'Quite apart from anything else, the way the broken glass was left lying around, and the amount left in the windowframe itself, means that it would have been almost impossible to climb in that way, without the intruder getting badly cut in the process.' The policeman's voice was authoritative and assured.

'Thank you, Superintendent. I'll take it from here.'

'Let us know, Herr Murray, if we can be of any further assistance,' the policeman said, then saluted, turned and left the embassy.

Murray quite deliberately withheld this new information both from the ambassador and from Curran, and instead summoned the MI6 station chief, Anthony Fox, and told him what the German policeman had said. They both agreed that they would have to act very quickly indeed.

5

The British armoured personnel carrier with its new green paint, its powerful caterpillar tracks, its Union Jack emblazoned front and rear, and its full complement of crew in their high-tech, padded helmets, complete with inbuilt microphones and head-phones, was one of the most advanced vehicles of its type. But on that tour of duty some of the heaviest armour-plating, which slowed down the vehicle enormously, had been stripped off, since the threat on that particular stretch of border was minimal.

An average night in the deepest mid-winter on the Polish–Belorussian border can deliver a pitiless temperature of minus fifteen degrees centigrade. The snow and the mist outside did not allow the soldiers to see further than about ten metres, but inside the vehicle an intelligence officer scanned a bank of monitors as a periscope-like lens on the roof slowly scoured the eastern horizon. The thermal imaging camera could pick up the warmth given off by a human body up to several miles away. So sensitive was it that at half a mile it could actually distinguish whether the person was male or female. Made by British Aerospace, it helped NATO provide a thermal curtain right along the border with the east, twenty-four hours a day, three hundred and sixty-five days a year. The technology was superb; human beings, however, are highly fallible.

With its engine still running, the APC came to a halt for two good reasons. One was because a large tree had been felled, partially blocking the border track ahead of the patrol, and the other was because Corporal Tate had eaten something that had seriously disagreed with him and he needed an emergency rest stop. He disappeared rapidly in among the pine trees just as the old peasant woman appeared. Shown up by the headlights, she was pulling a heavy sledge, piled high with anonymous bags, across the snow towards them. Had this been Londonderry or Sarajevo, the contingent would have been more alert. But here on the NATO border, any threat was not like that.

Inside the APC the intelligence officer frowned as he belatedly scrutinized the thermal image on the screen: no way was that a woman's body. *They have to be strong, these local women*, thought Sergeant Brace in a brief and futile moment of matching lucidity as he too peered at the figure from the vantage point of the observation hatch. He watched idly as the woman pulled the sledge close by the APC, wondering how long Corporal Tate's squits were going to delay their recce trip. He had a date with a German girl he had met in a *Gasthof* the other night. She had serious potential and he did not want to be late back at base.

Crouched low behind a bank amid the trees, Corporal Tate, with his immediate personal concerns, was only vaguely aware of the stooped peasant woman, until he noticed that figure suddenly straighten up, throw off the dark blanket it had been wearing, and a bearded young man in combat fatigues suddenly emerged and started running towards where the hidden corporal had just completed his intimate task.

It would have been impossible to guess who was more astonished. A huge explosion tossed the APC half into the air in a massive ball of fire that was silhouetted against the snow and the night sky. The young man, escaping from the destruction he had caused, was framed for an instant by the orange and yellow flames. The look of exultant excitement on his face vanished as he was unexpectedly confronted by a British army corporal, one hand desperately pulling up his trousers, the other holding an automatic pistol. That weapon immediately blazed away in fear and fury at the terrified young man until he crumpled forward and lay in a writhing, hideous, bleeding heap less than a yard away from where Corporal Tate stood. White-faced and shaking, the latter paused for only a moment, before turning and plunging into the safety of the undergrowth. He had served in those two cesspits of religious sectarianism, Bosnia and Ulster. He knew a successful ambush when he saw one, and he was quite determined to live to tell the tale.

A full twelve hours elapsed before the BBC World Service newscaster, his voice as passionless and as authoritative as always, announced: 'Reports are coming in about a serious incident involving NATO forces on the Polish–Belorussian border. European foreign ministers, currently meeting in Brussels, have expressed their outrage and have demanded an urgent report . . .'

From the low ceiling of the dank, dismal cellar, drips of condensation drained in dirty brown rivulets down the once whitewashed walls. Why was it always so cold? Why could they not find some decent heating? If this really was to be a modern, vibrant party, leading the new Russia, surely they could drum up sufficient money to set themselves up in more prepossessing surroundings. Why did Vladimir always want to meet down here, like some leader of a secret revolution?

This time he did not have to wait long for Vladimir. The leader arrived only a few minutes late; the ten men and two women already gathered round the long deal table stood out of respect as he came down the concrete steps and strutted into the cellar. Today he was sober. Today he was in a good mood, smiling deliberately, walking round the whole room, shaking hands with everyone. He wanted everyone on his side. This was to be a key strategy meeting. The agenda: how should they, the National Party of Russia, under Vladimir's charismatic leadership, use the starving masses encamped along the border for their immediate political ends?

How different it had all seemed all those years ago back in London, as Ivan or Ian had monitored, with increasing excitement, the rapid changes in the Soviet Union that had followed the Chernobyl catastrophe. That disastrous leak from the nuclear reactor was, in its deathly way, a trigger both for *glasnost* and for *perestroika*. When that nuclear contamination floated across many national frontiers, the leaders of the Soviet

Union, faced with the fury of those democratic nations, had at long last to come clean about what was going on. Chernobyl released Mikhail Gorbachev from the rigid secrecy of past habit, and allowed him to exert his growing influence. A new, more vulnerable and unstable image of Russia was rapidly exposed to an astonished outside world. That unstoppable flow of information began to do what the massed western armies had signally failed to do for four long decades: to force the Soviet state to relinquish its steel-clad hold over its rotting empire. High hope was in the air.

Against the background of these ever-accelerating events, Ian Carter, now increasingly slipping in and out of his dual role as Ivan Katerski, and inspired and encouraged by his new-found friend, Professor Dimitri Platov, grew more and more excited by the news from eastern Europe. Even the most far-seeing Kremlin watchers could not believe that the end of communism was nigh, but here, surely, were the cracks that might usher in some new beginning. In personal terms, this was an opportunity for Ivan to throw off convention and find his destiny. In his British career, he knew what he had achieved. He had found success, he had so much money that he had even bought, from an extra bonus he had just received, the flashiest of flashy Ferraris. He was an extremely eligible bachelor, and women fell over themselves to fall into his bed. Yet increasingly he dreamed of new horizons in a barren land of which he knew so little.

Perhaps he would have left it as a dream had not Professor Platov been there to inspire him. One night, the latter bluntly proposed that he ought to go on a fact-finding trip to Moscow, to see what was going on. He might pick up a few contacts, particularly in nationalist circles, since events were beginning to look as if they might herald not just the end of communism, but also of the Gorbachev era itself. Platov played cleverly on his idealism and emotions. He thought about it overnight, then rang the professor to tell him that, at last, he had found a proper purpose to his life.

That was then; this was now. Looking back, he marvelled

at how easily, on that first trip, he had been able to engineer a face-to-face meeting with Vladimir. Ian, Ivan, had offered his services, his contacts, his enthusiasms, even some money. Vladimir had taken the lot, recognizing the use that this young, idealistic westerner might be to his long-term cause. And now he was stuck in this vile, freezing basement, with a dozen fellow-conspirators, listening to the leader telling them what would, what must happen. How different it had all seemed then. Gradually his naivety, his expectations, his hopes were eroded, to be replaced by all the gritty realities of modern Russia. He soon came face to face with the corruption and the political idiocy that swept the country, all too quickly replacing the unlamented past. But somehow Vladimir appeared to rise above it and to offer him an honourable, noble alternative to fuel his dreams.

Which was why, in this dismal cellar, it all seemed so worthwhile once again. Why? Because as soon as the charismatic Vladimir rose to his feet, talking, exhorting, explaining how he was going to continue to build up tensions on the border to help the cause, Ivan Katerski found himself swept up once more in the great wave of enthusiasm that gripped each and every man and woman in that cold, bare room.

Paul Fawcett came into Murray's room on the way to the ambassador's morning meeting. 'There's been a minor incident on the Polish–Russian border,' he said breathlessly.

'Incident, Paul?' asked Alex.

'Five British soldiers, part of the NATO forces, blown up in a bomb attack.'

'You call that minor, Paul?' asked Alex, looking up at him.

'You know what I mean, Alex. It's not actually World War Three, is it?' Fawcett shrugged and glanced at his watch. They were going to be late for the ambassador.

Murray stared uncomprehendingly at Fawcett, then led him out of the room in the direction of the ambassador's office. It wouldn't be minor as far as those soldiers' relatives were concerned.

Sir Edward Cornwall's attention, like Fawcett's, was concentrated on other, more local matters. 'Are you fully up to date on the Plenzdorf case, Alex?' he asked abruptly. It was the weekly coordination meeting and Murray was seated at the table in the ambassador's office flanked by Fawcett, Brigadier Dicks and Anthony Fox. It was the day after the so-called break-in and everything had already been put back in meticulous order, as if nothing had happened.

'I've seen the most recent report, sir,' said Murray. 'Archives are digging around for the rest.'

'You better get a move on,' said the ambassador. 'I'm convinced it's going to erupt. Brigadier, why don't you take us through the story from the beginning, please?'

'I thought you'd want to hear about that very nasty incident on the Polish –' the brigadier began.

'First things first, please,' responded the ambassador testily. He had his agenda and he was going to stick to it.

Brigadier Dicks spoke rather ponderously, like a policeman giving evidence in court. 'Colonel Plenzdorf, once a wartime SS *Oberleutnant*, long stood accused of having ordered the massacre of over eighty British prisoners of war in a barn in Normandy, shortly after Dunkirk. It breached every term of the Geneva Convention. Only a couple of survivors were left to tell the tale. For years the story was forgotten about, but recently, Plenzdorf, now in his late eighties, was discovered living on the outskirts of Hamburg and the whole thing has flared up again in a big way. Photographs of him trying to hide from reporters have appeared in the British press and there now is a permanent contingent of journalists camped outside his house. The *Mail* tracked down one of the survivors, who gave them an exclusive: he told the story in graphic detail of how they had been herded into the barn which was bolted and locked and then the whole thing was set on fire. Those who tried to flee were blown to bits with grenades or shot dead as they ran away.'

When the brigadier had finished his summary, Murray asked, 'Are we certain that's what happened?'

'As sure as we can be. There are discrepancies in some of the witnesses' statements, but a former SS corporal, who was under Plenzdorf's command, has sworn an affidavit to the effect that it's all basically true.'

'Back to the age-old quandary: unearth the past or leave it buried. My own option would be to –' Fox began.

He was interrupted by the ambassador. 'Our business is keeping Anglo–German relations on the best possible footing. This one will fester until it's dealt with. We're going to have to force the issue with the German Foreign Ministry and get Plenzdorf brought to trial as soon as possible. Now they've got their teeth into it, the British tabloids won't leave this one alone.'

For once Murray found himself agreeing with Sir Edward. Whatever HMG's views, the inevitable pressures in the media would lead to questions in the House of Commons, and demands for rapid government action.

Fox again briefly attempted to argue the case for delay. 'What good will it do?' he began. 'If, as you say, sir, our job is to promote good Anglo–German relations, then stirring up this – I'm sorry to say – relatively minor historical incident, involving a frail, geriatric man, is hardly going to warm up our mutual regard for each other.'

'I hear what you say, Anthony,' said the ambassador, 'but I'm afraid you misjudge the ability of Her Majesty's Government to withstand a concerted media outcry. Number Ten govern by reacting to what they think tomorrow's headlines are going to be, even at the best of times.'

'I'll put a call through to Otto Klingenfeldt. Talk it through with him this afternoon if he's free,' volunteered Murray.

'Good idea. Keep me up to date,' responded Sir Edward, for once showing appreciation of Murray's suggestion.

'Stress that it's really more his problem than ours,' added Murray thoughtfully.

'Good approach, Alex,' Sir Edward added. They were the very first words of praise he had offered his deputy in all the weeks since his arrival.

After the meeting, Fox and Murray retired to the latter's office to discuss the break-in. 'You're playing a dangerous game, Alex. Why have you delayed telling the ambassador what the police said?'

Fox was curious. Behind that cold exterior, there beat, as someone once had said of him, a heart of ice. Fox's surface charm could be switched on at will, all part of the act that comprised much of his work. Good intelligence operatives like him had skins like an onion: the more that was peeled away the more the tears came. Fox would have made a good apparatchik if he had been born in another time and place. He usually seemed emotionally neutral. This time his concern was beginning to show.

Murray trod carefully. 'I'm beginning to know His Excellency. He'll dispute it out of hand without proof. You and I need to try to identify the culprit before we go to him. Don't worry, he's off to Hamburg until the day after tomorrow. I'll tell him then if we haven't come up with something.'

'How are your investigations going?' asked Fox. He gave no sign of either approving or disapproving of Murray's tactics.

'Quite a long way,' responded Murray quietly. 'Sylvia Watt has become quite an ally. She's gone through all the ambassador's personal possessions and *objets d'art* that were lying around his office. The old man already had an inventory and not one thing is missing. Strange, isn't it? Next we went through every paper and file together.'

'And?' Fox looked across enquiringly at his colleague.

'One thing out of place. A red folder of confidential personnel department letters to and from him, on senior staff like you and me, ones too sensitive to be kept by administration. It could have been gone through.'

'Ah,' breathed Fox. 'You think I can help?'

'You have means of telling whether a sealed envelope has been tampered with?' Murray thought he knew the answer.

'You wouldn't expect me to admit to anything like that, would you?' responded Fox with a wisp of a smile.

'Not asking for anything special.' Murray paused, opened the top drawer of his desk and produced a large brown envelope, and handed it over. 'This one. Have your guys look at it. Tell me what you think.'

'May be difficult.'

'I expect it will,' said Murray softly.

Diplomacy is often like bartering. One factor in international relations is played off against another; a subtle and unspoken weighing of advantage and disadvantage goes on all the time. To help this process, before Murray went off to see Klingenfeldt, the brigadier came in to remind him that the UK defence procurement company, the Strad Corporation, was in the middle of brokering a major deal between one of the big German communications firms and the RAF, for a new advanced air defence system. Lord Simms, the chairman of Strad, had only recently been on the phone to the ambassador to lobby him for his support.

'When you see Klingenfeldt,' said the brigadier with a grin, 'you could always drop a hint that the British government, particularly the boys at the Ministry of Defence who have to approve the deal, will be much less sympathetic to the German bid if the Plenzdorf matter isn't resolved one way or another.'

'Hardly in the same league. Germans won't like the implied threat.' Murray shrugged. He was far from convinced.

'Since when did that matter in international diplomacy?' the brigadier responded.

'OK, if it comes up, I'll ensure Klingenfeldt grasps the potential linkage,' said Murray reluctantly. He had too many other things on the go to play games like this.

Klingenfeldt received Murray with his customary charm. They sat facing each other, sipping cups of well-brewed coffee, keeping the main issue until the last. 'You had a break-in at the embassy, I hear,' the German began.

'Well-informed as always, Otto. Yes . . . thought we did, anyway. Your police believe it could be an inside job. We're working hard on that. It has serious implications.' Murray suddenly felt very worried: Klingenfeldt knew all about it, yet he still hadn't told his own ambassador about the police superintendent's suspicions.

Klingenfeldt smiled politely. 'Do keep me informed. We have to make sure our diplomatic guests are well protected. Now, what else was it . . . ?'

'It's touch-and-go over whether Germany wins that RAF radar contract.' Murray gently wheeled into attack mode. 'The Strad people are getting nervous.'

'I guessed you might say that.' Klingenfeldt's smile remained enigmatic.

'We're in the same game, Otto?' Murray grinned back.

'We are.'

'So you know what other matter I am going to raise?' Murray looked across expectantly.

'Another part of the Anglo–German diplomatic balance sheet? Yes, I believe I can guess. The Plenzdorf case? His house is besieged by British journalists.'

'And Germans, and French.'

'They've got their story.' Klingenfeldt's smile had suddenly completely disappeared. He stared down at his hands which were clasped together in front of him as if in prayer.

'What d'you mean, Otto?'

'I trust the radar deal will go through unhindered.'

'I'm sorry. You've lost me.' Murray was genuinely puzzled. 'If we don't get some rapid movement – '

'Rapid? Colonel Plenzdorf shot himself this morning,' Klingenfeldt interrupted softly. 'That term "balance sheet", Alex. In the end he may have done his country a service.'

The day ended well for Murray. Coincidentally, an advance party from the Foreign Office's inspection team had arrived and was firmly installed in the embassy, going through papers and files, checking on work-loads, preparing time and motion studies, working out, for the benefit of the Treasury, where staffing levels might be adjusted, which, in practice, meant cut. Murray and his staff were plunged into preparing the briefing material for them but he kept being interrupted by the ambassador who rang from Hamburg wanting to know how the inspection was progressing.

'No cuts, Alex. Do you understand?' said the disapproving voice at the far end of the line.

'You've made that absolutely clear, sir.'

'Briefed all the staff accordingly?' Sir Edward persisted.

'As instructed, sir.'

'If they and Treasury get really nasty, have we anyone we could throw to the wolves? As a last resort?'

There was a pause as Murray thought about it. 'An assistant military attaché; number three in the cultural section? Nobody from chancery,' he volunteered.

'I should damn well hope not. What about consular section?'

'Karen Deighton and her staff are very overworked as it is,' responded Murray. 'No question of cutting commercial section, you'll agree, sir? Every resource goes to industry these days. If they actually asked for *more* staff they'd probably get them.'

'Which leaves admin?' The ambassador waited for his deputy's response.

'Let me think about that, sir. I'll have a view by the time you get back,' said Murray reflectively. He believed he might have the solution.

Certain problems in life have a way of sorting themselves out. Anthony Fox came to Murray just as he was leaving for the night, with clear evidence that the envelope had indeed been tampered with. He gave the details, clinically and without emotion. The sealed brown envelope had definitely been opened and badly stuck together again. The metal staple holding the papers it contained had also been removed and replaced. Fox hadn't had the resources locally to check for fingerprints, but suggested that it might not be necessary. He went on to give his verdict; the envelope had almost certainly contained a highly sensitive report, written by Murray's predecessor, Douglas Young, on Peter Bennett, the administration officer. Young had suspected that Bennett had been dipping into the embassy travel account for which he had responsibility. Some six months previously, with Fox present, Young had privately confronted Bennett, who had vehemently denied the allegations. Because the amounts of money were small, Young had decided to take no further action but none the less had, Fox guessed, put a record of his suspicions on Bennett's file, in the sealed brown envelope. Then Young himself had upped and left and no one else had followed it up. The envelope now only contained Bennett's CV. The incriminating report was missing.

'Are you certain there was such a report?' Murray asked.

'I'd be in the wrong business if I wasn't,' came the enigmatic reply. 'For all his sins, Young confided in me.'

'Are you going to tell me about Young's sins?' Murray ventured. Fox merely smiled and shook his head.

Anxious to get the solution to the ambassador as soon as he returned from Hamburg, Murray wasted no further time, and had Bennett, a scruffy little man who always looked as if he could do with a good bath, wheeled into his office. He did not beat about the bush.

'Been talking to the police about the break-in, Peter,' Murray began deliberately, staring hard at the admin officer.

'Any news?' asked Bennett. He looked flustered and shifty, realizing that this must be a serious interview.

'Good news and bad news. Good news for the embassy, bad news for you.' Murray opted for the up-front approach. Fox might just have got it wrong, but it was worth the risk. 'We know it wasn't a break-in, don't we, Peter?' he continued. 'We both know who needed to get at one of H.E.'s confidential files. I suggest that unless you've got anything to say, you go now and pack your bags. I want you out of the embassy and on the plane to London within twelve hours.'

Bennett's response took Murray by surprise. He looked deeply shocked for a moment, then pulled himself together rapidly. 'I don't believe you can have put this to the ambassador,' he said in a low voice that trembled with emotion. 'I don't think, knowing what I do about the Douglas Young affair . . . and the fire for that matter . . .' he looked around Murray's office as he spoke as if looking for any remaining signs of damage, 'that he'll want me to go off to London and tell everyone just what's been going on out here.'

Later that evening, after the ambassador had been told the whole story and had coolly informed his deputy that he had decided to suspend Bennett rather than send him home, a furious Murray went and confronted Fox.

'For Christ's sake, if Bennett gets away with this . . .' he began. He was deeply troubled by what was going on. 'What the hell was Douglas Young up to, Anthony? What's the hold?'

'Ah,' responded Fox enigmatically. 'That's quite a story.'

'I'm not going to let go this time, Anthony. I want to know what happened.'

'Ask the Old Man,' Fox shrugged and looked away.

'I will. But I'm asking you first. I want everything out in the open.'

'OK, you really ought to be told,' came the curiously evasive reply. 'I'll just have to clear it, then I'll be back to you.'

Reports from the eastern borders were getting grimmer by the day. One night, a long stretch of razor-wire fence was pulled down, and several hundred more refugees swarmed through. The Poles, backed by NATO troops, had quickly rounded them up and forcibly repatriated them. The press were quickly on to the story, but despite their strident protests, they were not allowed to get close enough to the action to get tear-jerking pictures of starving families being driven at bayonet point on to their buses and back into their refugee camps, by the neatly uniformed armed forces of the western democracies.

'It's just the beginning,' Murray reported to the ambassador. 'That's now our NATO working group's unanimous view.'

'The Polish government won't be able to keep the media away for ever,' said Sir Edward. 'Stifling democratic freedom and so on.'

'The working group's meeting again in half an hour,' Murray said, looking at his watch. 'We've been in almost permanent session, with breaks only for meals. There's no doubt in our minds that the bomb attack that killed the British soldiers was deliberately planned to increase tensions – and it's succeeded in that, but we still don't know who . . .' He paused. 'I'm not sure, sir, whether we're working at a high enough level. All we do is make recommendations. Would you consider calling an emergency meeting of western ambassadors?'

'Certainly,' said the ambassador, relishing the action. 'No need to cancel your own meeting, though. And don't get a fraction out of step with the thinking back in Brussels, especially with the Secretary of State arriving so soon.'

'Sir.'

'For that visit we want no problems. I rely on you, Alex.'

'The embassy press officer is briefing the media that we're in continuous session. News of lots of activity behind the scenes gives them something to write about.' Murray stood to leave.

'And,' added the ambassador, 'with all your other preoccupations, Alex, don't take your eyes off those damn inspectors.'

'No way,' said Murray. 'Oh, one more thing, sir. Can I ask about the Bennett–Young link? Just what happened to –' As he spoke, Murray was aware that the ambassador had turned his head away as if to hide his reaction.

'Leave that alone, Alex,' said Sir Edward firmly, without looking at him. 'You've got quite enough to be going on with.'

Henry Kissinger once remarked that there couldn't be an international crisis next week since his diary was already full. Amusing as that sounded, it is a feature of diplomacy that problems tend to hunt in packs. It seemed like a small incident at the time. The consulate was closed for the day, and so the stooping, elderly Jew, a Mr Jacobs, in his long frock coat and black Homburg hat, accompanied by his pretty granddaughter, turned up instead at the main entrance to the embassy. Another man, who had accompanied them to the door, waited discreetly outside. The old man went in and presented himself to the security guard at the desk. Mr Curran was not a sympathetic man at the best of times and did not like what he saw. He was abrupt. No, the embassy could not help. No, there was no one available who could see him. The visitor could come back tomorrow and talk to the consul if he wished. The embassy was a busy place. Mr Curran more or less pushed the elderly Jew and his granddaughter out of the door. Thereby a number of mistakes were made. Curran, watching suspiciously from the doorway, saw the couple being joined by the other man who had been waiting for them on the doorstep. Curran thought he recognized the latter, and for a moment a flicker of anxiety triggered something at the back of the security guard's unimaginative mind. But he was heavily preoccupied in supervising the workmen who were fitting bars to all the downstairs windows, and so it was not until very much later that he realized the full significance of what he had done.

That other man was one of Fred Cree's press colleagues, a local Brit who acted as a stringer for the *Mirror*. He was covering Mr Jacobs' campaign to reclaim certain family properties that had been sequestered by the Nazis. Under recent German legislation it had become somewhat easier to process such claims, and one or two prominent court cases that had ended satisfactorily for the claimants had been widely reported in the press. Mr Jacobs was in possession of title deeds which appeared to prove that his family had once owned a large house in the Charlottenburg district of Berlin. It had been forcibly expropriated after *Kristallnacht*, when as a young boy he had only just managed to escape with his father and mother. The rest of his family were presumed to have perished in the concentration camps. The house had been seized, first by the Nazis, then, after the war, by the East German authorities, and for years it had served as a hostel for young people. Now, ironically, it was temporary home to a group of Turkish immigrant families. In trying to press his particular claim, Mr Jacobs had so far received little help from the German authorities and he had consequently arrived at the embassy looking for British support. The *Mirror*'s correspondent had his story. Was anti-Semitism alive and well at the British Embassy, or was it pure incompetence? The next day the tabloid ran the story all over its front page. Because the granddaughter was very pretty, there was a particularly heart-rending photograph of her standing forlornly outside the embassy gates. The planned apologies, including a personal letter to Mr Jacobs from the ambassador, might well have killed the story, had not the door and walls of the disputed property in Charlottenburg been daubed overnight with red painted swastikas. Whether they were directed at the Turkish occupants or the putative Jewish owner, no one knew. But as a picture story it provided further highly emotive material.

The ambassador was apoplectic. 'You mean to tell me that this man was turned away at the door? Why the hell wasn't he seen?'

'I've interviewed Mr Curran. He's deeply troubled, sir. Realizes he should have referred Mr Jacobs to someone senior. He said that the man didn't fully explain himself. All he said was to come back the next day and see the consul. He now admits he thought he recognized that journalist standing outside with Jacobs and his granddaughter.'

'Haven't the security guards got full instructions on how to handle visitors?'

'Of course, sir,' said Murray.

'Then why the hell did that idiot . . . ?' The ambassador paced angrily round the room as he spoke.

'If you don't mind, sir. The damage is done. I'll deal with Curran later. What we have to do is to contain matters before the Foreign Secretary arrives tomorrow or it'll run and run. I've left a message for Mr Jacobs at his hotel. I'll try to deliver your letter to him personally.'

'All far too bloody late.'

'We'll be seen trying to make amends,' said Murray hopefully.

'That's what the Germans always say,' said the ambassador drily.

When the Foreign Secretary stepped off his official RAF VC10 the following morning, he looked confident and relaxed. By the time he had been bombarded with dozens of questions about the Jacobs story from the undisciplined press that were waiting to greet him at the VIP suite, he was far from pleased. The embassy had requested minimum fuss so there was no guard of honour drawn up at Tegel Airport, just a team of protocol people from the German Foreign Ministry to bring the impromptu press conference to an end after a bad-tempered twenty minutes, smooth out the other formalities, and direct the Foreign Secretary and his team to their motorcade. Murray felt that the Foreign Secretary, an arid man with piercing blue eyes and arrogantly dismissive style, made Sir Edward Cornwall appear rather warm and cuddly by comparison. After the mauling from the journalists, he was glad that there was no room in the minister's Mercedes for him as well. The ambassador took the can, and what he had to put up with in the motorcade, Murray had thrown at him later when they all arrived back at the embassy.

'He's seething. Absolutely bloody furious,' said Sir Edward, who looked much the same. 'Here he comes on this major visit to Berlin, with a huge work-load to get through on the NATO front, and all the bloody press are interested in is the Jacobs case.'

'Human interest stories always get top billing, even in the broadsheets,' said Murray acidly. 'Course we could easily drive Jacobs' beautiful granddaughter off the front pages if we gave the press access to cover what's going on over on the Polish border. Plenty of poignant scenes there. They'd be out of our hair in a flash.'

'Thanks for nothing, Alex,' barked the ambassador. 'Have you seen Jacobs?'

'I've apologized to him on the telephone. He's had your letter and was perfectly polite about it, but he refused to see me. Said there was no point. He knows we've got the Foreign Ministry working overtime on his case. Their lawyers have, miraculously, managed to trace most of the relevant papers. They're trying to avoid him having to go through the German courts. That way, it could take years and the old man knows he would probably be dead before the whole thing was settled. We can't fault the Ministry on speed. The only real problem we're left with is the impression we gave that we were indifferent when he turned up. Our statement saying it was all a misunderstanding, that we're working hard on his behalf behind the scenes, etcetera, is OK, but, as always, apologies don't make headlines.'

'Get a bloody grip, Alex. You're responsible for Curran and his staff. You're responsible for the way visitors are received.' The ambassador needed to explode at someone. 'I get it in the neck from the Foreign Secretary so I'm going to sit on your neck till you get this embassy working much, much better than it has been ever since you turned up here. Get Karen Deighton up to see me straight away. Perhaps she can sort this mess out.'

'Sir, she's up to her eyes in meetings with the Berlin police over Saturday.'

'What Saturday?' Sir Edward was temporarily puzzled.

'The football match, sir,' said Murray, wondering in what ivory tower the ambassador lived. 'We're about to be engulfed by thousands of English football fans and a supporting cast of beer-swilling, tattooed thugs.'

'Jeez . . . I'd quite forgotten,' said the ambassador turning a little pale. 'Thank God the secretary of state will have gone . . .'

Throughout his professional career Murray had found that diplomatic solutions usually emerged from within the embassy itself. In this case, however, it was when he got back to his apartment and was putting his feet up, intending to catch up on the British newspapers, and enjoying a well-filled tumbler of whisky, that Frau Müller appeared at the door and coughed discreetly.

'Yes, Frau Müller?' He spoke to her, as always, in German.

'Forgive me, sir. I hear you have a problem concerning Mr Jacobs.'

'It's all over the press, Frau Müller. Taken up a lot of time. We weren't trying to be unhelpful. It's hit us at a bad time, with the Foreign Secretary here.'

'I understand, Herr Murray. My husband, before he died, was a civil servant. I know about bureaucracies. Truth and the story that hits the newspapers are not always the same, are they, Herr Murray?'

Murray stood up awkwardly, clutching his whisky glass. In his brief experience of Frau Müller, this was a surprisingly extended conversation. He asked what she was driving at.

'It's like this, Herr Murray, and I apologize for bothering you. It's that . . .' she paused. 'Mr Jacobs and my husband used to correspond over the years. My husband was partly Jewish, you see. His mother was ethnic German, so he didn't have too much of a problem during the war. He did, however, feel responsible for so many things. You know what it's like . . .'

'You *know* Mr Jacobs?'

'If I arranged for you to meet, I'm sure something could be worked out.'

Murray placed a hand round her shoulder. 'You are very astute, Frau Müller,' he said. 'Please . . .'

Late that night, following an amicable drink with Murray at his hotel, Jacobs personally rang Reuters and issued a statement in which he declared himself fully satisfied with the actions that the British Embassy were taking on his behalf. By midnight, the ambassador was mollified and that particular crisis looked as if it was almost over. But in the life of a busy embassy, problems never come singly, particularly with the media pack in hunting mode.

The secretary of state's concluding press conference was held the following day in a crowded conference hall in the chancery. Half a dozen television crews and thirty or forty other assorted journalists and photographers were crammed in around the room. The secretary of state sat at a raised table, the ambassador on one side of him and the head of the Foreign and Commonwealth Office news department on the other. Murray watched anxiously from the wings.

As soon as he had read out his prepared statement about his visit, the minister faced an expected barrage of questions on the Jacobs case. He waited until there was silence.

'I'm delighted to say that it has been satisfactorily resolved. By now you should have seen Mr Jacobs' own statement on this matter. The German authorities have worked very hard on the case over the last twenty-four hours, and, depending on a final judgement from their legal department, the ownership of the property appears not to be in question. Additionally . . .' He paused and looked around. 'I am happy to tell you that the ambassador and Mr Murray have personally apologized to Mr Jacobs and his granddaughter for the rather cavalier treatment they received the other day. It was a misunderstanding on the part of a very junior member of the embassy staff. He too has apologized directly to those concerned.'

'That will take the wind out of it,' thought Murray. It did. Some journalists looked disappointed. They had come ready for blood. They turned to the much bigger news item, the refugees massed on the border, but on that there was so little to go on and no pictures or TV footage. No lenses, no story.

'Can you comment, Secretary of State, on unconfirmed reports that a large group of Russian and Ukrainian refugees, including several hundred women and children, broke through into Poland some time over the last few days, and were driven back by force, by armed NATO troops?' asked the man from *The Times*. 'The incident is said to have taken place near the town of Przemysl.'

The secretary of state, hoping he might get away with it, tried an anodyne reply. 'There are frequent incidents involving illegal immigrants – I am not sure to which one you – '

Fred Cree was already on his feet. 'Minister, does HMG support the Polish authorities in enforcing a rigid press exclusion zone in the border area close to what is increasingly becoming known as NATO's new Iron Curtain?'

'I refuse to accept any comparison with the Iron Curtain,' said the secretary of state with a decided lack of conviction. 'National security in any border area is a sensitive issue. Customs and immigration officials must be free to carry out their often difficult tasks away from the public gaze, for the sake of the would-be immigrants as well. We, as NATO members, are trying to help control events and not inflame them. HMG fully supports the Polish – '

'With respect, this isn't the odd illegal immigrant,' Cree interrupted the minister. 'Why are you, why is NATO, conspiring to keep the press away if there's nothing to hide?'

'I repeat: a tense situation prevails along several borders at present. We do not wish to do anything . . . I understand that the Polish Government does not wish to do anything . . .' he corrected himself precisely, 'to further exacerbate the . . . er . . . highly volatile conditions that – '

'You mean that if the press and television could record the brutalities being perpetrated on defenceless, starving men, women and children, there would be a widespread public outcry?' Cree was again on his feet, scenting blood. His questions met with varying degrees of approval from the other media people present.

The secretary of state flushed. He seemed surprisingly unprepared for such aggressive questioning. 'I can assure you, I and my NATO colleagues are not treating this situation lightly. You must realize the enormous difficulties involved. We in the West, along with the Red Cross and other non-governmental agencies, already supply most of the food to sustain these people where they are. HMG's view, the unanimous view of NATO members, including Poland, is that it is far better to look after them in their countries of origin, than to take any action, or lack of it, that might merely lead to setting up vast refugee camps over here.'

'Why?' asked another journalist, pertinently.

'If you start, where do you stop?' The minister was now getting angry. 'You'll have millions of people camped semi-permanently in the West. HMG has every sympathy with the German and Polish Governments – '

'So all Europe is doing is what it did all along in Bosnia: sitting on its butt, wringing its hands in despair?' suggested a belligerent CBS correspondent.

'It's all very well for America to –' The secretary of state spotted that he was on a potentially slippery slope and checked himself. 'Europe's problems are the world's problems. We need to try to remove the root causes of such attempts at economic migration. We need to tackle the problem at source. The Russian Government are at one with us on that.'

'Are you sure, Minister?' asked another journalist cheekily. 'We hear stories that the Kremlin is not doing anything on their side of the fence because it puts more pressure on western governments to provide even more financial and food aid. And it defuses the pressures the Kremlin cabal are under from extremists like Vladimir.'

The secretary of state moved into full non-committal mode, but questioning on similar terms went on for about ten minutes until the head of news department, who was looking increasingly unhappy, on a signal from the minister, insisted on a change of subject. And change it did.

'What arrangements have the English and Berlin authorities made to ward off potential trouble with the influx of fans coming here for the match on Saturday?' asked the *Sun*'s correspondent.

The secretary of state produced a thin smile. 'I'm delighted to be able to pass that question to the ambassador.'

Sir Edward looked grave. 'We are, as always, in the closest possible touch with the German authorities. As some of you may know, British police representatives are already here to help identify those who may be bent on causing trouble. The embassy is particularly concerned by reports in some newspapers of links between English neo-fascist fans, if I can call them fans, and young Germans of similar persuasion.'

'Were attempts made behind the scenes to ban English fans from coming?' asked another journalist.

'No such request was made via the British Embassy,' said Sir Edward evenly. 'It would be a retrograde step for the British or German Governments to involve themselves in what must be a decision for the respective football authorities.'

'Is the British Consulate on standby to deal with the inevitable arrests?' Another journalist pressed the point.

'Many of you know Miss Deighton. I have the fullest confidence in her ability to handle the situation.' Sir Edward was particularly courteous and smooth.

'Are you worried about the bad image this gives Britain?' a German journalist asked.

The ambassador measured his words. 'I'm always alert to anything that might harm Britain's image. Sadly, certain so-called soccer fans have not been our best emissaries in recent years. I can only hope that the event will pass off peacefully as befits a purely sporting occasion.'

The Foreign Secretary stood up and addressed the press corps with a few final, practised words. 'I am conscious that the forthcoming football match is a game of sport. I only hope, though England's recent record has not been a good one, that we will win here on Saturday.' With that, and forced smiles all round, the press conference was over.

Later the ambassador took Murray aside. 'I completely ad-libbed on the football question. Is everything in hand?'

'Karen tells me the Germans won't stand for any nonsense. Riot police with dogs – the lot.' Murray shrugged.

'Very unpleasant,' said Sir Edward waspishly. 'Will you be going?'

'I'm not a spectator, sir.'

'Some of us ought to be there.'

'I believe Brigadier Dicks and Bobby Sofer are going. Will that do?' asked Murray.

'I'll take my phone off the hook for the weekend,' Sir Edward said, then added, 'I suppose a soccer game is marginally better than World War Three.'

'I'll only trouble you with a real crisis,' Murray responded with something approaching a smile.

As it happened, the gods were kind to Anglo–German relations, to the consul and to her long-suffering staff at the British Embassy. On the morning prior to the match, Berlin was hit by one of the worst blizzards in years. Both Tempelhof and Tegel airports were closed. The bulk of the fans were left stranded in Britain; the England team got through, however, and the Germans worked hard to clear the pitch, since a match postponement would have caused considerable upset. In the event, the handful of England supporters present were subdued by the bitter cold. The match ended in a draw, there were no arrests to speak of, and the ever-vigilant foreign press corps were denied another story. It was one small piece of good news for the Berlin Embassy in a sea of bad.

Almost a week later, in the aftermath of a long, tempestuous evening spent in the company of Carol-Anne, Murray was less than alert when the ambassador woke him from a deep sleep at around six-thirty in the morning.

'Get in here as soon as possible,' he said. 'One hell of a serious problem's blown up and I need your help. Pull Bobby Sofer in as well.'

'Can I ask . . . ?' Murray began sleepily. Apart from needing more sleep, the only serious problem he knew about was the Russian refugee threat and the fact that there was to be a crisis meeting at the Foreign Ministry at ten that morning.

'When you get in,' Sir Edward said curtly, then put the phone down.

Murray woke Sofer. The commercial counsellor was more alert. 'Ah. So it's broken at last,' said the calm voice at the other end of the telephone.

'Enlighten me,' said Murray. 'Never known the Old Man so jumpy. War broken out, has it?'

'War's not my department. My guess: the Scase affair.'

'Lost me,' said Murray.

'Heard of Sir Randall Scase?' responded Sofer. 'Rumours floating around for a long time. Insider dealing case I mentioned.'

'Why's the ambassador so steamed up?' Murray stifled a yawn and looked longingly at his crumpled bed.

'Old friend, that's why. They hunt together. Tell you the rest when we meet.'

When Murray arrived at the chancery half an hour later, Sofer was standing waiting for him at the doorway. 'H.E.'s already here,' he said. 'Yes, it's the Scase case.'

'What does he want? What's it to do with us, with Germany?' Murray asked. 'Can't he ever get his priorities straight? There are real crises to be dealt with.'

'All will become clear,' said Sofer with a grin. 'For the record, I'm told Sir Randall's as guilty as hell.'

The two men sat in silence, watching as the ambassador paced around his study. 'I've known Randall for forty years. As honest and honourable as I am,' he said. 'I cannot believe . . .'

Sir Edward Cornwall's vices he perceived as virtues. His tunnel-visioned focus on the minor at the expense of the substantial blinkered him in everything he did. He would have objected strongly if accused of ignoring what was going on at the Polish frontier, and indeed Murray knew that he read the reports and telegrams on that subject assiduously. But when it came to the pecking order of a day's action, the minutiae of protocol and placement, of who was to sit where at his glittering dinner table that night, came first. And when a rich and important friend such as Sir Randall Scase was involved, his potential fate, headline-grabbing though it might become, took precedence over the plight of a million predatory refugees from the Wild East.

'Can you tell us more about him, sir?' interrupted Sofer, hesitantly.

'Senior partner at the Corporate Bank. Been that for over

ten years. Lives here in Berlin half his time, as you know. See a lot of him socially. His German wife and mine get on extremely well. Indeed they're planning to go off on holiday to Switzerland together later this month. Sir Randall's wife rang me at midnight. Very distressed. He's been arrested by the German fraud squad.'

'British passport?' Murray questioned.

'I understand it's been impounded,' Sir Edward said crossly.

'Anyone warn us before his arrest?' asked Murray.

'No way,' said Sofer. 'I knew something was bubbling. Mentioned it once at your morning meeting; then there was that comment in *Der Spiegel* last week. *Die Welt* had a follow-up last Monday. Mentioned Sir Randall by name.'

'I want him released,' said Sir Edward emphatically.

'Dangerous business, sir, the embassy getting involved with the German police, with a possible criminal charge pending,' warned Murray. Sofer nodded in agreement.

'Then get him bail. Karen Deighton ought to be able to pull some strings,' Sir Edward persisted.

'Embassy must keep a hands-off stance, sir,' echoed Sofer. 'The Germans will know you're personal friends. Don't want to embark on anything underhand.'

'I don't mean anything underhand for Christ's . . .' exploded Sir Edward. 'Once he gets bail, once he's out, I'm sure he can handle his problems perfectly adequately on his own. And clear his name.'

Murray looked at his watch. It was still only eight-thirty a.m. 'I'm meeting Otto Klingenfeldt on the refugee crisis at ten. I'll catch him beforehand: ask his advice. He'll give me a feel as to what to do.'

'I'll ring around my contacts in the Trade Ministry. See what I can pick up,' volunteered Sofer. 'One contact in Finance owes me a big favour. He'll tell me what he knows. We should drop in the point that somebody with a knighthood is going to get a lot of coverage in the British media.'

'I'm not sure that will influence German justice, but you can try,' said Sir Edward, now more cautious. 'I'm most grateful to you both,' he added unexpectedly.

Late that afternoon Sofer and Murray met to review progress.

'How do we break it to the Old Man?' asked Sofer.

'You must have got the same steer as I did,' Murray responded.

'I guess. Pretty damning. Man's as guilty as hell.'

'Klingenfeldt could not have been more open,' Murray went on. 'He repeated that phrase about the Anglo–German diplomatic balance sheet. Knowing him, he'll want something in return later. Right now, they have a bulging dossier of ex-Stasi information about Sir Randall Scase's shady East–West dealings over the last three decades. This insider trading accusation is just the tip of the iceberg.'

'Exactly what my contact said,' added Sofer. 'Suppose we'd better get it over with. What's our line?'

'The truth. But the truth coupled with what should be good news for the Old Man. Klingenfeldt said more than he should: they've picked up on avoiding the embarrassment of bringing a British knight to trial in Germany. He's to be expelled, sent home with a complete package of information on what he's been up to. Leaving it to the British financial regulators to sort him out.'

'Good news? The ambassador won't shoot us mere messengers,' suggested Sofer.

'You know him,' Murray grinned. 'Given half a chance he will.'

6

When he had completed his period of compassionate leave back in Colchester, and after promising his wife Betty faithfully that he would definitely come to a decision about leaving the army before the summer, Sergeant Tate flew back to rejoin his regiment. He had been promoted in the meantime for his fortitude in making the long way back to base on foot despite the atrocious weather conditions, and there were strong indications that a Military Cross was also on the way for him. At the base he found everything very different and everything very much the same. Colleagues and superior officers alike were all kind and considerate and he was allotted a desk job in admin as a temporary measure, to give him time to readjust to the loss of several of his closest companions.

He learnt that he had missed several more lacklustre briefings from Major Oldfield about who was believed to have been responsible for the outrage. NATO chiefs, in their wisdom, had decided at ministerial level not to overreact, since intelligence reports indicated that the ambush had almost certainly been intended as a provocation by Russian or Ukrainian extremists, either to encourage a further mass breakout or some form of retaliation from the West that they could use to their advantage. Who or why was beside the point; they had not succeeded, though all patrols were now much more on their guard. Calls for action in the House of Commons, fuelled by outrage wheeled out by the British tabloid press over the deaths of several brave young British soldiers, were met by political caution, due to a lack of any agreement as to what countermeasures could be taken against whom. As Tate bluntly explained to colleagues in the sergeants' mess, it was once again a case of asking: who are the enemy? The Foreign Secretary said the same thing at rather more length in the House of Commons the same day: retaliation could, after all, only take place against a clearly identified foe. So far, no one had claimed responsibility.

Admin had few attractions for Sergeant Tate, and his adjutant quickly recognized a talent in need of harnessing if the army was not to lose one of its brightest NCOs. So, shortly afterwards, Tate was transferred to the regimental intelligence section, fortunately for him in the very same week that Major Oldfield was posted back to the Ministry of Defence in Whitehall. A replacement for the major was slow in arriving and thus it was Sergeant Tate himself who was on duty, decoding the classified intelligence reports, when the sensational news first broke.

The enciphered flash message came in from Warsaw, via London, copied to NATO Brussels. The codeword at the beginning indicated to Sergeant Tate that he had to seek clearance before taking any further action. He tried to reach the adjutant but he was on weekend leave, and the second-in-command was not answering his telephone. So, in some trepidation, he did as he was meant to, and had his commanding officer dragged out of a formal mess dinner.

'Well done, Sergeant,' said the CO over the telephone. Tate guessed from the voice tones and slightly slurred vowels that the colonel had been dining well. 'You have my authority to open the safe and the sealed envelope inside,' he said. 'I hope it'll all wait till the morning, but if you must ring back, you must.'

Left to himself once again, Sergeant Tate went quickly to the safe in the communications office, unscrambled the combination dials, opened the safe, extracted the sealed envelope labelled 'Top Secret: To Be Opened Only by a Designated Officer', tore it apart with scarcely a qualm, read off the meaning of the codeword which also spelled EMERGENCY in no uncertain terms, quickly decoded the message, then, pulse racing, again rang the officers' mess. A mess orderly answered, then a drunken captain came on the line. The subsequent telephone conversation was brief, tense and bordering on unpleasant.

'No, sir. I can't give you the message. This is for the colonel alone.'

'Just because of what's happened, you're not immune you know, Tate. I'll have you charged,' said the angry voice at the other end.

'Your prerogative, sir. The colonel, please? Immediately, please. This is an emergency, sir.'

'Impertinent, overpromoted bloody . . .' said the captain, then put the telephone down on Sergeant Tate.

Sergeant Tate was left with no alternative but to pick up his cap, straighten his tie, lock the comms office door securely behind him, and run all the way up to the officers' mess. Barging past an orderly, he walked straight into the dining room. The drunken captain stood up and tried to block his way.

'I warned you once, Tate,' he said, red-faced and swaying.

Tate ignored him and marched up to the head of the table where his commanding officer was seated, brandy glass in hand. He saluted smartly.

'A word, sir.'

'This better be bloody good, Sergeant,' said the colonel, standing up and moving to one side with him.

'Bloody bad, sir,' said Sergeant Tate, whispering gently in his ear. The colonel sobered up immediately. The twenty or so officers seated around the table watched the two men in curious silence.

'You're absolutely sure, Sergeant?'

Tate handed his CO the deciphered message. The colonel read it quickly, then turned to his fellow-officers. 'Gentlemen,' he said, 'this dinner is over, as of now. Sergeant Tate, you come with me.'

The drunken captain belched a little. 'Panicky bloody NCOs,' he said rather too loudly. 'Spoiling a perfectly good evening. Put him on a charge, I would.'

'Captain Neil – go to bed. That's an order. Immediately,' said the colonel angrily. 'I want your written apology on my desk first thing tomorrow morning. Now,' he said, turning to the rest of his officers. 'Gentlemen, no more drink. Sergeant Tate will come with me. I want the rest of you back here in full battle gear, with all your men not off duty, within the half-hour, d'you hear?' Then the colonel, followed by Sergeant Tate, rapidly left the officers' mess.

He could not stand the living conditions in his so-called apartment any longer, so one night he travelled across Moscow and checked into the most opulent of the western hotels to get a decent bath, a warm bed and a couple of substantial meals inside him. Within half an hour of his arrival, his telephone rang.

'How did you know I was here?' Ivan Katerski asked, astonishment showing in his voice.

The man on the other end ignored the question. 'Where have you been? I've been looking everywhere for you.'

'Out and about. Building contacts. Trying to find my roots.'

'Meeting up with your chums?'

'That too.'

'Love a chat . . .' The English voice was urbane. 'Are they interested in what I have on offer?'

'Perhaps.' Ivan hesitated, then, 'At your disposal,' he added reluctantly.

'With you at nine tomorrow. Meet in the lobby or shall I come up to your room?'

Ivan Katerski stared out of the window into the cold grey Moscow night. 'Wouldn't it be better to go for a walk?' he suggested.

'Good idea,' said the voice at the other end. It was amazing how cool he sounded.

At precisely nine o'clock the next morning, Ivan stood waiting by the main door of the hotel. The other man was prompt or maybe he had been there already, watching him, biding his time. He emerged from a large black Mercedes that was parked just a little way across the street and gave a friendly wave. It had begun raining quite heavily and Ivan pulled the collar of his raincoat up as he walked over to greet him. They shook hands politely.

'In filthy weather like this,' his visitor drawled, 'rather than that traditional walk, maybe we should go for a drive. What d'you think?'

'At your disposal,' Ivan shrugged.

They got into the car, his visitor drove off, then immediately turned right along a quiet side street. Eventually he pulled into the kerb beside a loathsome pile of bags of rotting domestic garbage.

'Symbol of modern Russia,' said the man.

'Very indiscreet, ringing up, arranging to meet just like that. Aren't you scared they'll find you?' Ivan was more than a little suspicious of this other Englishman and what he was selling.

Sprawled nonchalantly behind the wheel, the man shrugged his shoulders dismissively. 'Depends who you mean by "they". In the old days so many things were different. I wouldn't have used the telephone, that's for certain. But now, I suspect the grey successors of the KGB know exactly what I'm about.'

'They do?' Ivan was amazed.

'Sure. They'd be very stupid if they didn't already know what I'm marketing. But I'm well-protected, and so long as they don't tell the Brits what they know, and there's no reason why they should, I'm pretty relaxed. They'll certainly understand why you might be interested.'

'I suppose so.' Ivan began to relax. 'So won't Russian intelligence be worried at us getting together?'

'Worried? To what end? Half the people working for Russian intelligence can't know who they're working for any more, or for what reason. One day's suspect is next day's government minister.' The man laughed emptily. 'Right, left, centre. If I was them I wouldn't know where to position my loyalties. They're probably more curious about you, a Brit working for Vladimir. They've got far more troublesome people around than me – my friends, the Mafia guys, for example.'

Ivan did not fully understand. 'You come along with your goods, your expertise, your absence of loyalties. Surely . . . ?'

'Loyalties? That's a good word. D'you know where *your* loyalties lie, Ivan Katerski?' asked the other man softly.

'Maybe,' Ivan breathed, glancing sideways at his companion.

'That's reassuring. So shall we leave the dialectic and get down to business?' A trace of hostility had crept into his voice.

'Of course. What precisely have you got on offer?' Ivan asked. 'This car . . . ?' he added.

'Bug-free. I have it swept every day. Your friend Vladimir; he makes all the decisions, I take it? Does he want to talk?'

'He wants to talk. Yes, I know he wants to talk.'

'Soon? It's got to be soon. Either that or I go back to the hoods.'

'Soon, I promise you. Or it'll be too late. He's talking about using the masses at the border,' Ivan volunteered. 'He fantasizes about personally leading them in a great march westwards. "The Starving Army", he calls them. Your thing fits in so well.'

'He's serious?'

'I think so. He can be very . . . hypnotic.'

'Are you hypnotized by him?'

Ivan Katerski hesitated for a moment and then, for the first time, was not entirely honest. 'No,' he said. 'No, I can see through him. He has a huge number of personal weaknesses – as much an alcoholic as Yeltsin, for example. As I said, he is a powerful demagogue.'

'Powerful? Will he succeed?'

'Succeed? Harnessing his masses? Perhaps. As much as Russia's masses can ever be harnessed – or united. D'you know that there are an estimated hundred and fifty ethnic minorities in this great country of ours?' Ivan paused, then continued, 'If he controls his drinking, and his temper. He doesn't have much opposition, does he? Not with that bunch of corrupt illiterates who are floating around the Kremlin at the moment.'

'You're very committed, aren't you, Ian?' The Englishman deliberately dropped in his westernized name.

'I'm here to find my roots. I commit once I have something to commit to,' Ivan responded, he hoped with conviction.

'So how's the search for your family home you told me about progressing?' asked his contact, little interest showing in his voice.

Ivan told the other man as little as possible as they drove together back to the hotel. It had not been a satisfactory meeting for either of them. No deal had been done. He did not fully trust him nor his rotten loyalties. As they parted, Ivan thought about how little his search for his roots, the estates that his family had once owned, had really been progressing. How had his search for all his pasts been getting on? The answer was: not very far. Commitment had been getting in the way.

The moment his visitor had driven off in the Mercedes, Ivan entered the hotel foyer, and spotted Anatoli, one of Vladimir's senior henchmen. He must have been waiting for him to return. How the hell had he too known where he was: was nothing secret in Moscow?

From Anatoli's excited expression, Ivan knew instantly that something dramatic had happened. 'What is it?' he asked.

'I've never seen him so calm,' responded Anatoli, as they cursorily shook hands.

'What is it?' Ivan repeated.

'He'll tell you. He'll tell us all how he sees it. Let's go.' Anatoli made for the hotel door, then paused briefly. 'That man you came with just now. The Englishman?'

Ivan nodded. It seemed an irrelevance right now. 'He wants to talk to Vladimir,' he explained.

'Maybe it is unnecessary now. Maybe it's too late.'

'What is? Tell me, Anatoli, what the hell's happening?' Ivan begged.

'The balloon has gone up, that's what. Now come. Come quickly. Vladimir does not like to wait for us.' Anatoli turned on his heel and Ivan obediently followed him from the hotel.

Vladimir's aims and strategy were straightforward. He read the western democracies all too well. He knew how they would react. 'Democracy is alien to Mother Russia,' he said when all the members of his inner council had finally assembled. It was a full and powerful lecture. 'Our people need authoritarian rule. They prefer to be told, not asked. They want the security of knowing what is going to happen, where their next meal is going to come from, and that someone will look after them in old age. The Tsars realized that. Stalin and his successors knew that. The post-communist so-called liberal democratic leaders brought only poverty, insecurity and starvation. The Washington-controlled World Bank and the other development and aid agencies have tried to tell us how to behave, and what to do and not to do with our economy. All politics is about power. The power to govern Mother Russia must lie in Moscow, not Washington, nor London, nor Brussels.

'Yes,' Vladimir went on. 'They have bribed our former allies in eastern Europe by offering them a meaningless membership of NATO. What good has it done them, any of them, having their military forces run by Belgian, Dutch and Danish politicians. Soldiers from Luxembourg and Norway patrolling *our* borders, for God's sake! What kind of world is that? But I, we, are about to prove them wrong, and, more importantly, prove them totally impotent. We are moving, the masses are moving, and I promise you, NATO will not know what to do. They are already agonizing and bickering and that is before their western liberal media have begun to whine and carp and offer powerless advice, which will just make their politicians dither even more. Then, in a week or so, in return for us pulling our people back within our present borders, they will sigh insincere sighs of despair but relief. The air will be full of their lamentations and the wringing of hands and the shrugging of shoulders and the weasel words of politicians saying, "What else could we do?"

'And then,' Vladimir continued to his captivated, spellbound audience of apostles, 'they will come to us in secret and will conclude a treaty with us that is not written on paper but is fully understood right down to the last detail by both sides. That treaty will set out quite clearly that, while the West will be able to say glorious, heroic, democratic things about how much they deplore the return of authoritarian rule to Mother Russia, and how greatly they dislike that despot Vladimir –' He paused briefly as some colleagues laughed in cautious moderation, looking from one to the other to ensure that it was permissible to do so, then continued. 'They, the great democratic nations, under the wise guidance of a corrupt American administration, will connive at and condone what I, at what *we*, are doing to bring order to Russia. All this in return for our secret guarantee that we will take back and forcibly contain our people once more within our historic national boundaries. They will do nothing, because they will not be able to do anything. They have the military power and superiority in every way. That is regrettable but true. But what they do not have is an enemy. Our Russian army will have the same function as theirs: to control our people: a happy convergence of strategies, my fellow Russians. A happy, secret unity. Ah, what it is not to have an enemy any more.'

Such is the nature of diplomacy that, as the Jacobs case had demonstrated, little issues often sweep aside even the greatest matters of international concern. That said, there was little or no time for routine business before the storm broke. Murray had admittedly had a few weeks, with the help of Frau Müller, in which to settle into Berlin life, his apartment, and, in the meantime, pursue his physically exciting if intellectually demanding relationship with Carol-Anne Capaldi. They became good at minor dissimulation, believing that their affair was little remarked upon in their respective embassies. Murray also dealt, to the ambassador's if not to his own satisfaction, with the Foreign Office inspectors, who wrote their report recommending only a minor trimming of embassy staff and a modest, if infuriating, fifteen per cent cut in the ambassador's expense allowance.

On the political front, with the weather gradually improving, NATO leaders believed that the problem of the mass of refugees camped on Russia's and its allies' western borders was being better contained if not solved. There had been one major incident in late March when over three thousand men, women and children had pushed through the wire with the help of a stolen forklift truck, and had advanced, in a media-hyped, tear-jerking column of misery, almost twenty-five kilometres through Poland in the direction of Germany, before being rounded up, fed and reclothed by the International Red Cross, and then bussed (rather than in the cattle trucks which had been the first suggestion) back to their countries of origin. NATO just managed to live through the subsequent barrage of liberal media criticism and the self-seeking protests from a variety of politicians far removed from the scene of the action. In the nature of such issues there was, as Vladimir gauged only too well, the usual degree of inaction and confusion in Brussels and at the UN in New York, but the alternative, agreeing to allow a greater quota of immigrants into western countries, was never a serious option. Murray followed closely the background reports and telegrams from the British Embassy in Moscow about Russia's political and economic instability, which fomented, or at best tolerated, so much of what was happening. An appearance of total anarchy was the world's perception of life inside the Kremlin itself. No one seemed to be in charge, while Russia's generals and admirals were too preoccupied with finding enough money to pay their own rebellious soldiers and in quelling insurrections in the Caucasus and beyond the Urals, to give much thought to controlling what was happening on their western borders.

'Come the spring,' Murray had continued to argue at the strategic meetings he attended, 'extreme nationalists like Vladimir could easily stir a marginally better-fed people to march westwards. With no snow and ice on the roads and fields to hinder them, by the time we got round to responding, they'd be halfway across western Europe. We would be faced with an army of locusts that guns would not be able to stop because we would not be able to give the orders to fire. We must plan *now* how we would handle such an invasion.'

Murray was distracted from following such theorizing after the apparently unrelated suicide of an attractive young German journalist, one Heidi Kempner, who wrote largely on humanitarian issues. Stories appeared in the Berlin tabloids speculating on why she had done it: a broken love affair, a financial scandal or personal depression. Here seemingly was an internal German story of little concern to the British Embassy, until one Wednesday morning, Murray took a phone call from a man who introduced himself as Simon Bricker, a well-known human rights activist, who told him that he had come to Berlin to follow up claims that Kempner had been murdered because of her investigations into the activities of a British–American chemical company, which had for years been dumping highly volatile toxic waste in the former East Germany. Its communist government had turned a blind eye to what had been going on, particularly since the company had paid for the privilege with huge amounts of hard currency.

Bricker said he had hard evidence that Heidi Kempner had unearthed some highly sensitive correspondence which, if she had revealed it, would have shaken the company to its very foundations. He refused to be more forthcoming on the telephone, demanding to be received immediately at the embassy, otherwise he would give the whole story to the press. Angered by such a blatant attempt at moral blackmail, Murray none the less reluctantly agreed to meet him. Later that day, Bricker turned up with a scruffy colleague in tow, clutching a brown cardboard file which, when he was shown it, seemed to Murray to contain only a number of unsubstantiated press articles and typewritten allegations from unnamed sources, largely showing that Heidi Kempner had been threatened with legal injunctions by the company concerned.

Murray, who had taken the precaution of having Paul Fawcett present to act as witness in case things turned difficult, flicked through the file, while his visitors stared at him with undisguised hostility.

'Sorry, but there doesn't seem to be anything substantial here,' he said after some minutes. 'I can't possibly act on unconfirmed reports. If you like to leave this material with me, however, I'll go carefully through the file and write to you with our official views.'

'There's massive evidence in those cuttings of the disgraceful behaviour of British–American companies in general,' Bricker responded indignantly.

'That's as may be,' said Murray cautiously. 'I've only had a few moments to look at all this. You must understand I can't take any action without some proof, some evidence.'

'What more proof do you need?' Bricker was becoming increasingly aggressive. Beside him, his colleague nodded his vigorous agreement.

'You know, Mr Bricker, what I mean by proof.' Murray threw a look of frustration at Fawcett: he now deeply regretted having agreed to see them in the first place. 'I repeat,' he said, 'if you like to leave this file with me, I'll see how or if I can help. As to whether Miss Kempner committed suicide, or, as you allege, she's been silenced by someone, that's entirely a matter for the German police. The British Embassy has no role – '

'You're refusing to help?' threatened Bricker, his face flushing with self-righteous anger.

'I've been a diplomat too long to be pushed into that sort of corner, Mr Bricker,' said Murray calmly. 'I'm absolutely *not* refusing to cooperate. I'm saying that you've not given me a shred of evidence.'

'The press'll hear about this,' said Bricker standing up. His colleague rose with him.

'You're welcome to use that ploy, Mr Bricker. It doesn't make any difference to me or the British Embassy.'

'Bloody diplomats,' muttered Bricker.

'If you're reducing the argument to that level I'd be grateful if you'd leave right now and take your file with you,' said Murray standing up. 'I'll make it equally clear to the press that you came here and attempted to resort to blackmail. If you've got facts, use them.'

Murray's tough reaction elicited something approaching an apology from Bricker's colleague, who said they'd come back when they had more information to go on.

When Bricker had left and Fawcett had gone off to draft a report both to the ambassador and to the Foreign Office in London about the accusation, Murray put in a call to Carol-Anne Capaldi at the US Embassy.

'Official or social?' she teased.

'Sorry . . . business,' he responded. 'What d'you know about Heidi Kempner's death?'

'You've been pushed on that too, have you?' Carol-Anne asked. 'Tell me.'

'Had a human rights activist in just now, claiming she was bumped off to stop her revealing that some Anglo–US chemical company has allegedly been illegally dumping toxic waste.'

'Something about her came in the other day from the State Department,' said Carol-Anne cautiously.

'That it *was* murder?' Murray's astonishment showed.

'I didn't say that,' Carol-Anne said quickly. 'If you like conspiracy theories: OK. Illegal dumping certainly went on in a huge way; undoubtedly highly unethical in terms of current international law, and very, very hazardous. Heidi Kempner's articles would probably have been damaging to a lot of people, but that's a long, long way from murder.'

'So?'

'Ask Klingenfeldt. He's been looking into it. It's more for them than us,' she suggested.

'If the press gets stirred up . . .' Murray began.

'Even they won't touch it without some evidence.'

'When did truth get in the way of a good story?'

'Sure, the environmental lobby, given half a chance, might try to use Heidi Kempner's death to further their cause. The uncomfortable truth is that many unscrupulous western companies dumped highly toxic waste in a far from ecologically sound eastern Europe for years. It happened in East Germany, Czechoslovakia, Romania and Bulgaria. Huge sums of hard currency changed hands. It's a fact.'

'I know all that, Carol-Anne. So what're you suggesting?' asked Murray.

'I'm suggesting her death is nothing whatsoever to do with environmental issues,' she replied cautiously. 'Kempner's been in eastern Poland recently and, my highly reliable sources suggest, slipped across the border on a number of occasions. She was going to run a huge story about which Moscow-based extremists were whipping up the mood in the refugee camps and that was making some people very angry indeed.'

'That makes much more sense,' said Murray reflectively.

'As it affects both of us, I suggest we discuss all this, quietly and professionally,' she said dropping her voice a tone. 'How about tonight? My place or yours?'

Fortunately he left her bed at around midnight that night, to return to his apartment. The phone was ringing as he came in the front door. It was Anthony Fox. He was terse and to the point.

'There's been a huge breakthrough,' he said. 'H.E. wants an emergency meeting at once. I was at the same dinner party as him so he got me to ring round everyone.'

'Where have they come through?' asked Murray, his sleepiness dropping from him.

'Where have they not? Everywhere,' said Fox and hung up.

Murray got to his desk in twenty minutes flat and began reading through the reports as they came in. The breakthrough was huge: the estimate of numbers involved varied enormously. The Berlin working group was to meet at eight in the morning. NATO reinforcements were on their way to man Poland's entire eastern border but the suggestion was that it was all too late. Member governments were already under attack from both right and left, blamed for taking too soft a stance on those illegal immigrants who had already managed to get well beyond Poland, or accused of human rights abuses where they were forcibly repatriating people.

Meanwhile, according to news reports, the right-wing leader Professor Dieter Krauss had dramatically hardened his line. He had issued a statement calling for the immediate explusion of all illegal immigrants, wherever they originated from. Equally worrying was a telegram from the Moscow Embassy which suggested that Vladimir – he was always just known by his first name – was out and about exploiting the crisis for his own political ends. That was against the background of a chilling American report that there had been an attempted Kremlin coup which could, if it were successful, usher in a neo-fascist dictatorship with the backing of a demoralized but all-too-willing army leadership.

Murray knew from first-hand experience what dire circumstances had at last provoked the invasion he had long feared. Some weeks earlier, while Brigadier Dicks and the other NATO military attachés went on frequent reconnaissance patrols to see developments along the fortified borders for themselves, there had been some criticisms that diplomats like Murray and Carol-Anne Capaldi had little first-hand experience of what it was like on the ground. At key meetings they had been forced to discuss the problem in the abstract, without seeing the human dimension, and a number of them had consequently been instructed to participate in a three-day fact-finding mission, made up of a number of middle-ranking diplomats from Berlin, Budapest and Warsaw. Murray vividly remembered standing exposed to a bitter March wind, on a bare outcrop of rock overlooking the border between prosperity and chaos. He recalled how well the fence was maintained, with close-run strands of rust-free razor wire, all of it monitored by remote-control cameras. On the western side, a swathe of ploughed and carefully raked earth, an old East German trick, immediately showed up any footprints leading from any gap cut in the wire. Every kilometre or so, there was a lookout post on stilts, each one linked by a bulldozed cart track, along which well-marked NATO vehicles constantly patrolled. Beyond the fencing, even without binoculars, the diplomats had been able to make out the encampments of the refugees. They could hardly be missed: at places, the canvas covers of the tents had actually been attached to the border fence posts for additional support.

Later, Murray and his colleagues had driven right up to the wire to peer guiltily at the teeming humanity beyond. To him, it had recalled old film footage of concentration camps, though in this case the refugees who waved and shouted at the visitors through the wire had not looked particularly ill-fed. The diplomats had seen one clear reason why: at regular intervals, pristine Red Cross flags flew over the white tents and steaming chimneys of the food kitchens. While he had tried to prepare himself for what he would experience, Murray would never forget the pinched faces of the children, hands outstretched, begging for who knows what, towards this group of antiseptic, diplomatic tourists.

At around two in the morning, when the ambassador and his staff were in the middle of excitedly deciding what their line would be at the next morning's NATO working group, while Paul Fawcett, who was monitoring the reports as they came in to the embassy's communications room, kept them up to date with the latest intelligence on how many had got how far across Poland, a flash telegram came in from the Foreign Office that disappointed them all. NATO ministers, meeting in emergency session, had decreed that to avoid any country getting out of step, all tactical discussions were in future to be concentrated in Brussels and Warsaw. The British Embassy in Berlin was in future to confine itself to keeping informed of current developments. Other NATO embassies were being sent similar instructions.

'Klingenfeldt called the damned meeting,' Murray exploded. 'Why the hell can't they get their act together? Are Warsaw and Brussels still going to coordinate when the mobs reach the German border?'

'An instruction is an order,' responded the ambassador though he was obviously equally disconcerted. 'Well, everyone, I think we can stand down for now and await developments.'

By the next morning, the overnight sense of deflation had spread throughout the entire embassy, and Murray was driven back to dealing with more trivial domestic matters. One curious little story was reported deep on the inside pages of all that morning's newspapers, which otherwise carried column after column reporting on the mass invasion of Poland and the widespread looting that had taken place. The previous morning, the story read, a concerned German businessman had, with police back-up, broken into an apartment he owned in the Charlottenburg district of Berlin. His tenant had stopped paying the rent and had disappeared. Had he done a bunk or had there been an accident? The subsequent news was that the body of Heidi Kempner's lover had been found in the apartment. He had been strangled and the police were putting the story around that both of them had probably been murdered because of what they had found out about neo-fascist activities in the refugee camps. Someone in Moscow didn't like the truth getting out. When, coincidentally, the unpleasant Simon Bricker telephoned later that morning to repeat his earlier allegations, Murray had the greatest satisfaction in telling him to go and study that morning's press, and, thereafter, to get lost. Then he put the phone down on him. But the call left a bitter aftertaste: things were very serious when journalists were murdered for attempting to reveal the truth.

7

Vladimir was running for the Russian Presidency in all but name. He was high on the campaign trail, using the great international storm that the vast influx of starving peasantry had caused, to further his own political ambitions. Many of the illegal immigrants had, admittedly, already been returned to Russia and the Ukraine, bribed by western promises of yet more aid. But Vladimir's line was one with which many at NATO would have agreed: the battle was over, but the war still had a long way to run. His case was cleverly argued and people came from miles around when they heard he was going to speak. His motorcade consisted of two buses, a back-up van, a rag-tag of press cars, and two flashy four-wheel-drive trucks, one at the front and one at the rear, carrying the leader's undisciplined but well-armed bodyguards. There had only been one serious attempt on his life so far; but, as he kept saying, once was often enough. Ivan Katorski had been given the key task of importing a dozen of the best bullet-proof vests from London for the main members of the party; wisely he also bought one for himself.

That night Vladimir's campaign team had based themselves at a school on the outskirts of a nondescript village about twenty-five kilometres west of Smolensk, very close to the Russian border with Belorussia. On Ivan's reckoning, though the maps he had managed to scrounge were old and largely out of date, that meant he was now only a mere sixty to seventy kilometres east of where his family estates had once lain over towards Minsk.

The political rallies over the weekend had proved a great success; everyone in the party was particularly pleased both by the turnout and by the vast television and media coverage they had achieved. A euphoric Vladimir had taken Ivan aside the previous night and had personally gone out of his way to thank him for his help in handling the foreign journalists and TV crews that, given the circumstances, pursued him everywhere. But today, he was rumoured to have found a new woman and was celebrating with her, and as there were no more rallies planned until Tuesday, he gave his team the rest of that Sunday and the whole of Monday off. Ivan seized his opportunity. With the help of a wad of US dollars, he persuaded Vladimir's head bodyguard to let him borrow one of their vehicles and, early on the Sunday, he set off across the agricultural landscape, armed with his maps, an ancient address, and a few faded photographs of a once-proud stately home. The oldest of the maps, which had the house clearly marked on it, he had brought out with him from London. With difficulty he had then cross-related it to a modern map he had bought in Moscow. It proved far from easy to cross-check them with any accuracy; where tiny villages once had stood, there were now sprawling industrial townships; elsewhere, farms had been bulldozed into huge collectives, while some settlements had been wiped out of existence by the ravages of Stalinism and its long and ugly aftermath.

He did as he had long planned, and followed one main road until it crossed a river, the Dnepr. His assumption was that the latter's course at least would not have altered significantly over the past sixty or seventy years. By mid-afternoon, to his pleasure, he identified an old bridge over the river which he had been looking for. From one of the old photographs he had with him, he could see that the lay of the land along its banks had not changed too much over all these decades. It remained largely farming country; the villages were still backward and under-developed; the through-roads, the railway and the industrial complexes that besmirched so much of the rest of the country he had travelled through had spared this little enclave, sheltered as it was within an embracing arm of the river. Then, what made him convinced that he was close to his goal, was coming on one additional vista, where, beyond the bridge, a small tributary met the main river. There stood a battered Orthodox church with four onion-domed towers, sited on unusually high ground and surrounded by birch woods, just as his father had once described it to him. If he was correct, then the house itself would be a short two kilometres further to the north.

He considered asking for directions, but when he reached the largely deserted village beside the church, he decided against it; even in these relatively peaceful days, the villagers would be wary of any stranger. So he again pulled into the side of the mud-tracked road and examined the faded sepia photographs. To the left was the river; to the other side were long rows of trees flanking a driveway which had led to the sprawling, low-built house with the ornate Palladian façade at its centre. If it still existed, it would be unmissable in that otherwise rustic, peasant landscape.

Another kilometre, and he came to two massive, rusting gates supported by broken pillars, capped with heraldic beasts carved into the stone. The gates were locked, chained and thickly overgrown with weeds, while the road itself wound easily round them through a gap in the wall on the left-hand side. Beyond, he saw the remains of the two lines of trees, and what must, at one time, have been a well-kept drive. The path was well used and even showed signs of having been recently repaired. Many of the trees had disappeared, however, doubtless lopped down for much-needed fuel in times of past hardship. But about a hundred of these still stood as gap-tooth sentinels stretching towards his destination.

He did not know what to expect. He had dreamt about the place for so long, had spent many a night thinking back and cursing himself for not having questioned his father more closely about the house and what had taken place there over the previous centuries. He did not even know when it had been first built nor how long his family had owned it. He half expected it to be haunted. He knew so little about so few of its former inhabitants: grandmothers, grandfathers and what seemed like hundreds of brothers, sisters, cousins and nephews, who had peopled the house, eaten, quarrelled, worked and played there. Some of the other faded photographs told their own stories; men and women, boys and girls, sitting around happily in quaint, old-fashioned costumes, the ladies in wide-brimmed hats, the little girls in long pinafores, the boys in knee breeches with silk shirts and jabots around their necks. He had embarked, largely unprepared, on this uncertain journey in search of his family's past; now, amid the unchanging landscape and the permanence of the river, he was about to set this past against the harsh reality of his current life. Would the vulgar present damage the image of his dreams?

His heart beat in unusual anticipation. There was no sign of life as he pulled his four-wheel-drive truck to a halt outside the main door of the big house. The whole edifice was in a highly dilapidated state, yet in places he could see that some extensive repairs had been made to the walls and windows. In bygone times it had been a very grand house, full of prosperous people, served by countless servants. Decayed though it now was, it still dwarfed any other house nearby. The steep roof was patched and broken, covered with moss and with a sizeable tree growing from a neglected gutter. There had once been shutters to protect each window but most were now gone or hung at drunken angles on rusted hinges. As he stood for a moment and stared at it, he thought that only an all-embracing blanket of snow would paint it into what it once had been. The surrounding grounds, once doubtless so well tended by a legion of gardeners, now looked more like a farmyard than anything else; a broken tractor stood askew at one side, while to the other, concrete and wooden outhouses appeared to serve as pigsties.

He climbed out of the truck and walked slowly around the house. Suddenly, at a side entrance, a burly man in his sixties appeared, and asked aggressively what the nature of his business was.

'I'm looking for the present owner or occupant, please?' Ivan replied politely.

'Who are you?' came the surly question.

'I'm a property dealer. I'm looking to buy land,' he lied freely.

'There's no land for sale around here,' said the man threateningly. He held a pitchfork in one hand and swung it round, as if ready to use it if required. Then suddenly the man came up and stood too close to Ivan for comfort. He stepped back a pace, having spotted the small boutonnière, in the Russian national colours, that was fixed in the top buttonhole of Ivan's greatcoat. Noting the direction of the man's glance, Ivan cursed himself. It was careless of him. He had totally forgotten to remove it, the symbol of Vladimir's National Party of Russia. He expected to face any sort of violent reaction; to many of the old left it would be like a red rag to a bull.

But the other man's tone changed dramatically. He became much more welcoming and stretched out his hand in genuine greeting. 'I see you are of the party,' he said warmly.

'Why, yes.' Ivan hesitated.

'You perhaps work with Citizen Vladimir himself?' he was asked. The word 'citizen' had as many connotations as the word comrade, but Ivan ignored that.

'Yes,' he admitted. 'I do.'

'And I am secretary of our local party,' the older man said proudly. 'For the last two triumphant years,' he added.

'Delighted. In that case can I introduce myself?' Ivan drew himself up and smiled back. 'My name is Ivan Katerski, Ivan Ivanovich Katerski. I am personal foreign policy adviser to Vladimir himself. He is, as you may know, on the campaign trail and only about sixty kilometres away at this very moment.'

'And I am Secretary Nabakov. So have you come to visit me officially? Am I invited to meet Vladimir personally? Do you bring greetings from him, perhaps?'

'Of course I do.' Ivan smiled graciously, bowing slightly.

'Then come in, sir. Come in. Let me offer you the modest hospitality of my house. You are most truly welcome.'

*   *   *

To outsiders, embassies are either the play areas of fops living the high life on champagne and caviar at the taxpayers' expense, or the breeding grounds for spies and pederasts. More informed opinion realizes that they are often the focal point of one crisis after another, while a huge amount of routine, very boring work goes on, well hidden behind the chancery walls. But because an embassy is the meeting point or centre of friction for almost all relations between any two nations, there is, in any morning's newspapers, bound to be some issue or story that concerns or affects the diplomats who staff it. Sometimes it is a world-shattering issue of state; sometimes small, tragic or funny human-interest incidents attract the bored headline writers' attention. Sometimes a mixture of all these confuses the eventual outcome.

Looking back over the few months since the unfortunate circumstances of his arrival in Berlin, Murray remembered so many seemingly intractable problems that had come across his desk. The refugee crisis was, as far as it had affected them in Berlin, contained for the moment, if far from solved. Other problems had proved more transitory, had been quickly dealt with, and were now largely forgotten in the embassy files, like the insider-dealer case with the ambassador's friend Sir Randall Scase which was now firmly London's preserve, or the Plenzdorf affair which was merely another footnote to history. But each and every one of them, as they meshed in, had one common factor; they all had, for a brief moment, threatened the generally even-tempered nature of Anglo–German relations.

His pending tray was still far too full of items of potential friction. Despite Frau Müller's best endeavours, the case of Mr Jacobs and his property claim, for example, still took up an inordinate amount of his and Karen Deighton's time. Again, Bennett, the admin officer, was, in Murray's view, most wrongly still merely suspended from duty, a fact that continued to prompt his curiosity about the circumstances of his predecessor's hasty departure. He was convinced that he had still not heard anything like the full story.

That Monday began routinely enough at the ambassador's

morning meeting, with a lively discussion, first about whether the Bundesbank would lower German interest rates still further on the following Wednesday, then about the currently dormant problems over on the Russian border, and finally how Britain should react to German calls to site a future Olympics in Berlin. How far would Britain push its own case? How important were the faded memories of the 1936 Olympics, when Hitler and his cheering Nazis caused such threatening images to be dispatched around the world? Was a full six decades, and that long-remembered film of the Allies blowing up the great swastika that had once dominated Berlin's Olympic Stadium, still too short a time for world athletes again to compete in this city of greatness and of infamy?

'We shouldn't even consider the past,' said Murray aggressively. 'We'll be well into the new millennium. We should look at Berlin and Germany as it is today, and ask whether it is a better setting than Buenos Aires or Peking or Chicago.'

'I can't disagree more,' said Sir Edward coldly. 'I know that the events of the thirties stray away beyond any of our memories, but those images linger on. The Berliners would run things extremely efficiently, certainly. My view, we should stand well back and not get involved.'

The meeting moved on to other routine matters. The ambassador worked his way around the room asking his staff to raise what issues they wanted, and Murray mentioned that morning's press reports about the Heidi Kempner murder, and the new revelation that Simon Bricker, the British activist, had been secretly paying her to work on the toxic dumping story. 'The press are doing their usual,' said Murray, with some satisfaction. 'They started to build up Bricker when he came up with his allegations. Now they're assassinating him with sleaze allegations. Not sure there's much for us to do beyond indulging in a little malicious pleasure.' He looked at his watch, wishing that the meeting would soon be over.

'Anything else, anyone?' asked Sir Edward, again glancing round the room.

'Sorry to bring this up, sir, but I ought to . . .' began Karen Deighton hesitantly. Murray sighed, audibly. He had so many other things to get on with. 'An odd one,' Karen continued, waving a piece of paper at those seated round the room. 'German police report I've just received. Wouldn't usually bother you with a mere consular case but . . . a British subject was arrested for being disorderly outside a sleazy nightclub last Saturday night. In prison, now, because he assaulted a number of police, with one officer ending up having to have five stitches put in a head wound.'

'So?' queried Sir Edward, equally impatient to get on with his day's work.

'It's called the Black Whip Club. It's . . .' she paused. 'It's a transvestite club. Homosexuals for the most part. The first person that this Brit apparently accosted was an off-duty policeman, and by accost I mean – '

'I'm sure you don't need to explain,' said Sir Edward rapidly. Someone, possibly Fawcett, stifled a vulgar laugh.

'When two uniformed men arrived, he hit them,' Karen Deighton went on.

'So? Bees make honey,' said Sir Edward coldly. 'One more drunken Englishman misbehaving; neither here nor there.'

Karen Deighton persisted. 'He's given a fictitious name. He had no papers on him. Now he's demanding to see me.'

'What d'you normally do?' Sir Edward asked, tapping his fingers irritably on his desk.

'See him when charges are brought,' she said quietly.

'What's stopping you?'

'Putting two and two together,' she said, producing that morning's *Daily Mail*. The ambassador looked even more irritated. He disliked guessing games.

Karen Deighton opened the paper. On page two was a prominent story about Eric Murphy, a missing British MP. His family, friends and constituency chairman were worried. He had totally disappeared.

'I've reason to believe the prisoner and the MP could be one and the same person,' said Karen Deighton with quiet satisfaction. She suddenly had the rapt attention of all her male colleagues.

'Why?' breathed Murray.

'Police sent round a mug shot. Not the sort of picture he would use in his election manifesto, but . . .' Again she waved a piece of paper.

'How exciting,' said Sir Edward, a sudden flush of amusement lightening his normally severe features. 'Let me know what you find.'

Later that morning, Karen Deighton, bursting with excitement, came back to report at a hastily summoned meeting with Murray and the ambassador.

'So?' asked the ambassador.

'Confirmed,' she said, suppressing a smile. 'Eric Murphy, MP, it is.'

'The chap, sir, who's been banging on about us not doing enough to deal with the tide of illegal immigrants.' Murray had, in the meantime, been doing a little homework.

'The very one,' said Karen Deighton brightly.

'Arrested in a transvestite nightclub in Berlin last Saturday night, you said?' The ambassador spoke precisely, wanting to be quite sure he had all his facts.

'Arrested, charged and coming up in court on Thursday,' Karen Deighton explained.

'You've been to visit him?' asked Murray, astonished.

'I went into his cell carrying a copy of the *Mail*. Went so white when he saw it, I thought he was going to faint. Almost felt sorry for him. He's absolutely petrified that the press will find out,' she added.

'Which they will,' speculated Sir Edward. 'Well, well . . .'

'He's desperate to get out, get home, and get his version of the story out before they have theirs,' Karen Deighton explained.

'We'd all do the same, I suppose,' said Murray drily. 'What are the chances of you being able to spring him?'

'On legal grounds, few . . . or none. The charges are serious.

He . . . if you don't mind me explaining the nasty details, sexually groped a male police officer and then, as I said, in his drunken state, clobbered two uniformed police. He could get a stiff prison sentence.'

'I'll report to London on a *Top Secret and Personal* basis. The Office will deal with the PM and the party whips, I suppose,' said Sir Edward, reaching for a pen and pad of paper. 'I'll show you my draft before I send –'

'Can I suggest, sir, that you talk to the permanent under-secretary on the telephone. The less that's set down in writing, the less can be . . .' suggested Murray quickly.

'Quite right, Alex. Stay while I make my call.'

The ambassador put a call straight through to the head of the Foreign Office, and explained the situation. Both men strove to avoid laughing as they discussed the incident. The ambassador was told to do nothing at all until instructed. The PUS said he would talk to the Foreign Secretary, to Number Ten, and to the chief whip's office.

When Murray returned to his office to await developments, Samantha was waiting for him with an urgent message to call Otto Klingenfeldt.

'We've got a British MP in Berlin central police cells,' said Klingenfeldt in a matter-of-fact tone, when Murray eventually got through to him.

'I've heard,' he replied.

'He refused to give his name at first. We've now discovered which hotel he was staying in and found his passport there.'

'Are the press on to it?'

'Not yet.'

'My ambassador's already asked London for urgent instructions. Can you get your people to sit on the story for as long as it takes? This is one of these incidents, Otto, where the quicker we can get it over with, the better.'

'There are serious legal charges. He assaulted several police-men.' Klingenfeldt sounded at his most bureaucratic.

'I realize that, Otto. But you and I know that the quicker we can sort it the better. If it were possible for him to be released on bail, we'd winkle him back to Britain, then pick up the pieces after the event.'

'I'm not sure . . .' Klingenfeldt hesitated. 'I have a call in to the Chancellor's office. I'll come back to you.'

'He was on a private spree,' Murray said, scribbling notes for himself as a record of their conversation. 'Look,' he added, 'it's not that you and I should be keeping that famous balance sheet of favours.'

Klingenfeldt laughed briefly. 'If we were keeping that, we'd have to bring the German Embassy in Belgrave Square into the picture . . . all our consular cases in Britain . . .' he hesitated.

'You were most helpful over the Randall Scase affair, and our Jewish friend,' Murray ventured.

'And the embassy break-in, and . . .' Klingenfeldt was teasing now.

'Very grateful. I mean it, Otto.'

'Gratitude doesn't come into it with the serious charges this man faces.'

'According to *Who's Who*, he's married with children,' Murray further volunteered.

'The worse for him, and them,' said Klingenfeldt drily.

'Probably have to resign,' Murray argued. 'All the ambassador wants to avoid is this becoming an issue in Anglo–German relations. The quicker we get him out the better.'

'Back to you within the hour,' Klingenfeldt promised.

Murray went along to the ambassador's office to bring him up to date on the telephone conversation.

'Not sure there's anything more we can do,' said Sir Edward, 'till we hear further. In the meantime I have been enjoying myself by reading up on how much of a nuisance Mr Eric Murphy, MP has been, complaining that diplomats as a breed are a complete waste of public money. Apart from being bloody-minded about NATO's policy on the refugee issue, he's been in the forefront of trying to get our overseas allowances cut. I'd been thinking of having a word with the German Foreign Minister on his behalf, but now . . .' Sir Edward smiled a pleased little smile.

Messages came into the embassy in quick succession. The permanent under-secretary rang, followed closely by the chief whip. Both had the same blunt solution. 'Let him hang. That's everybody's advice. We can't be seen interfering with the course of German justice,' said the PUS.

The chief whip was more explicit. 'He's been a bloody nuisance for the last three years. Let him dig himself out of his own mess. I'm sorry for his wife and family, but that's another matter. I've spoken personally to the Prime Minister,' the chief whip went on. 'While the Foreign Secretary doesn't want anything to rock Anglo–German relations, he doesn't think this one will. If the story breaks, it breaks.'

Klingenfeldt's call, when it came, was a fraction more positive. 'Our legal department has been in touch with the Berlin Justice Department office. We've also, between you and me, had a word with the chief of police. It's possible, now that Herr Murphy's cooled his heels in prison for several nights, that they may not press charges. He was very drunk.'

Late that evening, as Murray was thinking of going to bed, he got a further call from Klingenfeldt.

'Diplomatic balance sheet, Alex. It's heavily weighted in our favour just now,' said the smooth, almost unaccented voice at the other end of the telephone. 'Thought I'd tell you straight away that Herr Murphy is being released in time to catch the first flight to London tomorrow morning.'

'How'd you wangle that, Otto?'

'I explained the circumstances to various people. That's the solution they've come up with. No charges on condition that he leaves the country immediately.'

'The press?'

'That's the bad news. One of your resident journalists, Fred Cree from the *Guardian*, is on to the story. He's very excited.'

'They deserve each other,' said Murray with satisfaction. 'It'll make his day.'

*　　*　　*

Cree, who had been chasing around trying to pick up on the detail before he pounced, did not contact Murray on the Eric Murphy story until the next afternoon.

His question was to the point. 'Have you been keeping something from me, Alex?' he pleaded.

'I always keep things from you, Fred.'

'Eric Murphy MP?'

'Name's familiar.' Murray deliberately played it low key.

'He's in Berlin?' Cree asked.

'Not as far as I know,' said Murray honestly.

'Was here?'

'Something you'd have to ask him.'

'My spies tell me he got into a spot of trouble at some night-club,' Cree persisted.

'As I say, you'll have to ask Mr Murphy.' Murray doodled on a pad in front of him as he spoke. It was a stick picture of a man hanging from a gibbet.

'Not denying you know about it, then?'

'Deny nothing; confirm nothing. You know me, Fred.'

'Off the record if you like, Alex,' Cree pleaded.

'Off the record or on the record. Nothing to say.'

'My office says the chief whip's office got you to put pressure on the Germans to get this MP released.'

'I repeat: I cannot confirm nor deny anything.' Murray smiled happily to himself.

'Gay bar, wasn't it? Started fondling some policeman?'

'If you've a story, run it,' Murray said.

'Don't have the proof.'

'When did that stop a good journalist?'

'Not going to help, then?'

'Right.' Murray was now drawing a coffin on his pad.

Cree tried another angle. 'Put it this way; what if a British MP got into trouble in Berlin . . .'

'. . . Our consul would give him or her exactly the same assistance as we'd give any other British subject.'

'I tried to speak to Karen Deighton. She's not answering.'

'She's very busy; she would have nothing to add.'

'You know that my story will have to run on the lines of "An embassy spokesman refused last night to deny speculation that . . ."' Cree tried the oldest of old lines.

'Your prerogative, Fred. But have reliable lawyers handy,' Murray said, putting the phone down with considerable satisfaction.

Back at his office, Cree sighed briefly, but he was not someone who stayed down for long. If the MP story was not going to run, he had plenty of others up his sleeve, for example the one that Simon Bricker had thrown at him about some British-born fanatic currently working for Vladimir. It was all a bit half-baked, but apparently Heidi Kempner had come across some unusual background on this guy that might just be worth following up.

8

Macmillan, once asked what he most feared, replied 'Events, dear boy, events'. The next event was first reported to a wider world by a very unlikely source. It was all unplanned. Hannelore Riese, a discontented seventeen-year-old's permanent pout on her unsophisticated face, was brushing her fair hair in front of her mother's full-length mirror. She brushed it powerfully and purposefully, savouring the needles of the brush on her scalp, relishing the hiss of bristle and nylon through her long, much-admired hair. It had just been washed in the most fashionable of shampoos; it was an advertiser's dream. It glistened thick, cascading, full of sensuous highlights, on to her fetchingly plump shoulders, and, if nobody but her could see the sight, sensuously over well-formed, deliciously provocative – fantasy words from her erotic dreams – breasts.

Hannelore's mother had died just before Christmas. She was briefly sad, but in practice, since the old lady had nagged in the desperation of her final sickness, it was a great relief to her. Her older sister had, with a quick bound, immediately upped and offed straight after the funeral and was now living with her plumber boyfriend in Charlottenburg. Her father, if he was currently sober enough to have been let in, would at this very moment be with his long-term mistress, Helga Frittpunct – terrible name – in her apartment beside the station in the run-down, once socialist paradise town of Königslager. So Hannelore was left alone with her hair, her thoughts and her resolution to ring her so-far one-night-stand friend, Helmut Wassertopf, whom she had met recently at a local beer festival and whom she now knew, but did not care, was a much-married disc jockey with the local pop radio station.

As she continued to brush hard and erotically through her golden tresses – her words in her mind – something reflected in the corner of the long mirror caught her attention. She did not fully comprehend at first. Perhaps it was a stray cow broken through the fence from Hochutsland. Perhaps it was . . . She put her ivory-backed brush down on a little gilded side-table, sighed, then turned to look out of the window. She could be excused for her uncontrolled fear at what she saw. A very few minutes later, having reluctantly taken her hysterical phone call at the radio station, her casual boyfriend, Helmut Wassertopf, broke into the big time by telling the world across the airwaves what his eye-witness girlfriend had just screamed out to him, and what, until then, Polish and NATO ministers had been trying to conceal from the outside world: the greatest mass of humanity in world history had started moving relentlessly westward.

It had not been his scene, indeed he wished he had not become involved, but Vladimir's word was his command. It was a quite extraordinary international meeting which took place in the leader's opulent dacha some twenty-five kilometres east of Moscow. Ivan had never been invited there before but he had heard a great deal about it, and how different it all was from the disgusting surroundings in which the party staffers normally met and worked. Surrounded by a high security fence, the dacha was set amid pleasant woods of birch and pine. It was sometimes disloyally referred to as Vladimir's Pleasure Palace; indeed, when Ivan arrived there, driven by one of the team of permanent bodyguards, his first impression was that the house appeared to be almost totally staffed by underdressed peroxide blondes. The glimpses he had of the other facilities away from the great dining room where the meeting took place, further lived up to its reputation as a house furnished mainly with huge beds and well-stocked bars.

But there was little to be seen of all this when the eclectic delegation of foreigners arrived. They came together, the diminutive, goatee-bearded Professor Dieter Krauss, the leader

147

of Germany's far-right political party, and the shaven-headed East End of London thug, Matt Huggins. Each had a phalanx of aides with them and Vladimir fielded a team of four, including Ivan, all of whom, after the formality of greeting, settled down round the huge table. The agenda was precise: how to play to best advantage the huge westwards invasion by starving pan-Russian hordes. It was like a mirror of the events of 1939, without the tanks and guns. How could there be any meeting of minds over anything as petrifying as this? Ivan thought. Stalin and Hitler had arranged to carve up Europe; would they be laughing in hell now? How could such events possibly lead to any cementing of relations between right-wing groups throughout the new Europe? Their Austrian and Italian counterparts had been invited to come to the meeting as well, but had, for one reason or another, failed to show up. Perhaps they realized that, even though the meeting was in secret, little was to be gained by consorting with someone as mad and extreme as Russia's Vladimir.

It was an extraordinary gathering, conducted by Vladimir with sweeping abandon. The invaders were nothing to do with him, he claimed, but they would be withdrawn soon, leaving Krauss and others of his ilk to further strengthen their support in banning all future foreign immigration. It was a thin argument and it held little or no water. In the end, nothing was agreed and it was easy to see why. The London bruiser, the neat, clipped German fascist in his spooky, rimless glasses, and the vodka-pickled Russian, might, to outsiders, have similar ideals and goals, but these were totally overwhelmed by their own extreme nationalisms. Any fear that some sort of mega-European right-wing movement might be founded, was strangled at that meeting. There was no anger, little acrimony, only a total lack of a meeting of minds. Ivan worked hard throughout, translating for the benefit of Vladimir and Huggins, but also for the German, whose English turned out to be almost faultless. They talked on in a desultory way for several hours, they lunched together, then they parted. Liberal Europe could sleep easy. Perhaps Krauss did not realize that Ivan also spoke some German, otherwise he might not have remarked incautiously to one of his colleagues as he left that he would have to disinfect his hand, the one that had shaken Vladimir's. Ivan did not translate that to anyone.

After the visitors had gone, Vladimir dismissed his other staff and ordered Ivan to come and sit with him. He was looking for a drinking companion. A bottle of vodka was produced, opened and the cork was thrown away. Vladimir was in expansive mood. He wanted to talk. Ivan sat, sipped at his glass with caution, and watched the level of liquid in the bottle drop at a frightening rate. Vladimir began by saying how impressed he was that Ivan's English was so perfect. He had, in consequence, a new task: to try and influence the western press. It was up to Ivan to make sure that in future the jackals of the European and American media no longer concentrated on the negatives: his erroneously reported admiration for Hitler; his desire to create a neo-fascist state in Mother Russia; his contempt for the Jews; his resolve to widen Russia's borders to their rightful limits; his alcoholism, his violence towards women . . . 'It is all lies; lies made up by my enemies.' Vladimir slouched deep in his chair and shouted at him as if, in some way, it was all his fault. 'It is up to you, my good Ivan, to correct all this. Your fluent English . . .' He paused. 'Where did you acquire it?' he asked suddenly.

'I grew up in Britain,' Ivan explained. 'I thought you knew.'

'You cannot expect me to know everything. I have so many, many burdens on my shoulders.' Vladimir waved his hand expansively, and for a moment Ivan glimpsed the signs of the megalomania which so many great men acquire.

'I'll do my best,' Ivan promised.

'Good, good. I want you to cultivate them, entertain them well, feed them only good stories about me, about the party, about our goals. Tell them we are civilized here. This is no Wild West. Wild East, perhaps.' He laughed suddenly, then added, 'I want to talk to them all. A press conference – you will arrange it. Do you understand, Ivan?' He stood up, Ivan with him, and put his muscular arms round his shoulders and gave him a powerful, breath-expelling hug.

'I understand, Vladimir,' Ivan responded, more than a little flattered, despite himself, at being given such a crucial role in the leader's campaign team. After that Vladimir turned and left him. He heard the shrieks and the laughter of women, then he found his way out to where his driver was waiting to drive him back to Moscow.

In the days thereafter, he worked hard and conscientiously out of the cramped little office he had been allocated at party headquarters, finalizing the arrangements for the press conference. Because of the rumour that Vladimir had masterminded the entire human floodtide, a large number of requests had been received from western journalists, asking for exclusive interviews; this would be the opportunity to deal with them all together. Ivan went through the lists, checking and assessing which ones might conceivably be more sympathetic than others. There were too few of those. Vladimir was his own worst enemy and was consistently reported on as being unbalanced or a total menace by most of the European and American media. To top it all, Ivan himself had received a fax from a banker friend of his back in London, commenting on his own recent exposure on BBC television. Unbeknown to him he had become something of a celebrity because of his perfect, upper-class English accent and because he was the spokesman for such an extreme cause. As a result, famous names, David Frost, David Dimbleby, and John Humphrys from the *Today* programme and others had put in requests to interview *him*. It had been a vain hope to believe that his respectable past would not eventually catch up with him. Thank God his mother would no longer be hurt by it all.

Until then he had hardly met nor mingled with other British people: he preferred it that way. There had only been two exceptions to this: the man whom he had briefly negotiated with in the car on Vladimir's behalf, and one very elderly Englishman, a longterm Moscow resident, whom he had tried to help in another way; neither could be described as typical expatriates. Now, almost overnight, his anonymity vanished. In a copy of the *Daily Mail* he bought one day at his hotel, he read, to his horror, a feature about himself, quoting a former colleague of his from the City who claimed to know him much more intimately than he had really done. But at that distance, some of the invented stories they wrote about him, the 'Public School Fascist', as he was now nicknamed by the tabloids, made him laugh rather than angry.

Later that day, he was halfway through translating one of Vladimir's interminable speeches into politically acceptable English, when there was a knock at the office door and, to his surprise, in walked Mr Nabakov, local party secretary and the current owner of his ancestral home.

Ivan stood up, smiling. 'Glad to see you again,' he said. 'What brings you to Moscow?' He was genuinely glad to see him, since on his all too brief visit to the big house, he had never steeled himself to explain why he had really come. Now he might have an opportunity to take matters further.

'Among other things, to see you, Ivan Ivanovich Katerski. I've come to ask for help.'

'Party matter?' Ivan enquired.

'Business, if you don't mind. As an English-speaker I want you to assist me in a little venture.'

'I'm only in the business of politics at the moment, Mr Nabakov,' said Ivan cautiously.

'None the less I thought I might persuade you to have dinner with me this evening.'

Ivan hesitated: he had to prepare for tomorrow's press conference. 'I am afraid that Vladimir –' he began.

'I have my daughter Tatiana with me. She is a fashion model with *Novi*, Moscow's best-known fashion house. That is another reason why I am here. She is so much looking forward to meeting you.'

'In that case, I would be delighted,' said Ivan Katerski, bowing politely. He would probably end up paying, but, on the house front, the evening might prove fruitful in the end.

*　　*　　*

On her birthday Murray took Carol-Anne to *La Bohème* at the Berlin Opera House. In the interval, Carol-Anne excused herself and made her way to the ladies, and the moment she was out of sight, an elderly, grey-haired man came up to stand four-square in front of Murray.

'Mr Murray, British Embassy?' He was a head shorter than Murray and stood staring intently up at him with sad, round eyes.

'That's me.' Murray smiled remotely.

'I'm sorry to accost you like this. I wonder if we could have a private word?'

'You're British?'

'I suppose I am.' The answer was a fraction odd.

'Please give me a ring at the embassy any time, or come and see me and I'll try to arrange something.' Murray fumbled in his wallet for one of his calling cards. 'You are Mr . . . ?'

'I'm not sure I could do that. You don't, by any chance, recognize me?' asked the little man.

Murray looked down at the stooped figure, noticing how tired his eyes looked, red-lined and watery. Yes, there was something vaguely familiar about his features.

'I'm sorry. Your name . . . ?' Murray could not quite place him.

'My name is a name from the past, Mr Murray. Again I apologize for buttonholing you like this, but once you remember, you'll understand why I couldn't come . . . to the embassy, that is, just like that. You see, my name is George Pike.' He paused deliberately, then went on. 'I want to come in from the cold.'

It was one of those few occasions in Murray's entire life when he found himself totally and completely lost for words. His lower lip dropped in amazement. 'George Pike,' he breathed. 'My God . . . I thought you were . . .'

'. . . either dead or in a dacha somewhere outside Moscow, I bet.' The old man smiled a thin little smile.

'Well, I'm . . . yes, I'm afraid that's what I did think.'

'You see the proof in front of you, Mr Murray. I'm not dead. I'm very much alive. And now, I want to come in from the cold,' Pike repeated.

'You want to come in from . . . ?' Murray, normally so self-assured, felt foolishly inept as he stumblingly echoed Pike's words.

'I want to know what would happen to me if I returned to Britain. I want you to make enquiries.' The old man's voice had become urgent.

Murray continued to flounder, wondering what on earth to do or say next. He looked round nervously, wondering if Carol-Anne was about to return, as if in some way he would be caught out doing something not quite respectable.

'I see you are here with a young lady. It took me a little time to identify you, but we have a mutual acquaintance in Moscow who helped me track you down. Before your friend returns,' George Pike spoke rapidly in low, compelling tones, 'I'm going to ring you some time tomorrow or the next day. I will say my name is George and ask whether you're prepared to meet me. I will ask if you have discovered from MI6 or whoever, what will happen to me, what charges will be laid against me, whether I will be put on trial, whether I will be put in prison if I decide to come back to Britain.'

Murray hesitated. 'How do I know you are who you say you are?'

'You recognize me. I know you do. Anyone would recognize me, shown old photographs. Why else would I risk coming to you here in Berlin rather than going to the embassy in Moscow and asking the same questions? I tell you, I want to come home.' The old man hesitated. 'But if you don't believe me,' he added mischievously, 'you could always get hold of your brother. Ask him. We've met once or twice.'

Out of the corner of his eye a flabbergasted Murray saw Carol-Anne reappear and advance towards them through the throng of opera-goers. 'My who? Where?' Murray stuttered.

'Tomorrow or the next day, remember. George Pike is the

name,' said the little man, with a wispish smile. 'Enjoy the rest of *La Bohème*,' he added. Then, without giving Murray a chance to say or ask anything more, he turned and disappeared among the crowd.

'Whoever was that?' asked Carol-Anne curiously as she came up to him.

'Elderly British resident.' Murray looked away, then quickly collected himself.

'You look thrown. He must have been telling you something pretty sensational,' she prodded.

'Didn't understand much of what he was talking about.' Murray flushed and, glancing at his watch, started fumbling with his programme. 'Why don't we go in and sit down,' he added quickly. 'The next act is about to start.'

'For once, Alex, I don't believe a word of what you're telling me,' said Carol-Anne looking at him intently. 'Just who was that little guy?'

'I don't know. I really do not know,' said Murray with such vehemence that she did not pursue the matter further.

Alone in bed that night Murray lay back on his pillows and thought about George Pike. Pike, perhaps the most famous British spy and defector after Burgess, Maclean and Philby. George Pike, the one the press had dubbed 'The Last Man', who had sold more defence secrets than anyone else of his generation. One day, in the early sixties, Pike had quietly left his desk at the Ministry of Defence and, when next heard of, was sitting in Moscow singing like a bird. Murray could not remember all the details, but, in his absence, Pike had been sentenced to something like forty years in prison for treachery. He had betrayed a generation; now he was asking to come in from the cold. And Pike . . . and George Pike knew his brother.

Murray slept extremely badly, then, towards dawn, fell into a deep sleep only to waken late, when he heard Frau Müller unlocking the front door and starting to prepare his breakfast. He looked at his watch. It was almost a quarter to eight. In a panic, he slipped into a dressing-gown and went and rang the MI6 station chief, Anthony Fox, at his home. When Fox answered, Murray said breathlessly: 'A fun one for you, Anthony. I mean it.'

'I feel like a joke,' came the dusty reply.

'Not on the telephone. Get into the embassy as soon as possible.'

Fox was already waiting for him in his office when he reached the chancery half an hour later.

'What's so exciting? Unearthed a spy?' Fox was more flippant than usual for that time in the morning.

'Good guess.' Murray had begun to relish his task. 'Let's go through to the secure room.' It was a windowless box at the back of the embassy that had been specially built to ensure that there was no question of conversations being bugged.

'Tell me.' Fox looked nonchalant, almost bored, as he fastened the security door and sprawled down at the small table. His was a steely profession where it never paid to show too much interest in what ordinary people thought important.

'George Pike.' Murray looked at the other man, waiting for his reaction. It came.

'He's died?' asked Fox.

'I met him last night.' It was, Murray had to admit, quite a punch line.

'The deuce you did.' Fox was suddenly very awake, very attentive.

'I met him last night,' Murray repeated. 'He came up to me at the opera and introduced himself.'

'The hell he did. How did he know who you were?' Fox was totally taken aback, his sangfroid abandoned.

'He'd done his research. I was with Carol-Anne. She went off to the loo and he came strolling up for a few minutes' chat. Cool as – '

'Chat? The devil he did. So what did he . . . you say?'

'Once I got my jaw off the floor,' Murray hesitated. 'I didn't have to say anything. Pike did the talking. He wants to come in from the cold.'

'My God.' Fox almost fell off his chair as if, suddenly, his body had failed to support him.

'He wants to know what will hit him if he goes back to London. Didn't he get forty years or something?'

'Something like that.' Fox was in a total daze. 'Fed up with Moscow, is he?'

'Didn't say, but could you blame him?' Murray speculated. 'I imagine his Soviet pension and everything else dried up long ago. All the honours and awards he was given were under the old regime. I can't believe that whoever are the new masters in the Kremlin have any interest in keeping somebody like him on their payroll.'

'How did he look?' Fox had grabbed a sheet of paper and a pencil and was making furious notes.

'Grey, tired, as if he was on his uppers.'

'Maybe he would actually welcome a square meal and free bed in Brixton prison.' Fox was talking more to himself than to Murray.

'What would he get?'

'HMG couldn't ignore him. I'm guessing, but they'd have to put him on trial or something. What age is he now?'

'In his late seventies, probably. If I were HMG I wouldn't want to touch him with a long bargepole. Too many skeletons buried for too long. You guys at MI6: what would you want?' Murray was curious.

'He'd hardly even be worth debriefing any more. 'Cept for historical reasons. So, we'd opt for peace and quiet. You know us,' said Fox with a flicker of a smile. 'Are you going to report this through your channels or shall I?'

'Well,' said Murray with a sigh. 'First of all, I thought, against my better judgement I know, I thought we'd better share this little gem with the ambassador. What do you think?'

'I'll go get him.' Fox rose to his feet. 'It'll make his day,' he said emphatically.

Left on his own for a moment, Alex Murray resolved not to mention Pike's last remark about knowing his brother . . .

After all, until he knew what that was all about, why should it be of any interest either to Fox or the ambassador?

When the greatest wave of all started pouring through the barbed-wire fences and across the borders from Russia, Belorussia, the Ukraine, Moldova, the former Yugoslavia, as well as from Albania and elsewhere further south, it was hundreds of thousands strong. When it began, the first thing to go on one key sector of the NATO front line was the power. As luck would have it, the army's stand-by generators and other back-up power sources had recently been flown out to the peacekeeping force in the Middle East. This added to the confusion facing the boys on that part of the border who had no ammo of which to speak, and no authority to shoot in any case. They were totally overwhelmed by the sheer numbers, and while there was remarkably little real violence, most of the troops felt they were lucky to get away with their lives. As luck would also have it, the NATO warlords were celebrating some anniversary or another back in Brussels and they and their ladies were dancing the night away in one of the most glittering of Belgium's ancient palaces when that greatest incursion began. Shades of the background sounds of approaching gunfire in the 1812 Overture, except that the cries and shouts along the hundreds of miles of frontier never carried to these crystal halls until it was far too late. One emigration of the have-nots was swiftly emulated by another, as the whole of civilized, prosperous Western Europe was threatened by an unstoppable, overwhelming tide.

A few hours later a BBC television team captured, with award-winning camera skills, the total futility of trying to contain it. True to form, Sergeant Tate recognized the same thing long before the news item had reached the editors who were coordinating the mass of other equally sensational reports back at Shepherd's Bush. His small detachment, rushed up to the line, comprised himself, a corporal, and six men; they had been delegated to guard the main entrance to a huge shopping mall on the outskirts of a neighbouring town. Eight British soldiers waited with small arms and enough ammunition to defend themselves if they were attacked. There was no question of shooting even plastic baton rounds at unarmed civilians. In any case they were almost immediately overwhelmed and isolated, since, long before that huge human tide arrived, all the shop assistants and floor managers, even the mall security guards, had fled to protect themselves and their own property where they could. They had locked the doors of the shops of course, and set all the burglar alarms, but that proved little impediment to thousands upon thousands of determined looters.

Yet, by and large, when they came, they were remarkably peaceable, even orderly. Sergeant Tate had witnessed indiscriminate looting before in his life, when he had briefly been part of a unit dispatched to Zaire in West Africa, to rescue a group of trapped British citizens during some civil war out there. That had been ugly and totally destructive. That which could not be carried away by the looters had been smashed or defiled, just for the hell of it. By contrast, this huge mass of people, having little property of their own, somehow respected it more. Private houses were, by and large, left intact by that otherwise all-engulfing flood. They plundered the shops and supermarkets, the car showrooms and furniture warehouses, and, above all, that treasure trove of treasure troves, the great hardware and do-it-yourself hypermarkets, with their mind-blowing displays of power tools, kitchens, bathrooms and other delights of comfortable western civilization.

So Sergeant Tate and his men merely stood aside and watched. He cleared his strategy of total inaction with headquarters; they confirmed, through their own confusion, that he should keep a very low profile and take no action that might provoke any hostility. How could it be otherwise? Eight soldiers against, at a guess, in his immediate area alone, a hundred thousand men, women and children, with their supermarket trolleys, their stolen cars, their vans, their lorries, their carts, their wheelbarrows, full of food, bottles of alcohol, fridges and washing machines and television sets; of Black & Decker electric drills, sacks of sugar and crates of cigarettes and a thousand other luxuries.

That teeming mass of humanity, where they noticed the soldiers at all, stared curiously at them, gave them a clear berth, and, when they saw them taking no obvious counter-action, largely ignored them. Sergeant Tate and his men watched and waited and meticulously reported all the looting that they witnessed to headquarters, while keeping their fingers nervously on the triggers of their small arms. Only twice in the course of that first long day did they feel a sense of any real threat. Once a Polish police car drove quickly through the crowd, its siren wailing, and someone from among the looters half-heartedly threw a brick at it, which missed. More threateningly, a German television crew appeared on the roof of one of the supermarkets and started filming the wholesale looting that was going on below them in the mall. One of the invaders spotted them, pointed upwards, and started shouting, which provoked a minor riot and a pursuit of the TV crew across the rooftops, with the latter just managing to escape with their lives, abandoning cameras and equipment in the process.

By mid-afternoon, as the dark was beginning to close in, most of the mob began to disperse, either back across the border with their booty or, in gangs, mainly of young men, further into western Europe on the search for ever more profitable lands to plunder. At dusk Sergeant Tate and his men were recalled to barracks where he spent much of the night writing up a full report which would never be read. It was as pointless an exercise as the whole day had been. They had looked in vain for an enemy to fight that was not there.

There was only one story that the western media, packed into the stuffy little hall, were after that day. They were furious when Vladimir, who was now universally believed to have masterminded the entire unarmed invasion, did not turn up to his own press conference. It was left to Ivan to develop a line in dealing with their excitable queries.

'What's Vladimir's reaction to these massive border incursions?'

Ivan's answer was cautious: 'Vladimir is fully sympathetic to the demands and aspirations of these poor people. He is with them in their struggle for a better life.'

'Is it true that Vladimir and his henchmen, including all of you working in the party secretariat, have, as certain western press agencies have been reporting, been working your way along the border refugee encampments encouraging these incursions?'

'We are seeing,' said Ivan wisely, 'a mass movement over which neither we nor any other group here in Moscow have any control. These poor people have their own local leaders: their motivation is the hunger that sears their bellies.'

'You are denying –' someone shouted at him.

'I have said what I have said.' Ivan spoke with more assurance than he felt.

'What does Vladimir want the western powers to do?' asked a man from *The Times* of London.

'The West is as responsible for the tragic situation as anyone, for bolstering up a corrupt Kremlin regime that has allowed this to develop.' Ivan felt that was his most telling and plausible line.

'Where is Vladimir?'

'He is busy.'

'Is that all you've got to say?' came a testy final question.

'That is all,' said Ivan Katerski briskly and shortly after that, the media people drifted off in more rewarding directions.

No call came from George Pike on Thursday and by Friday lunchtime Murray had almost convinced himself that meeting him at the opera had all been a bad dream. With the ambassador's approval, Fox had sent a long and detailed telegram to London asking for immediate instructions. First reactions were predictable. 'Drag the negotiations out,' they ordered. 'Don't promise anything; don't threaten. Tell Pike that it's impossible to read what the legal position would be. Tell him you need more time.' Then came another suggestion from London. 'Would it be better to alert the German security authorities that he is somewhere in Berlin and get them to pick him up? We would use our bilateral extradition agreement to winkle him quietly back to London in no time. Why should we even begin to negotiate with somebody like Pike?'

By three o'clock, with still no phone call, Murray had decided that he had been the subject of a gigantic hoax. He as good as admitted as much to the ambassador and Anthony Fox.

'I might agree with you, Alex,' said the ambassador, 'were it not for the fact that London got so excited. I suspect they'd got confirmative vibes out of Moscow. Pike's not alone: he and his ilk must be feeling a lot of hardship with their state pensions drying up.'

It was not until six-thirty in the evening, when Murray was about to leave for a reception at the French Embassy, that the telephone call eventually came.

Pike began by apologizing politely. 'I didn't realize how devious deal-making can be,' said the surprisingly confident voice at the other end.

'I don't understand.' Murray pressed a button by the telephone to start a tape-recorder which Fox had wired up to record the call when it came. It also would alert Fox in his office.

'Yes, I'd forgotten what the capitalist system could be like,' Pike went on softly.

Murray thought he detected that a slight note of amusement had crept into the man's voice. 'Would you like to explain?' he asked.

'What have you found out?' Pike countered. His voice had now turned almost aggressive.

'We need more time. I can't give you a view straightaway. There are charges outstanding and, in your absence, a sentence was passed.' Murray paused.

'The old stringalong, eh? That's what you're giving me? I know that line, Mr Murray. Surely after all this time they wouldn't keep me for forty years, would they? Let's see. That would last me until I was a hundred and eighteen.' Something that could have been a bark of laughter erupted at the other end of the line.

'With remission . . .' Murray began, realizing how pointless his words sounded. Behind him, he heard Fox steal breathlessly into his office.

'Ah, yes. Remission for good behaviour. Look, Mr Murray, I'm sorry to have bothered you, but I've been in Berlin for a month or so now. I've seen what the new West has to offer and it doesn't impress me overmuch. Except the money. That, I like very much. What I've been doing, consequently, is negotiating.'

'Negotiating?' Murray asked.

'What every public figure, every decaying ex-politician, seems to do these days. I'm negotiating to sell my memoirs,' Pike said bluntly.

Murray suppressed an oath. 'To whom?' he asked innocently.

'That would be telling, wouldn't it? I seem to have acquired quite a long short-list of bidders from the British press and London publishers alone. They don't seem to mind paying an old man like me, even though I've been called a traitor to my nation. That's why I've taken a little time to come back to you. I've done a deal, at least my lawyers and my literary agent tell me I have. A very nice deal. It'll translate excellently into roubles even at the present inflated rate of exchange.'

'So you've . . . ?'

'So I've decided not to come back after all. I don't really like what I've seen of the West anyway. There's a helluva lot of excitement in Russia these days. I've met a couple of fellow-Brits in Moscow recently who feel the same way: oh yes, one was your brother. He'll tell you exactly the same thing, Mr Murray. Shall I give him your regards, by the way? There was another fellow, too, former diplomat as well, I believe. He likes money just as much as me. Gave him a few tips on Russian survival techniques – but I digress.' Pike ploughed on without giving Murray a chance to respond. 'The advance I've got signed and sealed should see an old man like me through the next ten to fifteen years in reasonable comfort. Even without a sequel. I won't have to sell my dacha after all. It'll keep me in vodka, and I might even find a nice, cheap, companionable young lady to share my last days.'

'My brother? What diplomat? What have you decided?' Murray searched for any device to keep Pike on the end of the line for a little longer.

Pike interrupted him. 'So sorry to have troubled you, Mr Murray. Hate to give anyone time to trace this call while I'm talking. You do understand, don't you?' Then the line went dead.

After Murray had explained the gist of what Pike had said, Fox asked, 'What was that about your brother?'

'Dunno,' said Murray vaguely. 'He also talked about some former diplomat.' He was quite relieved when Fox did not pursue the point, but naively forgot, in that mood of excited disappointment, that the tape-recording of the conversation would be listened to later with the greatest possible attention.

Bobby Sofer, the commercial counsellor, held a reception at his apartment that following Monday evening for a group of prominent Scottish hoteliers. Murray went along largely out of national loyalty. To his dismay Fred Cree was there and deliberately manoeuvred him into a quiet corner.

'What the hell are you dips up to these days?' began Cree aggressively. 'You seem to be on a full-time cover-up mission right, left and centre. We're meant to have open government these days, remember!'

'What are you on about this time, Fred?' asked Murray cautiously. He had had his fingers burnt twice by Cree; he was not going to be caught out again.

'The Murphy case; the whole business of Simon Bricker; the embassy didn't begin to be helpful when I asked about Sir Randall Scase.'

'I can fill you in a bit on that,' said Murray helpfully.

'Water under the bridge now, thanks very much,' said Cree sarcastically. 'To top it all, my paper missed out on last week's second-biggest story.'

'What?' asked Murray innocently.

'Are you so busy that you can't remember what happened last week?'

'Last week we finally got the inspector's report on the future staffing of the embassy. That's our big story.'

'Might make a diary piece. Are they going to cut your job?' Cree brightened perceptibly.

''Fraid not. But we're subject to budget cuts like everyone else.'

'So . . .' Cree paused. 'After the catastrophic way NATO's reacting to the illegal immigrants crisis you might at least have won yourself some brownie points if you'd let on about George Pike.'

'Ah. George Pike,' Murray sighed.

'Whom you met last week.'

'You're guessing again, Fred. You're all over the place. You don't know,' Murray teased.

'You arranged to meet him last week, didn't you?' Cree persisted.

'That I deny absolutely.'

'But you met him?' Cree pressed.

'Why don't you come straight out with it?' said Murray chirpily.

'Pike claims he approached you to ask whether you'd get him off if he went back to Britain.' Cree was blunt.

'He told you that?' Murray was almost caught off guard.

'Well . . . to be precise, he told some friends of mine just that, while all the time he was very busy, complete with lawyers and accountants, trying to sell his story to the highest bidder. Fleet Street went wild, you know.'

Murray was intrigued by how well informed Cree was, as the journalist continued: 'He was using you at the embassy as a negotiating tactic, far as I can judge. Pretending he was thinking of coming back and handing himself over to the British authorities. That would have killed stone dead the chance of anyone publishing his memoirs for years to come. It was a clever move. His lawyers secretly contacted seven British national newspapers; they were all sworn to secrecy and flew out here in droves within hours. Working from his hotel room he negotiated the deal like there was no tomorrow. Why the story did not break I do not know. The *Guardian* dropped out at the first fence but he's picked up several hundred thousand pounds from someone. And it was hard cash up front. Said he couldn't trust us. Can you believe it? Couldn't trust the British press! Can you believe it?' Cree repeated.

'Believe it, Fred? Believe it? Maybe George Pike and I have something in common after all,' said Murray with conviction. 'By the way – you said second-biggest story?'

'Western Europe's actually been overrun by one of the largest invasions in world history – case you hadn't noticed.'

'Ah yes, but the diplomatic action is all happening in Brussels and Warsaw. We in Berlin are only keeping a watching brief, Fred. I'm hardly involved at all.'

9

It was impossible to do anything about repairing or strengthening the border fences before a second wave of Eastern Hordes, as the press were now calling them, flooded over into a still totally unprepared Western Europe. The headline writers surpassed themselves with the words they used to describe the scene – cataclysm, torrent, tempest, typhoon, floodgates splattered themselves across the headlines of the world's broadsheets and tabloids alike. In the reports themselves, seismic shock, terror waves, and flash floods were terms also widely employed to describe the so-called starving vandals and barbarians who poured with such gale force across the map of Europe. While thousands of the original illegal immigrants had been rounded up in the meantime and had been more or less peaceably herded on to buses and lorries and driven back to Belorussia, the Ukraine or to Russia itself, serious problems arose when NATO troops, helped by local police reinforcements, tried to relieve them of their loads of ill-gotten booty. Fights broke out as the forces of law and order vainly attempted to impound the stolen goods, to little purpose since the original ownership of most of it was never clear. In any event, most of the food looted from the supermarkets, if it was repossessed, usually ended up over the border as well, to help stock the depleted Red Cross food kitchens. Again and again they came in their hundreds of thousands, most often to return home after a day or so's looting, many to stay and move ever westwards, camping, squatting, taking over schools and churches and offices, and setting up temporary refugee centres wherever they could. The Poles and Hungarians fared the worst from these human locusts; the Germans and the French had more success in stemming the tide, since by the time the immigrants reached their geographical borders the numbers had fallen to more controllable proportions.

As part of a concerted response forced upon divided western governments, Sergeant Tate was posted to help man a hastily established NATO central population monitoring unit. There he helped plot, on huge ex-Cold War maps, the main migrations of people as they marched like a plague across the face of Europe. Even the great economic migrations that had resulted from the Second World War were as nothing in comparison. Meanwhile, the continent's politicians met in continuous sessions in Brussels, Paris or Berlin, achieving little beyond demonstrating, once again, their blinding indecisiveness and inability to agree on any common strategy. Typically, some ten days later, Tate was posted on again, to be replaced by a team of women army reservists specially flown out from London. He meanwhile went to augment the complement in the military attaché's office at the British Embassy in Berlin.

Outside the hotel the atmosphere was heavy with menace. Dark-windowed limousines were lined up by the door, while bull-necked security guards lurked in the shadows eyeing up the hookers that filed in and out of the lobby. In the restaurant and bars the general line taken by western business people was either that 'we're well taken care of, because our local partner is an ex-member of the KGB' or, another commonly overheard remark, 'I'm paying 3,000 dollars a month for protection, but it's worth it because if you make it here, you can make a mint'. Modern, capitalist Russia was a minefield, with no map to go by. Most legal agreements were worth less than the paper they were written on. There were meant to be something like 3,000 new banks in Moscow in which one could put one's money, but as old hands would tell you, there was no means of telling if any of them would still be there the next morning. Contract killings happened every day, as frequently as in Chicago in the days of Al Capone. Yet no gang members ever came to trial because prosecution witnesses were murdered before they got that far. Wherever a businessman went, he needed someone to protect him. Bodyguards – Afghan veterans were said to be the best – advised their clients that the best protection was to keep one's head down. Knowing how to survive in Moscow was number one on everyone's personal agenda.

Stretched out fully clothed on the large double bed inside his comfortable hotel room, Ivan worried about his own security. He thought back over the previous few weeks and to his fatal dinner with Nabakov. From that moment on, his problems in dealing with an ever more critical western press corps, coupled with the constant stick he was getting from Vladimir because of the bad coverage the latter was getting, were left behind. His own personal predicament loomed ever larger by comparison. It had started to go wrong that very night. At the crowded, noisy restaurant, the Russian had talked business for most of the time; his half-formulated idea was to set up a vodka-bottling factory somewhere in western Europe, preferably in Britain. He wanted Katerski to help him. In his untutored way, Nabakov exhibited all the attributes of the new-style Russian tycoon; in particular, pragmatic avarice. He admitted to supporting Vladimir for the simple reason that he, of all the political leaders, seemed to offer the most lenient regulatory laws. At the same time, like everyone else, he was prepared to pay a certain amount of protection money to whoever was currently the most powerful local Mafia boss, so that he could pursue his business interests with the minimum amount of intimidation or interruption. As he said jokingly, 'It keeps them from causing me grievous bodily harm,' but it was no joke. He also admitted to forking out generously in the direction of the local bureaucracy to avoid some of the worst formalities in getting anything done in modern Russia. As both explanation and evening progressed, Ivan had found it increasingly difficult to concentrate on what Nabakov was saying because of his daughter, Tatiana. Dark-haired, sensuous, stunningly beautiful, with great wistful eyes, she sat silently watching them both, hardly ever uttering a word herself.

'What knowledge do you have of vodka-making?' Ivan feigned brief interest. Despite himself he found the answer surprising.

'Over the last few years I have built up one of the biggest vodka-bottling plants in private hands in our entire region. I own it, but profit little from it.' Nabakov snorted. 'More and more I'm being coerced and swindled by the local Mafia ginks who force me to sell only to them, then double the price before they sell on to the domestic and western markets. I want to bypass the bastards.'

'The Mafia are everywhere.' Ivan nodded in sympathy. 'People keep telling Vladimir he must do something about them, that they are worse than the communists. That is why they all rush to support the party.'

Nabakov hesitated, glanced round the restaurant, then dropped his voice. 'I hope you are not fooled, my young friend. Vladimir has his Mafia contacts too. He needs their support, or, at least, he needs to ensure they are not his enemies. He knows the old Russian proverb – "Free cheese only exists in mousetraps".'

All the time the two men were talking, Nabakov's daughter continued to sit in silence, watching Ivan closely. He was all too aware of her attentions and, equally, that he would rather be talking to her than to her father. She was tall and slim, with a pale, translucent skin. Her long hair framed a strong, attractive face: unlike most models he had met in London, she wore almost no make-up. She needed none: her eyes were naturally large, her cheekbones high, her lips full. Yes, Ivan desperately wanted to get to know her rather than hearing about some potentially dangerous and, doubtless, dubious vodka production deal.

Yet for that and several other good reasons, by the end of the evening Ivan Katerski had agreed to investigate the possibilities of opening up some joint venture in the United Kingdom. One was that Nabakov began talking about very large sums of money indeed; a second was that, as an apparently stalwart member of the party, he promised a substantial political donation if the

British deal went through; thirdly, though he still made no mention of it, there was the old house, which, when he got carried away by his dreams, Ivan thought he might try to buy and restore to its former glory. Above all there was Tatiana. He very much wanted to meet her again.

At the end of that evening – Ivan had scarcely taken in his surroundings in that big noisy restaurant, except when a roving gipsy string band played too loudly and too close to their table – Nabakov suddenly stood up. 'I must go now; I promised to call on your aunt early tomorrow,' he said to his daughter. 'Do you want to come with me or will you . . . ?' He paused, smiled, and she smiled back at him. Tatiana had stayed on.

In the following weeks, many things happened. Ivan and Tatiana met frequently; their mutual attraction overwhelmed them both, and soon they became lovers. When he rented a semi-permanent suite in his hotel, she moved in with him.

But with the pleasure that she brought came many dangers. In between continuing to work as a press spokesman for the party, he faithfully tried to promote the business proposition that Nabakov had put to him. He opened up direct contact with a large bottling company based in the north-east of England, and they, impressed by his enthusiasm and his apparent English pedigree, sent out a team to follow up his proposals and to scrutinize the draft business plan that he and Nabakov had drawn up between them. But the negotiations leaked as they always do in Russia, and when the deal looked as if it might take off and prosper, unpleasant pressures quickly came to bear upon him.

During his long months in Russia Ivan Katerski had often come across a species of men, bedecked with gold chains and other jewellery, who all seemed to wear sunglasses permanently. These were the Mafia. He had, fortunately, never had direct experience of them or their techniques, but media stories about the corpses they left in the wake of their activities were legion. He kept clear; he was, after all, a mere underling in Vladimir's team, and partially protected by that great leader. As Nabakov had explained, however, even Vladimir had to keep his options open. The Mafia had the brute power, they had the bullets, and they had the money. Vladimir had only his political support. Ivan's idealism was far from blind, but his trust in Vladimir and what he stood for diluted his appreciation of one natural fact: the criminal and the political were close and natural bedfellows in modern Russia.

Thus it should have come as little surprise to him when, with two or three other party workers, he went with Vladimir early one evening to what he believed was to be a meeting with potential supporters, who were intent on breaking away from another fringe party of the right. Their leaders had apparently indicated that they might welcome some sort of coalition. Ivan immediately became suspicious when he discovered that the meeting was to take place in the opulent presidential suite on the penthouse floor of the very hotel in which he now lived. This was not the natural setting for political power-broking in Moscow. The four men who were waiting for Vladimir and his companions were cold, powerful, and flashily dressed. One obviously wore a bullet-proof vest, like a fashion accessory, under his Gucci jacket. He had a pony tail and a large gold and diamond ring in his ear. He was known as the Kestrel and was reputed to run Russia's biggest laboratory for drug refining. He, Vladimir whispered with a sneer, as they waited to enter the suite along with their bodyguards, was a man who, single-handedly, was doing more via his drug running to destroy the fabric both of Russian and of western society, than Stalin and his cronies had ever been able to achieve.

In an adjoining bedroom, Ivan briefly glimpsed through a partly open door a number of scantily-dressed young ladies lounging about on sofas, waiting to do their duty. While he did not follow all that went on at the subsequent meeting, what he did understand he did not like. Even Vladimir, with his armed bodyguards standing tensely around him, seemed ill at ease. With allies like these, if allies they were, was this where Ivan's western, democratically-educated loyalties should lie? He believed in a greater Mother Russia with a strong and economically viable future, but did such a cause need such shadowy supporters?

He tried to blend into the background. He said nothing and no one spoke to him nor appeared to acknowledge his presence. His mind wandered. They were talking big money. They were talking deals about which he knew little. He was not sure why Vladimir had brought him along in the first place. Then, as the meeting was on the point of breaking up, one of the Mafia figures, a man of about his own age, with dark, shiny hair and a well-tanned face that showed up the thick gold medallion he wore on a chain at the open neck of his broad-collared shirt, came across to him, took him firmly by the arm and steered him into a washroom by the door of the suite, firmly closing the door behind him.

'How are things in Britain?' The man smiled through eyes that were as grey as flint. He turned and flushed the toilet, then ran the taps on the wash-hand basin and left them running. 'It helps drown conversations if anyone is trying to listen,' he explained helpfully.

'I haven't been back for several months.' Ivan was more than a little shaken that the man knew anything about him.

'I hear you're looking at a joint venture with a British company.' The man's pressure on his arm tightened perceptibly.

'What d'you mean?' Ivan Katerski briefly and unwisely played the innocent.

'You know precisely what I mean.' The man was still smiling. 'You've been talking to our close friend, Mr Nabakov. Sadly he hasn't shared all his plans with us, but we understand he means to set up a vodka-bottling plant in Britain. You are helping him, perhaps?' It was very much a statement and not a question.

'We have had some preliminary discussions . . .' Ivan heard his voice tailing away. He was not sure how to play this game, but he was all too alert to its underlying dangers.

'We hope it goes well. We wish you every success. We really do. We are sure you are a key figure in making it happen and that there will be plenty of money, or profit, profit that can be shared, if you understand my meaning. We want to be part of your deal. You understand clearly, don't you?' The Mafia man smiled again, this time showing a line of gold-capped teeth. 'We like to be very closely involved in any business deal like this with our friendly western neighbours. Do not keep us waiting. And, if you value your . . . business partner's contribution, make sure Mr Nabakov fully understands that as well.' The man kept smiling. It was not a pretty nor reassuring sight.

When the brief conversation was over, and the Mafia man left the washroom, Ivan emerged to look for Vladimir, but he and the other men had all vanished in the direction of the room where the girls had been waiting. Of all the bodyguards there was no sign. Ivan wisely decided not to go in search of his leader but to slip quietly away to the partial security of his own room. When he got there he collapsed in a chair and stared down at his hands. They were shaking uncontrollably.

Party political conferences do not normally provide highly romantic settings; if anything they are occasions for illicit affairs, usually but not always between self-important men and younger impressionable women. The Munich conference might have been otherwise. The city itself is an attractive, lively place with many exciting bars and nightspots that can cater to the entire range of human desires. Murray and Carol-Anne Capaldi, dispatched there by their respective ambassadors to cover the annual conference of the extreme-right-wing German National Party and to report back on the prospects of Professor Dieter Krauss picking up a sizeable percentage of votes in the forthcoming Federal elections, saw little of all this fringe activity. They did their work conscientiously and well, but then they were indiscreet enough to spend their nights together in a shared hotel room.

Because of this a tangential problem arose. It hit them when Sir Edward Cornwall tried to reach Murray late on the second night of the conference, to call him back because of the further mass incursion of starving refugees across Poland's eastern borders. It was Carol-Anne who reached across her friend's supine, naked body to answer the telephone. Consequently, when they arrived back in Berlin, the ambassador sent for Murray and demanded to see his hotel and travel claim, more or less accusing him of fiddling his expenses by booking in with Carol-Anne.

'I imagine your American friend's putting in an expenses claim for a separate room.' Sir Edward was terse.

'Sir. Before you say anything that you might regret,' said Murray, flushing with fury at the pettiness of the accusation, 'let me say that we have both only and exactly claimed for what we have spent. In addition, Carol-Anne and I have just decided to get engaged.'

Without another word, he turned on his heel and stormed out of the ambassador's room, rushed back to his office, and telephoned Carol-Anne to tell her what had transpired. 'I've told the Old Man that we got engaged,' he added, a trifle lamely.

There was a silence at the other end of the line, then, 'Have we?' she asked softly.

'Unless you've had further thoughts,' Murray said hesitantly. He was shaking with a mixture of pent-up anticipation and the flood of his anger.

'I *have* been thinking. We should talk further. We've everything going for us at the moment,' came the guarded reply.

'What d'you mean?' Murray asked. He knew too well what she meant.

'Just that we should talk some more,' said Carol-Anne, defensively. 'Don't worry, though. If I'm strung up, horse-whipped, cross-examined and made to confess, I'll stick to the party line.' She laughed emptily, told Murray to relax, then rang off, leaving him even more unsettled and confused than before.

In his office, the ambassador might conceivably have been found to be somewhat put out at having his accusation thrown back at him. But instead, he was metaphorically rubbing his hands in muted glee. Diplomatic spouses are almost never permitted, in such a nationalistic profession, to be serving members of another country's foreign service. He was confident that either Murray or Carol-Anne Capaldi would eventually have to resign. In the meantime their very public affair was in danger of becoming an intolerable conflict of interests in the professional confines of Berlin diplomatic life. He summoned Sylvia Watt and began dictating a *Personal and Confidential* letter to the head of personnel department asking for an urgent replacement for Murray.

Later, Murray bumped into Sylvia Watt in the corridor outside his office and she drew him to one side and whispered urgently in his ear.

'Watch your backside,' she said robustly.

'About?' he asked.

'Your American friend – your engagement.'

'I thought engagements were a cause for celebration,' Murray said lightly.

'The Old Man thinks so too. Conflict of interests and all that. He thinks he may have got the skids under you.'

'Got the point. Thanks, Sylvia.' He smiled.

'Oh, and by the way, can I add my congrats too.' With that Sylvia pursed her lips ever so slightly as befitted someone who had missed out on the engagement stakes, and left him alone with his thoughts.

The uneasy conversation with Carol-Anne focused Murray's mind. Was he really headed towards a second marriage? He had never thought of himself as becoming a family man; never had, never would. Apart from his all too brief months with his wife, Marcia, culminating in her wasting death from cancer, he had been self-sufficient. It stemmed, he supposed, from the remoteness and isolation of his adolescence. His father – how difficult it was to picture him now – had died when Alex was only four. Looking back, he had withdrawn into a hard defensive shell for years thereafter. His mother had of course been there, vague and unhappy after her husband's death, until she too was swept away from him into a new marriage and family of her own. That new, strange, Russian stepfather and a wayward, noisy, often violent young half-brother, had served to drive him even further into self-sufficiency. There were distant relatives of course, but his contacts with them were polite affairs, ruled more by occasional duty than by any emotion.

175

Was there emotion with Carol-Anne? There certainly was intellectual stimulation, there was even better sex, there was more laughter than he had had in years, there was a demanding companionship, a multiplicity of mutual interests. But was this the shape of their future together? Carol-Anne's dedication to her profession, her inner tensions and her resolute approach to life which sometimes bordered on the opinionated, seldom allowed him any relaxation while he was with her. At first he had welcomed the challenge; now he realized he might just relish the tranquillity of getting on with the rest of his life without always feeling guilty that he too was not operating in overdrive. Yes – he agreed with her. They should talk further.

As befitted a child brought up in the harsh, food-rationed, postwar years under the rule of the Allied occupation forces, Frau Müller was nothing if not resolute. Under that conventional, austere exterior, she was as sharp and street-wise as the Berlin urchin she once had been. She knew what it was to survive on a diet of potato soup, how to haggle and barter with contraband cigarettes for black market silk stockings. Frau Müller also had a degree of loyalty to her new employer that became her well. She knew it was her duty to inform Herr Murray immediately of what she had found.

He was sitting at the breakfast table browsing through the *Berliner Zeitung* when she came in carrying his usual tray with coffee pot, toast and two boiled eggs. He put down his paper as she set them out in front of him.

'Thank you, Frau Müller.' He glanced up at her.

'Did you have a good evening, yesterday, Herr Murray? The French Embassy, wasn't it?'

'Cooking superb, company boring.' He smiled.

'Fräulein Capaldi was not there perhaps?' she asked sympathetically.

'Correct. You might as well know – I'm sure you'll hear – Carol-Anne and I are thinking of getting married. Just thinking; nothing definite yet.'

'I am most pleased for you, Herr Murray. Congratulations,' said Frau Müller cautiously. She was hesitant about how far she should go.

'Nothing firm. No dates. Just to warn you,' Murray added, wondering at his caution.

Frau Müller seized the opportunity to broach her subject. 'I have been tidying up the big store cupboard behind the kitchen,' she began. 'You know the one – '

'Yes, yes. I leave all that to you,' said Murray, turning back both to his breakfast and to the *Berliner Zeitung*.

'I've thrown out a lot of old boxes, newspapers and bottles, left over from Herr Young's time here,' Frau Müller persisted.

Murray again looked up at her, curious as to why she should wish to chat. She knew he liked peace and quiet over breakfast, before the turmoil of his long office day. He none the less took the opportunity he was offered. 'You knew Mr Young?'

'I thought you were aware, Herr Murray. I worked for him for about nine months but . . . we did not get on . . . and his lifestyle . . .'

'His lifestyle?' Murray questioned.

'I'm not one to gossip, Herr Murray.' Frau Müller looked away.

'Of course not. But?' Murray prompted.

'Some other time, perhaps,' she added a little stiffly. 'But before I leave you to get on with your breakfast, I must . . . I should tell you that, under all that rubbish in the storeroom, I found this. In the rush, when he had to leave so suddenly, Herr Young must have forgotten about it.' Frau Müller walked back to the door and returned carrying with difficulty a heavy, grey, metal-bound case; she laid it triumphantly on the floor beside him, and looked at him expectantly. It was an unusually long shape and there were two metal clasps holding the lid shut. They were made to hold padlocks but the case was unlocked.

As soon as Murray opened the case and saw its contents, he knew that something highly significant had been uncovered. In a flash of recall, he also remembered that his predecessor had spent much of his career in the passport office in Petty France in London, and that, before his posting to Bonn and Berlin, he had been promoted to head of migration and visa department in the Foreign and Commonwealth Office. As such, Young would know the very heavy penalties for taking away from the office, indeed for stealing and hiding large bundles of blank British passports at his home, along with a wide selection of official stamps, embossing equipment and rolls of the transparent security tape that was designed to prevent passport photographs from being tampered with or replaced. Here, in this abandoned case, was all the equipment needed, not to *forge* British passports, but to issue ones that would be, to all intents and purposes, entirely genuine. No matter what infra-red scanners immigration officers might use to look for the correct water-marks or the other high-tech devices employed to detect pages that had been split so as to insert a new photograph without breaking the security film, the possessor of one of these would walk straight through the checklines fully in the clear. The going rate for such a forged-genuine British passport, quite apart, Murray noted, from the large bundle of blank visa forms and other official stamps in the box, would have ensured that Douglas Young had a very tidy pension nest-egg. What else had he taken that all this could so lightly be abandoned in the haste of his departure?

Frau Müller might have been reading his mind. 'I remember seeing them before,' she said uncertainly.

'Them?' he asked quickly.

'Yes. They are unusually-shaped cases are they not? I remember: there were two of them. They arrived one day, separately from his other heavy baggage that came out from London. I remember that Mr Young was most concerned. They arrived unexpectedly; I took delivery of them. I told him that to my surprise, the man who brought them did not want any delivery slip signed. I thought that a little odd.'

To Frau Müller's interest and only slight annoyance, her find and her subsequent remarks caused her employer to abandon his *Berliner Zeitung* and boiled eggs – she would make the latter into a tasty salad for his supper – and, lugging the heavy grey case with him, leave rapidly for the embassy. Frau Müller was a percipient woman. She understood only too well the extreme importance of her discovery.

Alex Murray walked into Anthony Fox's office carrying the case, put it down on a table and shut the door firmly behind him. Fox knew from the expression on his colleague's face that he had come on serious business.

'Found by my cleaning lady,' said Murray, dramatically opening it to display its contents. 'Would this, by any chance, have anything to do with why Douglas Young left in such a hurry?' He would have taken his find straight to the ambassador, but the latter was giving a speech at an Anglo–German trade conference in Cologne.

Fox gave a sudden intake of breath, bent over, picked up a bundle of blank passports, then quickly examined the other contents. 'Well, this is the works, isn't it? All the additional proof I needed. All much too late now,' he added, staring grimly at Murray.

'According to my housekeeper, there once were two of these –'

'The devil there were!' Fox broke off for a moment, then continued. 'Sorry to have been so secretive about Young, Alex, but if I tell you that this,' he waved at the contents of the case, 'is nothing in comparison with the enormity of what your predecessor appears to have done . . .' His voice tailed off as he again stared down at the contents of the case. 'I asked permission, as I promised, to tell you what happened, but London said no. So now I'm telling without asking.'

'Spying, was he?' Murray probed. Espionage had always been the most heinous of all crimes in the diplomatic service. The other man was dismissive.

'On what; for what?' said Fox bitterly. 'Only commercial espionage is of any real monetary value to traitors these days. This is . . . Look, what's the single most important task you've been dealing with since you arrived here, Alex?' he prompted.

'I suppose . . . the refugees crossing.'

'Exactly. So if any or all of them had access to, say, tens of

179

thousands of perfect, non-forged British passports, each one in immaculate order, each one undetectable, because every detail of the high-tech security devices we currently use to stop forgeries were known to those who bought them, and . . .' Fox paused and sat behind his desk. 'And if there was another more organized break-out, one that was carefully orchestrated and encouraged, one that, because of the professionalism involved, we were not able to stop for some hours or even days, how could anyone prove, with documents as real as these,' Fox held one of the blank passports up and shook it, 'who was legitimate and who not?'

'The results could be incalculable; the great march of the starving masses would become a permanent reality,' breathed Murray. 'Where did Young go?'

Fox spoke quietly. 'Appears to have gone to Moscow, or has recently been there. You surely remember Pike mentioned to you that he had met a former diplomat – probably him. One contact suggests he may have already sold himself, or what he has to offer, to some clever Mafia entrepreneurs. They'll be well capable of doing the rest. In Young they have someone who knows as much about the security details of the passport business as anyone else in Britain.'

'Why isn't this known? Why hasn't the story leaked, become public?' asked Murray, bewildered. 'Has Young been formally charged?'

'A whole bunch of questions there, Alex,' said Fox with unusual tolerance. 'The answers lie in the fact that when we first had our suspicions, when we uncovered the tip of what Young was up to, that he might be selling a few genuine passports for beer money here and there, to cover his gambling debts, we pulled him back to London to confront him. We were very slack. We underestimated the nature of the man. He had grander plans. All we did was scare him. He came back briefly, then did a flit, probably destroying a bit of evidence in the fire he started in your office on the way, in his haste leaving this case of passports behind in your flat.'

'Two cases.'

'I told you, news to me,' responded Fox, 'until now, that is.'

'And Bennett? What did he know?'

Fox shrugged. 'Too much to be sent home in disgrace where he might try to get his own back by talking to the papers. Which is why the bugger's still here. But it's Young's whereabouts that are critical. Not to put too fine a point on it: we don't know where the hell he is or who he's with. Our most trusted contacts in the Russian intelligence community, particularly the FSB, their security service, are trying to help us track him down, or say they are, but he's totally vanished. And – '

'In the meantime, HMG can't possibly admit to anything, or the press outcry would be enormous. The floodgates would be opened,' Murray speculated aloud, suddenly realizing the enormity of what he had been told. 'Our immigration controls would be worse than useless, wouldn't they? The masses wouldn't need to push down those razor-wire fences, they could just walk through immigration.'

'We have emergency plans almost in place,' Fox explained. 'The experts back in London are at it flat out. But most of the immigration people who are working on the solution can't be let into the real secret, so it all takes time. It's a huge operation. Just think of the chaos at every airport and dock, let alone the Channel Tunnel, if all genuine British passport holders had to be verified in other ways, checking home addresses and so on, before they were allowed through. It's not just here in Germany that immigration controls are a hot potato. In the UK, the right wing, and the left wing, and everyone else for that matter who realizes that jobs would be at risk, that pressures on housing would be enormous, the burden on the health service and social security system and so on, would go bananas.'

'Even if only a tiny proportion of them hid till the fuss died down. I see it all now,' echoed Murray in a small voice. 'So this . . . ?' He pointed to the case and its contents.

Fox was cynical. 'It may be the only hard evidence we have if we eventually find him and try to nail him. But I suspect it's the other case and what it contains that really matters now.'

The rest of the day was particularly hectic as, by chance,

they were for Carol-Anne Capaldi at her embassy. Both she and Murray were dog-tired when they came together late that night, though not sufficiently so for them to quarrel openly. But things had changed, and it was totally without tears and without recriminations that, in bed around midnight, they decided not to get engaged after all. They slowly came to recognize, in weary reflection, that they were both too firmly wedded to their careers. 'Why don't we keep on the way we've been going. It suits us both,' was what each of them more or less whispered to the other. Their relationship had developed so easily and so rapidly that both had thought it inevitable that they would get married. But faced with the blunt reality stirred up by Murray's much regretted face-saving announcement to Sir Edward and what havoc such a move would cause to both their prospects, they stepped gently back from that brink. What they did agree was that they would leave it for some time before Murray, swallowing his embarrassment, would pluck up sufficient courage to go back and tell Sir Edward Cornwall that the engagement that had never been on, was off.

There was one brief plus point in the grim day that followed. Murray had, some time in the distant past, read an article about the theory of coincidence. Chance happenings occurred in everyone's lives, and he had always felt he had experienced his fair share. Thus it was that at the end of a day's hard work, followed by a formal diplomatic dinner at the Malaysian Embassy, he took a taxi back to his apartment. The driver took a route through the centre and, in between Schönhauser Allee and Hermannplatz, stopped briefly at some traffic lights. Murray, idly looking out of the window, suddenly sat up very alert, as he spotted that constant thorn in his flesh, Paul Fawcett, emerging furtively from the doorway of something called the Black Whip Club. It was a well-known nightspot that Sir Edward, quite apart from his politically correct wife, would certainly not approve of his adored first secretary frequenting. The taxi moved on through the heavy traffic and Fawcett was soon lost to view. But Murray had seen enough.

The next morning, when Fawcett strode in bumptiously as was his wont, and started instructing Murray about something the ambassador had told him he wanted done immediately, the latter was able to make his mark. Without looking up from his desk, he said, 'You sound a bit jaded today, Paul. Spent too long in the Black Whip last night, did you? Don't worry. Unless anything untoward happens, your secret is safe with me.'

Fawcett turned grey, his mouth opened and he started to say something, then he checked himself and quickly left the room. From then on, Murray knew that his unspoken, gentle blackmail would ensure that he had little further trouble from his mischief-making deputy.

10

It was the best speech he had ever heard Vladimir make. The audience was small, but it was select. They were the men and women with the metaphorical megaphones, who would let a world audience hear his every word. After the abortive press conference, Ivan had at last persuaded fifty of the world's press to come to listen to Russia's most unpredictable politician again; he did not fail them. It was his best speech and by far his most dangerous. They listened in spellbound silence.

'The official crest of Russia, my friends, is the double-headed eagle,' he began. 'There is a huge symbolism about that, since one head has always looked inward at our ancient Russian despotisms, while the other stares longingly westwards to your so-called European progress and civilization. The tension between these two Russias of ours has always marked our history. This dichotomy has produced the best and worst out of Russia: anarchy versus dictatorship, heroism versus corruption, where only the strong, the dictator, can really rule effectively. Without our Catherine the Greats, our Genghis Khans, or, as Trotsky said of Stalin, Genghis Khan with a telephone, Russia seems to pursue a perpetual death wish.' His audience laughed at that last anecdote. Was Vladimir going to compare himself to these greats from the past?

'Lenin is laughing in his grave,' Vladimir went on, with no trace of humour in his voice. 'The cowboy economy we now have has got right out of hand. Crony capitalism fulfils his prophecy of huge inequalities, high-level corruption, higher prices, the enrichment of the few at the expense of the weak and the old. Russia is like your America a century ago; it is completely dominated by a frenzied race to get rich. There are no rules of market nor of society. What Mother Russia needs now is financial transparency, fair competition, clear laws and a proper taxation system. And strong leadership. Instead we have a Wild West free-for-all. A flashy plutocracy rules. In the Duma, deputies, as like as not, have criminal pasts. A friend of mine in the Interior Ministry has a list of fifty sitting members who have been in prison, who claim parliamentary immunity to keep them out of jail again. What sort of nation is this? This stirring giant must be harnessed for the national good lest it destroy us all.' Vladimir paused and sipped at a glass of what looked like water that stood on the table in front of him. Ivan knew it was neat vodka, but for once he was not worried. Vladimir in full flow needed more than a bottle of vodka to stop him.

The speaker stared contemptuously round the room at the assembled journalists, then continued. 'Once again there come whimpers from the Kremlin giving so-called notice to Russia's criminals and profiteers that their days of plundering the nation's wealth are over. Bah! They merely laugh at that. Yet Russia has reached a turning point. We must crush organized crime or die. Criminal elements in pursuit of easy money have infiltrated this present government at every level. They sit there, bloated at the feeding trough. Currently, ladies and gentlemen, no fewer than eight generals and admirals, and a matching number of senior officers from customs, the tax inspectorate and the procura- tor's office, have been convicted of serious crimes. In the Urals and in western Siberia, Mafia gangs have taken total control of local government and are running a terror campaign over the lives of tens of thousands of ordinary people. Look out- side: Moscow's vile streets are jammed with the BMWs and Mercedes of the new rich who are buying up million-pound apartments in London, New York and across western Europe. I know for a fact that organized Russian crime syndicates have joined forces with Colombian drug traffickers in a deadly trade of high-tech weapons in exchange for cocaine. According to your own *Washington Post*, Russians suspected of having ties to organized crime have set up more than a dozen banks on

Caribbean islands, in particular on Aruba and Antigua, which enable them to launder money without their profits being identified or seized. These are not petty criminals; these are big Mafia boys, backed by former KGB agents with access to the most sophisticated information. They are almost impossible to control. Any arrests that have been made by your American cops have merely been the tip of the iceberg.'

Vladimir was coming to his conclusion. There was a total silence in the room. 'You all know something of this great country of mine,' he said softly. 'Much about Russia is still magical. The Golden Ring, the holy cities of Russia, still pre-serve their medieval Kremlins, their fortified monasteries, their beautiful cathedrals. Great lakes and rivers still adorn a Russian countryside of timeless beauty. Even Moscow itself, with its multi-domed St Basil's cathedral out there, its Red Square, even the Kremlin, which itself contains three whole cathedrals, may seem to you to rise above the ugly squalor of our streets. I will not let corrupt politicians and Mafia hoods destroy my country. That, ladies and gentlemen, is why I am fighting this great campaign. That is why I will triumph in the end.'

When the stunned applause, unusual at a press conference, had died away, Vladimir sat back in unusual silence, watching as Ivan tried to field follow-up questions from the western press corps. Each one was pushing, interrogating, demanding, looking for an exclusive, a slant, a piece of mischief-making, that would add to the headlines in tomorrow's press that Vladimir had declared open war on the Mafia. That was real news. That was brave, very brave. Vladimir, his speech over, no longer had to stay sober and his tumbler of vodka held firmly in his right hand was constantly refilled. Surrounded by his sinister, equally silent bodyguards, was Vladimir laughing at him or mocking or decrying his efforts? Tomorrow, would he praise or condemn Ivan? A man from the BBC World Service was being particularly insistent. He demanded an interview with Vladimir for the Russian service. It would, he promised, be honest, sincere, unprejudiced. By contrast, a journalist by the name of Fred Cree, sent by his paper from Berlin to Moscow to cover the immigrant flood story from the other side, wanted to do a joint profile: Vladimir and his spin doctor, his British public-school-educated mouthpiece. Ivan gave a glance across at Vladimir, as if looking for guidance or reassurance, but Vladimir only smiled. No, he said, by new-learned instinct, Vladimir had said all he was going to say. So, of course had he, Ivan Katerski. He was merely an unattributable spokesman for the greater cause.

Eventually he pacified, or placated, or put them off. The western press wandered away to file their stories. When they had all gone Ivan turned to where Vladimir and his bodyguards had been sitting, to find that they too had disappeared. As things turned out, he would never see Vladimir again.

Ivan did, however, meet Fred Cree once more, or rather Cree set it up so that they bumped into each other later that night, when Ivan had been drinking with some friends in the hotel bar. Cree waited until Ivan was on his own, then strolled up to where he was sitting at a corner table.

'Hello there, remember me, Fred Cree?' he said. 'We met earlier today at the press conference.'

Ivan looked up, less than pleased at being disturbed. 'Can I buy you a nightcap?' Cree asked. Ivan shook his head. Even in his somewhat drunken state, he knew to be wary.

Cree shrugged. 'OK,' he said, 'but look, I do want to press this idea of doing a profile of you. You've built up a great deal of interest in the British press, given your background, who you are a spokesman for, and all that. I'd just do the human interest bit, you know. All nice stuff. You don't need to get worried. It would be very sympathetic both to you and Vladimir's cause.'

Ivan looked up and the ghost of a smile played across his face. 'No way,' he said. 'I'm just a spokesman, unattributable, like I said earlier on.'

'If you could just give me a little bit of background on your-self, where you come from, family, parents, brothers, sisters and so on, I could do the work myself, then come back to you to fill in with a few easy questions. How about that?' said

Cree. 'Are you sure you won't change your mind about that nightcap?'

Again, Ivan shook his head. 'No thanks, no nightcap and, talking of brothers, mine certainly wouldn't like reading about me after what I've been doing.'

'Why's that?' asked Cree casually, as if he wasn't really listening.

'Part of the establishment, my brother,' said Ivan.

'Really?' asked Cree. He kept his voice low, trying to disguise his excitement. This was the line he had been following, courtesy of that man Bricker.

'Yep, he's a diplomat.'

'A British diplomat?'

'Yep.'

'In the Foreign Office in London?'

'I think he's in Berlin.'

'Berlin? Like to give me his name?' asked Cree.

Suddenly all the warning lights were flashing. 'No way, no way,' said Ivan as he pulled himself to his feet. He waved jovially at Cree and made his way unsteadily towards his hotel suite and to the waiting arms of Tatiana Nabakov. In the meantime, Cree went back to his room, to telegraph his office to ask for a complete list of all the diplomats presently serving in the British Embassy in Berlin.

From then on, events took on a catastrophic momentum of their own. Nabakov had rung Ivan incessantly over the last few days, pressurizing him to get on with the deal. The next evening he rang him again at his hotel. This time he was very different, highly upset and emotional. Ivan was aware that he had often been threatened by hoodlums in the past, but Nabakov had always shrugged: he knew how to handle them, he said; he knew how far he could go and when he needed to buy them off. But now something had gone seriously wrong. Today his much-prized Mercedes had been destroyed by a car bomb: it was by pure chance that he had been late in using it that morning. At the other end of the line Nabakov sounded deeply shaken.

Suddenly he came out with his startling plea: he begged Ivan to get out of Moscow, to go home to Britain and set up the deal, while he tried to placate the Mafia. Nabakov had one other, even more unexpected request. Impressed by the urgency of the old man's plea, Ivan agreed to that as well.

They took the morning British Airways flight to London. Tatiana's father had insisted that she go with him for her own safety. Nabakov had underestimated the enemy. Until he had sorted out the mob, it was essential not to have any of his family around to be kidnapped, or worse. Tatiana, realizing only a part of the danger they were in, was only too delighted to oblige her father; she had never been to London, though she had, by good fortune, a British visa, obtained for a recently-cancelled modelling assignment.

Ivan himself needed little encouragement. There were many reasons why he was only too happy to return home then. First of all Vladimir was about to set off on a major campaign beyond the Urals, and it had been made clear to him that he was not wanted. Secondly, he had been badly shaken by his own brief encounter with the Mafia. Thirdly, while he was financially well enough off, his funds were far from limitless, and he needed to spend some time with the City broker who managed his investment affairs. In addition, he had, as he faithfully promised Nabakov, agreed to talk to other business contacts about the prospect of finding the necessary City finance for the vodka deal.

He arrived home in buoyant mood: seen from a British perspective, surely such a joint venture had many things to recommend it. The vodka market was expanding, the product was good, and there must be many opportunities for Russian vodka to be properly bottled and marketed in England. As to Nabakov's own safety, viewed from London the danger seemed so unreal: Nabakov was a survivor; he would sort things out better on his own, in his own way. He knew the Mafia boys: they were just trying to frighten him into paying them more protection money or to get a larger cut of the deal. But, as an insurance for the future, for him or for Tatiana should she ever need it, Ivan carried inside his briefcase a brown paper envelope in which was a very large amount of hard currency in used notes, which were to be banked safely in London. When Nabakov had turned up with the packet, he looked tired and drawn, but he had smiled bravely enough and waved after them with both hands when they parted. 'I'll be all right,' he had said. For that brief moment, Ivan believed him.

He spent the first day back opening up his South Kensington flat, getting in food and other supplies, and making sure Tatiana was comfortable and well provided for. She was, inevitably, bewildered by London, but he rang up an old girlfriend who turned up on the doorstep straight away and whisked the Russian girl off to show her the sights, promising to look after her until Ian had finished with his urgent business.

As a first step, he took a taxi to the City to call on a banker colleague to discuss whether they would invest in the joint venture. Ian Carter was ebullient and enthusiastic, the banker was, from the very outset, cool, distant and more than a little embarrassed.

'What's wrong with my proposal?' he asked, puzzled. 'I remember that last year you were all for this sort of East–West deal.'

'Vodka deal? Nothing much wrong there. But . . .' His City colleague smiled a dry smile that, for some reason, seemed devoid of all warmth. Then it all came out and it dealt Ian a sickening blow. He simply hadn't realized how much things had changed. 'I've seen you on television several times. You're the spokesman for that man, Vladimir?' his erstwhile colleague ventured.

'It's a much-misunderstood cause, you know; we're not fascists,' Ian explained, still cheerfully maintaining his optimism.

'Of course you're not,' said the City man, looking away uneasily.

'Will you help?'

''Fraid not, old man. Politically far too difficult, you know.'

The City man stood up. Their meeting was at an end. Just like that.

Ian Carter went elsewhere, to a number of other old contacts and drinking partners from his financial past. Their response was horrifyingly uniform. When he got back to the flat that evening, there was a note from his former girlfriend saying she had taken Tatiana off to a party. They had left the address, but by this stage Ian did not feel like partying. Bruised by the brush-offs from his former associates, he sat down wearily at his desk and tried to put through a call to Nabakov. There were lots of other avenues he could try, and in any event he was in no hurry to return to Moscow. Cursing the antiquated Russian telephone system, he tried to get through repeatedly all that long evening and again during the next day. He carefully hid his concern from Tatiana when eventually she returned from her partying, but she was so excited with her discovery of London life that she noticed nothing untoward.

Ian Carter, reverting firmly to his English style of address for the duration of his stay, returned one night to the Russian émigré club to talk to his old mentor, Professor Dimitri Platov. Even here his welcome was much less warm than he had remembered it. The other club members were polite; they too had seen much of him on television, they remarked. They said little else, but they kept their distance. Platov was more understanding, but very blunt, almost aggressive, warning him in no uncertain terms that he would be a fool to return to Russia until things calmed down. Vladimir was a dangerous man to be associated with now that he had tangled with the Mafia bosses, declaring open war on them. Anyone in his immediate circle would be equally at risk. If the thugs got really nasty, they would not stop at trying to extract money from him over a mere vodka deal. In response to a half-asked question, Platov countered with: 'As I read it, your friend Vladimir won't be any protection to you whatsoever, even if he wanted to be.'

For the first time in years, Ian Carter felt confused and deflated. Gone were the passion, the fervour, the brash certainties. What had he done to have everything he had worked for so suddenly upset? Had it all been a political pipe-dream? Had he merely been used? Of course he had, but . . . He was no coward but, suddenly, desperately, he needed help and advice, impartial advice. He wanted to know whether he should on such slim grounds abandon Vladimir, and Nabakov, and his secret dream of restoring the great family home, a dream he had shared with no one, least of all with Nabakov or Tatiana. If he had said anything to them about his family's claim to the house, perhaps they too would not have trusted him. It was his secret, his alone. All this, just because of one brief and unpleasant encounter with the Mafia, just because Nabakov had been threatened, just because Vladimir was, he suspected, tiring of him. And . . . and where the hell was Nabakov anyway?

Whom could he turn to? Professor Platov stood up. 'Do not go back, I urge you. Wait until things have eased,' he added. Then they shook hands, and left the club together. Carter felt the other members staring after him as he went out of the door. He thought of stopping, turning, shouting at them, telling them exactly what it was really like over there. But wisely he kept his own counsel.

As he walked back home to his flat through the deserted London streets, he thought about who else he might turn to for advice. Then, suddenly, he remembered someone, some-one from his distant past, from whom he knew he would get blunt, unprejudiced advice. Despite their past emotional tensions, his brother would surely recognize what Ian had been trying to do for the country of his blood. He looked up a number in the telephone directory and got through to the information desk at the Foreign Office. They confirmed that his half-brother, Alex Murray, was, as he thought, currently *en poste* in Berlin.

It took almost twenty-four hours for it to filter through the British intelligence system that Ian Carter and Ivan Katerski were one and the same person. MI6 were most intrigued that this dangerous man was wanting to meet the second most senior diplomat at Her Britannic Majesty's Embassy in Berlin. Thus it was that Anthony Fox came to Alex Murray later that day with some very personal questions. He was not apologetic; he was brief and to the point. 'Sorry to add to your burdens, Alex. You remember you mentioned to me that Pike muttered something about meeting up with someone you both knew in Moscow?' Murray nodded, a shiver of apprehension racing down his spine. He had mentioned no such thing to Fox. He must have picked it up from the tape of his telephone conversation with Pike. Fox had slipped up – or was he deliberately trying to trap him? It wasn't just someone he knew. Murray stared at Fox, waiting for what was going to come next. 'This Brit goes by the name of Ivan Katerski. We've been watching him closely because of the friends he mixes with. He's desperately keen to get in touch with you.'

For a moment Murray was genuinely fazed. 'Who?' he asked. Then he remembered that Ian had sometimes called himself by another, Russian name. 'Oh yes,' he said. 'I'd heard he was in Moscow working for that madman . . .' His voice died away. 'Has something happened to him? Has he done something stupid?'

'Not yet,' said Fox distantly. 'He wants to meet you. You know each other well?'

'It's been a long time since I've seen him. Years in fact.' Murray checked himself. 'He can ring me any time,' he said. As he spoke, his hand involuntarily reached up to the faint scar that ran down the entire side of his face.

'He's in London. Just back from Moscow. He's got serious problems. We were, as I say, watching him because he's got a British passport and because of what he's been doing. Now we're monitoring him, for his own protection, or maybe to recruit him to work for us in the future. He's in trouble with some very unsavoury types. They've got their people even in London. He's running scared. Now he seems to be planning to come to Berlin to meet you.'

'I'm not sure why you're telling me all this, Anthony.' Murray felt distracted and uneasy; he did not want to disinter that particular past. 'I told you: I haven't heard from him for ages. I've got enough problems on my hands at the moment. Tell you what: if he gets in touch, I'll see him in London next time I'm on leave. I promise, I'll keep you fully informed.'

'How well d'you know him?' Fox pressed.

'Recently, not well. Until Pike told me, I didn't even know he was in Moscow.' Murray was not dissimulating. 'It was all a very long time ago,' he repeated.

'Why would he be so keen to get in touch now?'

'I genuinely don't know.' Murray was being totally honest. He had not a clue.

Fox watched Murray intently, as if he did not believe him. 'Let me tell you what I know, then. We think it's not to do with the work he did for Vladimir. He's involved in some sort of messy business deal. He wants your help.'

'Not my scene. I tell you, we owe each other nothing at all.' Murray was about to explain his relationship with Ian or Ivan, and that his contact with his half-brother had scarcely lasted into adulthood, when Fox turned the whole conversation on its head. 'It's not like that, Alex. We need to know. We *want* you to meet him. As soon as possible. You see, we think he knows where Douglas Young is.'

Late that night, Fox rang Murray at home, just as he was about to eat the supper that Frau Müller had prepared for him.

'All options are off, Alex. For the moment at least. Your . . . friend, Ivan Katerski, has just flown back to Moscow. Very foolish of him: very foolish indeed.'

11

Why the hell had he come back? It was a question Ivan had repeatedly asked himself over the past few hours. Here he was in the intense climate of Moscow for less than a day, and already he was feeling pressurized to the point of panic. He carried his return airticket and his passport with him at all times, as if this offered him sufficient protection from any known or unknown enemies. He had left Tatiana to her own devices in London; he had ignored the warning that the professor had given him; now he realized that Platov was almost certainly right.

Maybe, just this once, it was his British blood, inherited from his old mother, that had made him return. He was back for the most honourable of reasons – to come clean: with Vladimir that he was going to pull out of his campaign team, with Nabakov about his failure to do a deal and about his long-term interest in the old house, with the Mafia, if he had the misfortune to come across them again, that he was not going to get involved in any business deals any more. Surely they would all understand. Inside, his idealism was still intact; externally he was surrendering to reality. This wasn't for him, none of it. He would come clean, then he would immediately return to London and get on with the rest of his life, with Tatiana, if she would still have him.

He went first to see Vladimir, but things had dramatically changed there too: security had been doubled and the atmosphere inside party HQ was immediately more menacing. The message to him was abrupt: Vladimir was far too busy to see him. The advisers, cronies and hangers-on round Vladimir, people like Anatoli, with whom Ivan had worked so closely in the recent past, were either suspicious or distant. From an indiscreet secretary, when he persuaded her to have a drink with him, he picked up a whisper of a potential coup, of a top-secret deal between Vladimir and a group of the more right-wing generals to control the Mafia, since there were those who were equally resolved to bring some order, or the disorder that suited them, back into Russian society. Who could blame them? The country was in a mess. It was anarchic; the people were starving; beggars were everywhere; people were devoid of hope. On the western borders, it was again rumoured that the people were massing, ready, waiting for the last and the greatest migration, the one that no one would be able to contain.

Again and again he tried to telephone Nabakov. Eventually he got through. Nabakov too seemed strangely distant and unforthcoming. There was no warmth of greeting, no questions about the deal. Nabakov did not even ask about Tatiana: that was particularly odd. At first Ivan wondered if he could be ill, but something told him to be cautious, to say little or nothing. Ivan demanded to see him. The reply was hesitant and stilted, as if Nabakov was being held against his will. He felt every word was being listened to by others. Why otherwise would he not have asked one single question about how his own daughter was? There was a pause and Ivan thought he heard whispering in the background as if Nabakov was being given his instructions. Eventually, reluctantly, as if Nabakov had had to suppress a sob in his voice, the faltering answer came: if he wanted to meet, Ivan would have to come all the way over to him at the big house. They would be safer there than in Moscow. Safer? The way the little word was uttered sent an added chill of horror through Ivan before the line went dead.

And yet it might all fit in. The house was over towards the Polish border, near Minsk. And it was to Minsk in Belorussia that Vladimir had also just departed. He might be able to kill two birds with one stone. He flew to Minsk, where, driven by his desperate resolve, he dipped into his diminishing private funds, hired two tough, ex-Afghan bodyguards and a four-wheel-drive jeep, and set off once again towards the house of his ancestors. He was fully resolved to be honest with Nabakov and tell him that no way could he go through with the vodka deal, because, in the present political climate, City funding was going to be impossible to raise. He would be economical with the truth, that his own reputation as a Vladimir aide had hardly helped. He would, however, tell Nabakov the other truth, why he had come to the big house in the first place. He would like to purchase it. Maybe, if all that went well, he would get round to mentioning his affection for Tatiana. Nabakov would surely understand. They would all understand what had driven him. He had, until now, told no one, not even Tatiana, about his family history, though one night the previous week he had nearly poured out the whole story to her over a candlelit dinner in a South Kensington restaurant. At the last moment he had held back. There would be time enough for all that.

He arrived at the house late that afternoon, having been further delayed by that most trivial of misfortunes, a burst tyre, coupled with the fact that they discovered too late that the spare tyre in the boot was also defective, and that there was no garage for miles around. At last he and his guards bribed a farmer to take them to a workshop of sorts, where a rough and ready repair was made to the tyre, and they were able to complete their journey.

The house appeared deserted. On his last visit there had been some other signs of life. This time there was no one; only the mangy dog he had noticed on his previous visit, tied up by a rear door. It barked piteously as he approached, then, whimpering, backed away as far as it could from him. He noticed to his growing horror that one side of its head was cut open and a back leg looked as if it was broken.

That sight alone produced in him a sudden overwhelming sense of dread. Yet, bolstered by the presence of his heavily-armed bodyguards, he went boldly up to the door and banged hard on it to announce his presence. As he hit it with his fist, it swung silently open in front of him. Moving step by step into the dark hall beyond, he turned cautiously to the left and into the big living room that he remembered from his previous visit. He stood still, transfixed, listening to the silence, aware that the two bodyguards, uncomprehending, had none the less sensed the danger, and had taken their automatic pistols from their shoulder-holsters, ready for what might come.

There is no danger from the dead. There, on the thinly carpeted floor in front of him, he saw the reason for the silence. Nabakov's hands were bound behind him with wire, there was a rough blindfold over his eyes, and the whole back of his head was shot away.

Ivan drove the long miles back to Minsk and checked into a hotel, hoping to track Vladimir down. Then he rang Tatiana in London. 'I'm coming back . . . very soon,' he said. He was shaking violently, but he forced himself to say nothing to her about his grim discovery. At the other end of the line she giggled a little. She had been out drinking with her new-found friends, she explained. She did not ask about her father.

A great deal happened before the next dawn. In particular he failed miserably to make any contact with Vladimir: he guessed where they would be holed up – in a magnificent dacha in the countryside to the south, but his calls and messages all remained unanswered. That in particular caused Ivan Katerski's remaining ideological convictions to desert him with great rapidity, as the reality of his predicament hit home. He requested his two bodyguards, who doubled their danger money from the moment they discovered Nabakov's body, to stay on with him and move into his hotel suite; they were instructed to accompany him everywhere he went, until he got back to Moscow and on to the safety of the plane out. To hell with his beliefs: Vladimir and his pack had abandoned him; he now realized that not only were they of no use, but, by having been so closely involved, his life would be in even greater danger now that Vladimir had declared war on the hoods. He was expendable. He had to get home. He would try to put behind him how foolishly idealistic he had been.

And as to reclaiming the family property, that too had been an absurd pipe-dream; that too would have to wait until another age, when law and order had come again to Mother Russia. But there was still Tatiana: she would be his new inheritance from what might have been.

He slept a little and when he awoke, the immediate panic he felt died away when he saw the reassuring presence of his two bodyguards bedded down in the hallway of his suite. Only a few hours more and the long nightmare would be over. But very late that night, after he had again fallen into a restless sleep, there was a sharp knock at the main door. He sat up rigid in his bed and felt a surge of blind panic shoot through him. His bodyguards rose, silently loosening their guns in their shoulder-holsters, and, with one of them standing behind it, the other unlocked the door and opened it cautiously. Outside were ranged five uniformed members of OMON, the elite branch of the Russian security police. There was some muttered argument between them and the bodyguards as Ivan, tying his dressing-gown around him, came through from his bedroom to investigate the disturbance.

'These officers want to talk to you. What do we do? They've got their cards. They're genuine,' said one of his bodyguards with a shrug, as he replaced his gun in its holster.

'I'm always ready to talk to the police,' said Ivan nervously. What the hell was this about? He pulled his dressing-gown even tighter around him as the policemen pushed rudely past the guards and into the room. One of them, the most senior officer judging by his gold-braided rank markings and epaulettes, said: 'We talk privately, through there.' He pointed to the bedroom. 'Your men and mine will stay together here. You will be safe.'

Ivan followed the officer through into his bedroom, where the man, a thin figure with a wisp of a moustache and a slight squint in one eye, shut the door firmly behind them. He sat down unasked, on the edge of the bed, produced a cigarette and lit it.

'Got a drink?' he demanded.

'Vodka?' asked Ivan. He was shaking violently.

'That'll do.'

'I've nothing to mix it with.'

'No need to mix with anything.' The officer did not smile. There was nothing warm about him. Light dawned.

'You're not from OMON, are you?' Ivan's voice came in a forced whisper.

The man shrugged. 'Does it matter?'

'I'm a British subject,' Ivan protested softly. He was not, he realized, in a position to make any real fuss. 'I've nothing to hide. What do you want of me?'

'You're a British subject maybe, but you're heavily involved here in Russia. Politically and . . . commercially. That's what interests me and my friends,' said the man in a tired voice. His squint was even more noticeable now, despite the thick cloud of cigarette smoke that hung around him.

'What d'you want?' Ivan repeated.

'Nabakov.'

'What of him?'

'You know he's dead?' asked the officer.

'You know I know he's dead,' Ivan responded. He felt sick with fear. He felt he might vomit, there, right there in the middle of the bedroom carpet. What the hell did they want with him? Why couldn't they let him just go home?

'You know why he's dead?' the man asked.

'I have no idea.' Ivan gripped his hands together to stop them shaking. He failed. He felt the sweat of pure terror running in rivulets down the small of his back.

'You are not naive, I think. You are involved with setting up some vodka operation for him in England.'

'I *was* involved. I was trying to raise capital in London to help him. I got nowhere. I went to tell him I'd failed to get any interest in London for the project. The idea is dead – like him.' Ivan tried to regain a sense of calm, but knew that his fear continued to show through.

'You have money for us?' The man's words were more a demand than a question.

'Why should I have any money for you?' Ivan stuttered out the words.

The man stood up slowly then deliberately flicked some glowing ash from his cigarette on to the thick bedroom carpet. It continued burning where it fell, causing a thin wisp of acrid smoke to rise from the singed fibre. He looked meaningfully at the glowing tip of the cigarette in his hand, then at Ivan. 'We want his money,' he said.

'I have no money except my own money. As you know I was here principally to work with Vladimir.'

'We know all about your connections with Vladimir. He was a friend of ours, we thought.'

'He will tell you –' Ivan began.

'He's already told us. He says it's up to us what we discuss with you, if you see my meaning. To him, you are nothing. Totally, finally, disposable.'

'I have no money.' Ivan's words came out almost as a whimper. 'Except what's in my wallet. You're welcome to that.'

The man took the wallet he was offered, removed the few roubles and British currency it contained and casually shoved it into a top pocket of his uniform, then threw the wallet on the floor. 'You know where Nabakov's money is? You know where Nabakov's daughter is?'

'I believe she is in London.' His voice came like a sob.

'You believe . . . Where is she being kept in London?' The thin man moved to stand over Ivan, then deliberately flicked some hot cigarette ash over his hand.

'I've no idea.' Ivan almost screamed the words as the hot ash momentarily singed his skin.

'We'd hate to think you are lying, Ivan Katerski. If you are lying and we find out, then, I promise, wherever you are, the consequences for you will be terminal.'

Ivan collapsed on to the other side of the bed, trembling and shaking uncontrollably. There was a long silence. Eventually he looked up, to see the officer staring down at him, a mixture of contempt and indifference in his eyes.

'That is not the main reason why I came,' the man said. 'We have work for you. You will come with us.'

'No!' The word spurted from Ivan's terrified lips. 'Why d'you . . . ?' They were going to take him away somewhere, then kill him.

'Don't worry. You will be safe with us for now. You may even earn a little credit from my colleagues if you help us. You translate well from English into Russian, I believe? We have someone whom we want you to help us talk to. He needs to be persuaded.' The officer moved rapidly to the door and pulled it open. 'On your feet,' he ordered. 'We go now.'

Abandoned in a dreary street near his hotel some two hours later, Ivan was in a blind panic. What should he do now? Where could he turn for help? How could he find out what to do? What did a foreigner do when caught up in a crisis in a strange environment? Of course, the British Embassy. Less than twenty minutes after he was set free from the terrifying ordeal he had just been through, he telephoned the embassy, and asked to speak to someone in authority. He quoted his British passport number frantically as futile proof of identity. The embassy switchboard were sympathetic but distant. They were quite used to getting urgent pleas from British business people who had run into trouble in the nasty world that was the commercial life in the Wild East. But Ivan turned out to be someone rather different. He had telephoned because he wanted help, but he had also called because he knew something that could be of crucial assistance to Her Majesty's Government. He knew something about what had happened to a man, a British diplomat called Douglas Young. But, as he explained to an increasingly bemused first secretary who sat taking copious notes of what he was being told across a bad line from Minsk, as part of the deal, there was only one person to whom Ivan was willing to tell everything.

Sergeant Tate's arrival on secondment to the military attaché's staff at the British Embassy in Berlin was hardly noticed by the senior members of the embassy diplomatic staff. Alex Murray, however, was aware that the brigadier's complement had been increased by one person and he had also seen the confidential report on the soldier who had so recently been involved in the attack over on the Polish border in which a number of his colleagues had been killed. Because of or despite that tragic event, Alex Murray and Sergeant Tate were to be thrown closely together in what happened thereafter.

Fox came in to Murray's office first thing next day. 'Ivan Katerski wants to see you,' he said abruptly. Was his tone of voice even crisper than usual?

'Happy to oblige,' responded Murray, cautiously.

'As soon as possible.'

'Where? London, Moscow, here?' Murray stood up.

Fox ignored the question. 'Says he knows where Young is, and what he's been doing.'

'The hell he does. So . . . I'll fly to Moscow if you tell me I must.'

'Worse than that. He's holed up in Minsk of all places. He wants you to meet him on the Polish border south-west of there. He is pretty convinced the Mafia will pick him up if he goes through another airport. He got through to us via the Moscow Embassy. He is terrified out of his wits.'

'If he can get as far as the border, why can't he get to, say, Warsaw? Meet at the embassy there.'

'No way he'd get that far, he says. It's all too delicate in any case. Our embassy in Poland don't know anything about all this. Afraid you're going to have to fly to Warsaw, then get driven.'

'Driven? By whom? Why? How? Where?' Murray was totally bewildered.

'By chance, we've got the perfect man.'

'In the embassy? Who?' The questions continued to flow unchecked.

'A Sergeant Tate. We've already vetted him.'

'Oh, him. Wasn't he – '

'The very man. Knows that border well.'

'And he's happy to take me?' asked Murray.

'He's certainly not happy to take you. He doesn't want to go back. It's too close to where all his buddies were killed.'

Despite all that, less than twelve hours later, two highly reluctant people set out from the British Embassy in Berlin to fly, first to Warsaw, then to drive by hired car which Fox had arranged, to Brest Litovsky, through the border into Belorussia, and up towards Minsk. They had been given very specific instructions as to what they were to do and where they were to meet.

On the four-hour drive, inevitably the two men got to know each other, particularly since they were forced to share so many terrible sights on the way. They had read the news reports, they had seen the TV pictures, and both had, in the past, seen refugee camps. But this was a horrific new experience. Thousands upon thousands of economic migrants were camped all along the roadsides and in and around any public building of any size: school, church, town hall, shopping mall, warehouse. At times, with the rude tents and the campfires, it was like some grim medieval battle-scene, at others like footage from a hellish Hollywood version of the Apocalypse. The faces denoted the range of their origins: Caucasians mingled with slant-eyed Mongolians, Asians and dark-skinned peoples from beyond the Urals and from the myriad Muslim states much further to the south. All, all of them, were pushing ever westwards, in a gigantic rollercoaster of humanity.

One briefly-witnessed scene captured something of the living hell it was. 'What d'you think's going on over there?' asked Murray as they drove past the ruins of a village church. A crowd of weeping women, children in their arms or standing disconsolately at their feet, huddled around the open door. Behind was an open truck filled to overflowing with what looked like black plastic sacks.

'Body bags,' replied Tate soberly. 'A hell of a lot of them too.'

Here and there were pockets of newly-pillaged prosperity for all to see. New tents, new cars, new lorries that had been looted from some showroom or depot. From time to time, they saw that the Polish security authorities, with the help of NATO troops, had rounded up sizeable numbers of refugees and herded them into football stadiums or industrial compounds, whose high fences were able partly to contain some of these illegal tourists. In many ways Murray thought that the refugees looked less abject than the local people they came across, who displayed a fear and loathing and had set up armed vigilante groups, the better to protect their homes or farms from the looters.

Some attempts at a system of cowboy justice were all too obvious. Murray and Tate passed one makeshift gallows where three bodies suspended on ropes, their heads covered by sacks, blew ceaselessly in the wind, presumably to discourage others from whatever crime they had committed. It was not a pretty sight. Later, close to the border, at a town called Grozod, they got caught up in a large crowd of people who completely blocked their way. Reassuringly, they seemed indifferent both to the car and its occupants, but were struggling forward to see whatever was going on in the centre of the town square. When their car failed to make any progress through the crowd, Tate switched off the engine and found an English-speaking local who breathlessly explained that some sort of public execution was about to take place. They got out and stood by the car, trying to see what they could over the heads of the crowd. Many of the people round about them were peasants and nearly a head shorter than Murray and his colleague, and they were, therefore, able to witness all too clearly what happened next. It was not at all clear which group was about to do what to whom, and what the victims' crimes had been. But the end result had a fearful inevitability about it all. It was only when five bedraggled men were dragged out, loosely blindfolded and with their hands tied behind their backs, that Murray and the sergeant noticed the heavy poles that had been driven into the ground in front of a blank wall to one side of an abandoned school building. Then a group of about a dozen ill-disciplined soldiers or paramilitaries, all armed with rifles, shuffled into view. Behind them came half a dozen officers in Cossack hats and neat uniforms, who moved to stand to one side, boisterously chatting and slapping each other on the back, as if they were at some society party.

Murray and Sergeant Tate watched with growing horror as the men were tied to the posts. Little time elapsed between that and the soldiers almost nonchalantly lining up in front of them and raising their rifles. It was impossible not to look away as the volley of shots rang out and then to look back and see the twitching bodies lying at the foot of the posts. Among the crowd, some wept, some looked pale, some cried out, but then Murray saw over their heads that the group of fur-capped officers were actually laughing.

'And what was that about?' a deeply shocked Murray asked Sergeant Tate, not expecting the soldier to have the answer.

'There's a sort of rough and ready self-discipline among these people,' he responded. 'They were probably caught looting the wrong shop or raping the wrong women. They've had strict instructions to leave all private property alone and go only for the big warehouses, garages and supermarkets. Heard about it from my army mates who saw summary justice just like this. Never thought I would, though.'

Murray turned and looked at the soldier with a new awareness. Here was an interesting and intelligent man. 'How long have you been in the army, Sergeant?' he asked.

'Too long, sir.'

'Find it challenging?'

'Sometimes, sir. Next you're going to ask me why I've stayed on when I am obviously able to think and all that.' Murray looked embarrassed but Tate merely smiled, then glanced at his watch and added: 'Sir, if you don't mind, the crowd's beginning to disperse. We'd better get going, or we'll miss your contact.'

The bar in which Alex Murray reluctantly waited had retained the greyness of the recent past, the long, tired decades of postwar communism. Apart from a poster of some forgotten soccer hero, there was little or no decoration on the walls; the wooden tables were scrubbed bare, the man behind the bar was surly, and the beer was thin and flat. Murray felt a deep unease. This was beyond his experience, what he wanted to be his experience. He knew that twenty yards away, around the corner, Sergeant Tate was watching and waiting, but he still did not like it. This was no job for a diplomat. This was something for MI6. He felt that in some way he was about to betray his past, and he was not proud of it.

Surprising as it might seem to a casual outsider, Alex Murray had almost forgotten that he had a half-brother. He never mentioned him, nor wrote to him, and seldom thought of him except remotely. They had long had nothing in common; no bonds of emotion tied them to each other. He had always been the dutiful one. It was he who, without fail, always rang their mother every week no matter in what far-flung part of the world he found himself. He remembered birthdays and Christmases and other anniversaries and what flowers and chocolates she liked. He was dependable, loyal, caring. Ian, by contrast, was intellectually and emotionally flawed. Yet Murray had long felt that despite or because of all that, until recently when she had fallen victim to Alzheimer's disease, he had always taken second place in his mother's affections. Because he was always conscientious, always there, would always fly home in any emergency, he was taken for granted. It was the other, the wayward, the unreliable, the prodigal, who came first. As in any love affair, it was the unsteady, the unpredictable, that inspired the sleepless nights.

And now, after such a long time, Ian wanted to see him urgently. Fox demanded the same thing. Ian: how well he remembered him from his childhood; even then he had been wild and unfathomable. When they played together, every time young Alex started to believe he knew him, Ian would do something outrageous that would shatter every childish illusion. Even after the incident on the Scottish beach when he had been hit so violently with that metal spade that it had left a physical and emotional scar which would stay with him for ever, he was prepared to forgive his temperamental half-brother. But then came long periods when Ian failed to keep in any contact with the mother who adored him. It caused her great anguish and heartache and that Alex could not forget. He had written to and confronted Ian on many occasions, but the latter had ignored his pleas or simply shrugged and walked away. That was something Alex could not forgive; it was cruel and unwarranted. In more recent times, when he had discovered that Ian had become richer than Alex would ever be, he had always half expected that one day he would wake up, open his *Times*, and read about some great financial swindle in which Ian Carter was inextricably involved. It had taken a very long time before Alex fully realized that Ian's Russian blood so greatly overwhelmed the Scottish that it dragged him into a way of thinking and behaving that could never be familiar. The two of them had kept in intermittent touch until Murray's postings overseas and Ian's involved businesses in the City led to a complete drifting apart. Alex sent him an obligatory Christmas and birthday card, but even those were futile gestures, and nothing ever came in return.

Every time Alex Murray had come across his half-brother in recent years he had felt himself ever further away from him in terms of ambition and lifestyle. At such times he wondered how there could possibly be any blood link at all between them, they were so completely alien to each other. It was not that he disliked Ian, it was that there was no empathy whatsoever. Yet every time that he thought of him, his hand would, unbeknown to himself, move automatically up to his face to touch the thin, almost invisible scar his brother had imprinted all those years ago.

Ian wanted to see him. MI6 wanted them to meet. That was why he was waiting in that scruffy bar, somewhere in the middle of nowhere, an in-between world close to where he had, for the first time in his life, seen men deliberately put to death.

Murray looked at his watch. Ian was twenty minutes late. How long should he, must he wait? As he was preparing to leave, the door opened and in walked a spare, slightly stooping

208

man whom Murray did not at first recognize. But then the stranger's face broke into a nervous smile and he saw who it was. How thin, how tired, how drawn Ian had become: and there was something else, something he had never seen before; the look in Ian's eyes suggested the fear of a hunted animal.

The two men sat at the scrubbed wooden table over glasses of untouched beer and talked generalities. At first they did not attempt to reveal their separate truths to each other. They had to find a way to reach out again, and that would take some time. Blood-brothers to the end, that was what they had once sworn as children. Now it was so very different.

Alex realized that he too had changed, but his was a marginal transformation, with age and with experience. With Ian, it was very different. He had always been mercurial, but confronted by the uncertainties ushered in by the end of the Cold War, he had altered beyond recognition. Here, in this run-down bar, a stranger had walked in. Alex, when he started talking of their childhood, talked of loss; Ian spoke only of the freedom he had sought from that past. What had captivated, motivated, driven him, was his Russian inheritance, or so he had believed. Now, he said, he was afraid. Now he wanted out. Would Alex help him?

They spoke of this and that and touched on the closeness that once had been. At last, Ian hesitantly asked about their mother's health. Alex replied to that coolly, suppressing the anger that threatened to well up within him. Ian made a pretence of reviving past intimacy, but it was an artificial thing and he quickly abandoned the attempt. Like those involved in an emotional divorce, what emerged was a deep schism. The bleak fact was, they owed nothing at all to one another. When there was a gap in the conversation, Alex volunteered that he had been deeply shocked by the summary executions he had just witnessed. Ian merely shrugged and said, 'That's nothing. That's a clean way to die. It's what they went through first that I shudder at.'

'What d'you mean?' asked Alex, looking hard at him.

'Old Comintern habits die hard. They like confessions, to keep the record clean.' Ian laughed emptily.

'Torture?' Alex breathed the word.

Ian shrugged again. 'They have ways and means of extracting what they want to be the truth,' he said quietly.

They talked for half an hour, perhaps forty minutes. Alex did as he had been bid and listened with a cold lack of emotion, while Ian poured out what he had been up to with Vladimir and with Nabakov. He talked, for the first time, about the ambitions he had briefly aspired to over his family home, and how Tatiana was now staying in his flat in London. Then he stopped, breathless, and totally silent for a moment, as he remembered the depth of his fear. He told Murray of the horror of finding Nabakov's body and something of his terrifying encounter later that same night when the Mafia men arrived at his hotel suite. Now he needed to escape, with Tatiana, to where the thugs could never find him. Would Alex help? Alex responded coolly: he would do what he could.

Without any compunction, Alex turned to the matter Fox had asked him to pursue. He began by saying how much easier it would be if he, Ian, helped him in return. He raised the subject gently, as he had been instructed to do. Had Ian, Alex prompted, met another diplomat in Moscow? An ex-diplomat, a man called Douglas Young?

Ian blanched and shook. Yes, he said, looking away. Yes, he'd met him once or twice. The Englishman had turned up one day, unannounced. He interpreted for him. It was – Ian became distraught and his eyes darted furtively around the bar – something to do with forged British passports. Vladimir had said he might be interested in getting hold of them in bulk, in hundreds, in thousands, as part of his mad scheme to drive the starving Russian peasant hordes into the lush lands of the West.

'And?' Murray pressed him. 'What happened to the deal? What's become of Young?'

'I don't know,' came the faltering, uncertain reply. 'One day he . . . he disappeared. That's all I know.'

Murray remembered back to his childhood. He recalled that he'd always known when young Ian had been lying about some exploit: who had tied up the cat, who had broken the window, who had scribbled with crayon on the walls of the elegant drawing room. Now too he knew that Ian was lying but somehow he did not feel like confronting him. An adult should know what damage lies can do. But it put an end to things between them. Ian suddenly announced that he had changed his mind. Perhaps he had panicked too much, over-exaggerated the danger he was in. Murray knew that he was lying then too. Both men smiled uncertainly, stood up, shook hands, gave each other an uneasy un-Anglo-Saxon embrace, then parted, agreeing to be in touch within the next few hours. Somehow both of them knew that, by that time, everything would be very different.

As Murray walked away from the bar in a direction opposite to the one Ian Carter had taken, Sergeant Tate appeared from a doorway and came up behind him. He too looked more than a little shaken.

'Message from Mr Fox, sir. Plans have slightly changed. We've got to meet someone else, sir,' he said, firmly. Murray was bemused by the disorientating conversation he had just had; otherwise he would have questioned the sergeant as to where they were going, how he had heard from Fox, why they were not simply returning to Warsaw. Instead his thoughts were still with his brother, and so he followed the soldier, got into the car and was driven a short distance to an anonymous building in the centre of the town.

No one else seemed to be around. It was only when he was politely ushered into a bare room and the steel door with rubber insulation round its edges was firmly shut behind him, leaving him alone with his thoughts, that he realized, to his growing bewilderment, that he must be in some sort of interrogation room. High ceiling, no windows, a slight air of mildew, and a hum from an air-conditioning vent, two chairs, one bolted to the floor, and a small army-style trestle-table. It was then that he saw the peephole in the door, and noticed that there was no inside handle to it.

He did not have long to wait. Sergeant Tate returned with a fractured smile, a tray of coffee, milk, sugar and biscuits.

'Sorry about all this,' said the soldier, firmly but politely.

'What's this about, Sergeant?' Murray was half curious, half angry.

'Don't know, sir. Mr Fox turned up out of the blue, as I was waiting for you. Told me to bring you here.'

'What? Fox here?' asked Murray, suddenly recognizing how naive he had been. On such a key mission, he would surely not be left only in the care of a simple soldier.

'He said to say, given the need for discretion, he'd best do business here. Quieter, he said.' Sergeant Tate could not or would not answer anything more.

'Business?' Murray's frown had returned: his irritation threatened to explode. 'Look, Sergeant.' He stood up angrily. 'Get Fox here. I want to speak to him.'

'If you wait, Mr Murray, he'll soon clarify things, I'm sure.'

The two men sat facing each other uneasily across the trestle-table. 'Let me pour,' said the sergeant with affected politeness. 'Milk? Sugar?' Murray shook his head in disbelief.

'What the hell is this all about, Sergeant? I do Fox a favour, agreeing to meet Ian. It's as if,' he waved at the bleak room, 'as if I was under some sort of arrest . . . being interrogated.'

The door opened then and Fox walked in. Sergeant Tate stood up smartly and left them together.

'What the hell's all this, Anthony?' Murray exploded. 'What is this building?'

Fox answered the second question first. 'Just a place I've borrowed. Somewhere quiet. We need to get to the bottom of things,' he added, drily. 'Best here, right away from the embassy.'

'What on earth?'

'What? You ask what?' Fox injected a sudden cold harshness into his voice. 'If you'd explained, from the start, Alex, that you and Ian Carter were *brothers*, OK, *half*-brothers, I won't quibble, it would have been very different.'

'I was going to clarify –' Murray began.

'You were going to clarify?' Fox seemed seriously angry. 'Look, Alex. You got an intelligence block? You're a senior British diplomat. Your brother – you never once admitted your relationship – has been working very closely with a fascist madman who may well become President of Russia at the next election. He's also in deep shit with a very nasty bunch of Russian hoods. Most important of all he almost certainly knows the whereabouts of Douglas Young, the most damaging British defector in years. And talking of first-order defectors; as you probably guessed, it was almost certainly your brother who suggested George Pike contact you in Berlin. And yet you tell me you *were going to clarify*. Wasn't all that being a fraction economical with the facts? Going to clarify – jeez, Alex.'

'You never asked,' said Murray lamely.

'Never asked? Come, come.'

'Look, I told you: we were never close, even as children. I haven't seen him for years. Until a cousin, who'd seen him on TV, wrote to me, I didn't even know he was in Moscow. Mother used to keep me in general touch with what he was up to. But for the last few years, with her memory gone . . . What the hell more do you want me to say, Anthony?' Murray said frustratedly.

'Until we get this clear, let *me* ask the questions, Alex,' Fox snapped back. It was an order and Murray, chastened, did as he was told. Fox had a point; he could have been more forthcoming, particularly since he had nothing to hide.

'Now,' said Fox. 'Why don't you tell me all about Ian Carter. Then we can go on to what he has just told you.'

As Murray spoke, Fox took detailed notes; he had also produced a small tape-recorder which he placed carefully on the table in front of him.

'Five years older than Ian,' Murray began. 'Only comparatively recently he's started calling himself Ivan. Always was a maverick. Mother, a fine lady, was very normal. Ian, by contrast, inherited a sort of madness from his Russian father. He is, not to put too fine a point on it . . .' he paused, '. . . eccentric, romantic, given to great swings of mood and emotion. I don't know him. Ian is someone of indifference to me. We neither asked for, nor gave favours to one another. I only have one thing, a small painting he once did, that he ever gave me, on my thirtieth birthday. By that time he was quite well off: he'd found his feet in some City job.' Murray stopped, stood up and began pacing round the room. He was more relaxed, less intimidated by his interrogation now. He would get it all out and that would be the end of it.

'After he left school, he showed more and more of his father's character, so my mother told me. She was desperately unhappy about him; she used to show it. It hurt me a lot, his indifference and that she could still care for him. He gave her a very hard emotional time. He went through a period of low self-esteem, and deserved that too. I was abroad with the service for several years, and then, when I met him again, he'd completely changed, had become a total egotist, committed to all this new Russian kick. But believe me, until you told me that he was trying to get in touch, I genuinely hadn't realized how extreme his ideology was.'

'I believe you, Alex. Talk. You don't need to try to persuade me,' Fox interrupted. 'Tell me: why was he so committed? He actually was Vladimir's chosen spokesman.'

'I heard he'd appeared on British television, but I never saw – '

'His father was a fascist?'

'I never really knew him either, but I don't believe so. Nor, probably, is Ian at heart. Romantic, idealist, nationalist, believing he has found a superior ethic. If you asked him, he'd probably be amazed that anyone thought he was an extremist. But . . .'

'But what?' asked Fox, curiously.

'In the end, Ian is like the rest of us. Impelled by passion, but, in the end, ruled by expediency. He's dead scared. He showed glimpses just now. He wants to run right away and hide like he did as a child when he had done something wrong. You see this scar?' He pointed to the faint white line down his cheek. 'He did that. We were building sandcastles on a beach. I told him he was doing something wrong. He got furious, hit me with a metal-bladed toy spade – ten stitches, I remember. He ran and hid then too.' Murray paused. 'What else do you want to know?'

Fox stared at him, taking in the faint line of the scar. 'We're curious. We want to know why he's so frightened.' Fox continued to look thoughtfully at Murray for a moment, then went on. 'What's happened to him that's so shocking? Something to do with Douglas Young?'

'That's my guess, too,' said Murray softly.

12

Factually briefed if not emotionally prepared, Alex Murray set out for his second meeting at precisely ten a.m. on that desiccated early summer morning. Two days later Ian had unexpectedly turned up in Berlin. Murray was told to see him again and offer him every assistance. He'd be helped to disappear into some safe environment in exchange for revealing where Douglas Young was. If Ian was cooperative and told him everything, he would be spirited away by MI6 to a new identity, immediately and with no further questions asked.

Berlin was *en fête*. Pretty girls strolled along the Kurfürsten-damm hand in hand with handsome men. Fat ladies sat at pavement cafés as they always had done, eating huge chunks of cake topped with layers of thick cream; old men sat on park benches in the sunshine, nodding and dreaming of past great-ness. The British Embassy was shut. It was a holiday weekend, and such weekends are sacred in Germany as in Britain.

To the east, away over on the Polish–Belorussian and Ukrainian borders, refugees had been largely herded back to where they belonged, but still camped out in their hundreds of thousands. The new western emergency aid programme was up and running, the Red Cross and the UN Commission for Refugees had got their act together, and the immediate crisis seemed to be being contained, as the well-established soup kitchens and the increas-ingly well laid out tent cities provided the basic necessities of life for the masses. Besides, it was moving towards high summer, it was warm and sunny, and that always made life a little more bearable. What the following winter might bring could wait until then.

Berlin boasts two zoos, the original Zoologischer Garten founded away back in the eighteen-forties, and the newer Tierpark, with its own range of exotic species. Berlin's older zoo, where the giraffe house still stands as a memento of the dreamy baroque style that once made it the most famous menagerie in the world, remains a favourite tourist destination. Alex Murray paid his entry fee at the kiosk then pushed his way through the metal turnstile. To one side, a boisterous group of children on a holiday weekend outing ran screaming past a cage in which apes played sedately: the children's behaviour as they set upon each other in a series of bad-tempered skirmishes seemed more primitive than that of the animals caged beside them.

Murray strolled down a path between two fenced enclosures; the notices proclaimed that they held various species of wild cat, but the occupants remained hidden, wisely sheltering from the fierce heat of the sun. Jacket off, he mopped his forehead with a handkerchief and advanced towards the high-fenced compound which contained the Siberian wolves. There, on a bench under the shade of a linden tree, he was to wait for Ian.

As he sat there waiting, he thought back over the last six tempestuous months at the embassy. With all that had been going on with Ian, he was unashamedly relieved that he would not have to dissimulate, or explain what he was involved in, to Carol-Anne. Just over a week ago they had had a light spat, their first; then she suddenly announced what she must have been thinking about for some time, that she had decided to go back to the States on extended home leave. It would give them both time to think, she added, but Murray already sensed what the outcome would be. His friend, Vernon Cranston, the American Ambassador, had taken him aside and confirmed it bluntly to him when they had met at an evening diplomatic reception. Judging or guessing that he would pass it on to Murray, she had indicated to Cranston that if a suitable post came up back in the State Department, she would seriously consider taking it. It would be a good career move at her age, getting to know the Washington scene once again.

'She's a very determined lady,' Cranston had added gently. 'Believe me, Alex, she's married to the Foreign Service, always was, always will be. She's not going to give up her career any more than you are. It's not the way either of you is made. You're too alike. The very day you got hitched the tensions would start. It wouldn't need your friend Sir Edward to have you pulled apart. You'd both do it all by yourselves.'

Murray was not surprised and rapidly became resigned to the news; he was resigned to most things these days. Carol-Anne would all too soon be remembered by him with remote affection, as someone of a moment that had gone; passionate, implacably enthusiastic, a degree over-earnest, with a professional life which had eventually, or perhaps had always, as Cranston suggested, come first. She had arrived late in his life and now she had gone, leaving surprisingly little feeling behind. That judgement, heartless though it might seem, was not in his mind a disparaging one; he had always recognized how much of a career woman she was, someone unusual for her gender, who liked her relationships, as many men did, fast, keen then over and out. He felt he was being swept along by events rather than influencing them. Maybe it was just a phase; maybe it was the male menopause; maybe he was getting old.

There was a movement to his left and a man sat down on the bench beside him. It was Ian. In the bright sunshine, he seemed even older and there was a new, manic look about him. He leant across and they shook hands.

'Why here?' Murray asked. Beside him sat a total stranger.

'Because here the wolves are caged,' answered Ian without a smile.

Murray did not press the point. 'How did you get out without them stopping you?'

'Three reasons: surprise; I came the unexpected route, via Berlin, rather than flying direct to London. Then . . . well, I'm not that important, am I? And, thirdly, money buys everything in Russia. It cost me a lot to get here, but it was worth every penny.'

'What can I do?' Murray asked.

'Help me out of this mess, Alex, please. I don't want to have to look over my shoulder for the rest of my life. I want to disappear.' A look of almost childlike panic had suddenly appeared on his face.

'Colleagues of mine have promised to help,' Murray said, increasingly wondering why Ian should be in such danger merely because of an aborted vodka deal and having been a spokesman for Vladimir.

Ian looked across at the other man. 'Why, what do they want in return?' he asked.

Murray hesitated. 'Tell me all you know about Douglas Young.'

'I was waiting for that,' Ian whispered. 'He was your predecessor, wasn't he? Strange coincidence, isn't it? Small world. You wouldn't have been posted to Berlin if he hadn't done a bunk.'

'Where is he?' Murray asked.

Ian again ignored the question, and pleaded for reassurance. 'You promise I'll be OK?'

Murray nodded.

'Douglas Young? You want to know about him? Very important, must be. First couple of times I met him he was cocky, almost arrogant. He was full of his own importance. He had this amazing passport deal on offer. He was a world expert, he said. He was on a real high.' Carter paused, swallowed, then falteringly continued. 'Later, he came running to me, pleading for help. I didn't . . . I didn't much feel like helping him. We had a pretty sharp exchange. Asked him how he could live with himself, selling out his country in the way he was proposing. He told me not to lecture him on patriotism or morality. Only thing he did say was that, by working with Vladimir, I was on the edge of a precipice too.'

'Why you?' Murray was fascinated.

'Because I was some sort of fellow-Brit, also on a razor's edge. He was scared out of his wits and wanted to scare me too. It was when I was still in a position of influence with Vladimir. He thought I would act as his ally, his agent, selling techniques, his passport manufacturing secrets, to Vladimir, to the party, or, if not to us, to the Mafia. They started leaning heavily on him after he tried playing one lot off against another. He had every reason to be scared.'

'What happened?' Murray asked.

'I told you, he first turned up at Vladimir's HQ offering to help us use the refugee problem for our own ends. Just like that. Give everyone a genuine passport to the West. He was mad. But he was speaking to madmen. For a while it looked as if it might work. Even if it had stood a chance, he didn't realize that that was the last thing Vladimir really wanted. Vladimir *doesn't want* a solution to the refugee problem. He wants it to escalate, to use the subsequent mayhem to his political advantage. He wants that constant pressure at the border. He doesn't want any further invasions, migrations, great marches west. In any case, the western powers, with all this increased food aid, tents, Red Cross services, have defused the crisis, at least for the time being. It was all a ploy played up by Vladimir. Now it's past its sell-by date.'

Murray did not argue, not entirely believing what he was being told. Coldly he returned to his task. 'What's happened to Young?'

'Told you. He did the worst thing. When he failed to get us excited, he tried to barter with two of the top Mafia bosses. Barter – can you believe it? They weren't interested in the politics or in humanitarian emigrations. They wanted to flog his passports for a hell of a lot of money.'

'They bought up his passports, his expertise?' Murray asked.

'Did they hell. They're not stupid, these guys. They soon sussed out that Young was the genuine article, and what a potential money-spinner they were on to. He came with one or two samples. He'd hidden the rest. He pushed too hard. Suddenly they saw him in a new light. He was just an English spiv trying to rip them off, playing one off against the other, looking for the highest bidder. That approach hasn't even got the soft option of Russian roulette these days. Do it that way and every cartridge is firmly in place in the revolver. They killed the golden goose.'

'Killed? What happened to him?' Murray took a sharp intake of breath.

Ian Carter stood up and stared emptily into one of the zoo cages. A couple of Siberian wolves stirred lazily at the back of their compound. 'Tell your friends that they don't need to worry about Young any more. I just said these Mafia people are not stupid. Correction: they are very stupid. It was obscene. I saw it all. I knew they were trying to frighten me too. I heard his screaming before I got to the room where he was being held.'

'Tell me.' Murray was shocked, though he did not yet know why. Then it came.

'I told you how the mob came, disguised as OMON Police, to my hotel suite? God, was that just last week? It seems like years. After they'd done the frighteners on me over the Nabakov deal, this guy, the chief – he had a thin moustache and a cast in one eye – insisted I went with him. He said he had somebody he wanted me to translate for. It was Young. They drove me a few blocks, I don't quite know where. Down some backstreet they stopped outside a derelict-looking building where they took me down into a cellar. It was the most horrible . . .'

Ian Carter paused and lowered his head into his hands. A little boy of three or four came running past, paused in front of the two men sitting on the bench, and stared at them. Carter sat up suddenly and the little boy saw this grown man with tears running down his face. He was badly frightened by the sight and ran away screaming. Neither man paid any attention to him, as Carter continued. 'They had him bound to a chair with wire. He was half-naked and his face was almost unrecognizable. His feet were in a tub of hardening concrete.' Carter paused to compose himself, then went on, his voice hardly rising above a whisper. 'They were beating the life out of him. Why I don't quite know, since he was ready to give them anything they wanted by that time. But they wouldn't let him alone. They were annoyed he'd been trying to barter between them and some other gang. They don't like that sort of thing. He was screaming. Crying and screaming, and when he saw me, he started pleading with me to help him, to tell them to stop. There was nothing I could do. I was shaking as well. I had tears running down my face too. I'd seen what they could do. There was nothing I could . . . nothing I could . . . Then . . . it's all a blur.' Carter paused and wiped his eyes with his sleeve. 'I suppose I did some translating from English to Russian and then back to English. It was difficult because it was almost impossible to hear what Young was saying, he was crying so much. His teeth were all broken; his nose and mouth were running with blood. He kept sobbing, telling me to tell them he agreed to do anything, anything, so long as they let him go. They were fools. They always were. They always will be fools. They killed the golden goose.'

There was a very long pause. 'What happened next?' Murray asked quietly.

Carter's head was bowed again and his shoulders were shaking. He was sobbing deeply. 'Don't remember,' came the faint response. 'Yes, of course I remember. I threw up,' he said suddenly, looking up and staring with bloodshot eyes at his brother. He wiped his eyes and face with the back of his sleeve. 'How could I forget?' he continued. 'That's why I'm here. That's why I'm running. That's why I am terrified. They took me with him as they dragged him up and up and up on to the roof of that building, the cement bucket round his ankles. They held him over the edge for quite a while before they threw him off, off the fourteenth storey of the building. They forced me to watch. It's cheaper than using a bullet, they said. I think . . . I hope . . . he had some sort of fit and passed out before they dropped him, poor bastard. Then,' Carter shrugged, 'his was just another anonymous, unrecognizable body, cleared away by the police the next day, another nameless victim of a gangland feud.'

Murray listened in shocked silence. He listened on and on without interruption, as Ian told him of the plan he had become so involved in, personally rallying the peasants, ready for their great march westwards, which their leader, Vladimir, had pretended to foment. Half a million starving men, women and children, breaking down the barriers, not at one point, not at ten, but at hundreds of points along the whole of the western borders would, if it had been carried out in its entirety, have produced an exodus that would have been totally impossible for NATO, despite its huge resources, to contain without bloodshed.

If Murray was shocked by what he heard, he also felt anaesthetized by guilt, by betrayal, because inside his shirt a tiny tape-recorder was strapped with surgical tape to his chest, recording all he was being told. He might have felt that guilt even more, had he not been so sickened at hearing what happened and what had been planned. But Ian, having told his full story, having got it all off his chest, was now more interested in talking about the future, about Tatiana, about selling his house in Britain, about disappearing with her into everlasting safety.

'What now?' asked Murray when he had finished talking.

'Look after Tatiana if anything happens to me,' Ian Carter said simply. Gone suddenly were his fear and tears. He spoke in a monotone.

'Nothing will happen to you if you keep your head down. Our people will hide you for a while until things cool down. Eventually you'll be able to go back to your City job, your clubs, your wonderful home in South Kensington, your Tatiana.' Murray at last tried to console him a little, though he did not believe his own words.

Carter changed mood once again. He seemed resigned to his fate. 'It's too late,' he said softly. 'I'm in it too deeply. I see it all now. I need to go back to Moscow, to Vladimir, to continue to help him. Not that Vladimir will help me, I know that. I'm the most expendable member of his whole team. In the last resort he doesn't care what the western press think of him. They don't affect one single solitary vote inside Mother Russia. He knows that. He doesn't care,' Carter repeated. 'You see, Alex, I love Russia. I want to help her. I believe I can have a meaningful life, working there in Moscow, building bridges between West and East.'

'So? Stick to politics,' Murray interjected. 'Why get involved with the Mafia at all?'

'You don't understand Russia, Alex. They're inextricably entwined. You *have* to play one group against the other. Money is what matters. Money is what buys and brokers power.'

'Is that really what you want, Ian?' Murray asked. At long last he was genuinely beginning to feel sorry for him.

'What d'you mean?' Ian looked back at him and, for a moment, Murray saw the insecure little boy he once had known.

'Money is everything?' Murray asked.

'Of course not. But money is the means to my end.'

'D'you aim to become a politician in your Mother Russia?' Murray pressed his point.

'Don't mock me, Alex. I don't aim so high. I want to help build a true democracy,' Carter responded woodenly. He stood up, indicating that their conversation was drawing to its close.

'Supporting Vladimir will lead there?'

'He offers some prospect of order. Particularly if he manages to destroy the Mafia warlords.' Carter walked round behind the bench and stood behind his brother. Murray looked away, embarrassed by their sudden physical closeness.

'What happened to Douglas Young's box – a metal-bound box of passports?' Murray was guessing wildly, but it worked.

'You know about that too?' Ian turned and stared at his brother.

'I know it exists. You know where it is, don't you? Perhaps it's your old-age pension now, taking over from where Douglas Young left off?' Murray watched and waited. Then, slowly, Ian Carter reached into an inside pocket, produced an envelope and handed it over to his half-brother. 'I came prepared for this,' he said. 'You'll find all the instructions you need. And now . . . if I live long enough, once in power, we'll sweep aside all the corruption.' Ian Carter's final, glorious words were belied by the hesitant tone of their delivery.

'That's what dictators have always said,' responded Murray carefully. Then he too stood, turned, they shook hands and parted uneasily, making no more promises which might have to be broken.

It happened as if in slow motion. Each frame became a still photograph in Alex Murray's memory. Ian Carter left him standing alone by the bench, next to the cage of Siberian wolves, under the shade of the great linden tree. He watched as his brother walked rapidly towards the entrance to the zoo. Then suddenly, along a path by the ape house, he noticed two men come out of nowhere. They moved up behind Ian as he was passing through the bars of the exit turnstile. The triple cracks of a silenced gun were hardly audible above the excited shouts of children and the exotic call of some strange bird in its aviary. The turnstile could turn no further as the body wedged itself, bloody and lifeless, between its heavy bars. And then no more.

It was not the only assassination that day. But the other one hit the world's headlines. It was also brought about by one deal too many, one too many challenges to the anonymous, multi-headed hydra that was the Russian Mafia system. Even Vladimir was not big enough to take them on. It wasn't that the hoods had shot many politicians before; most of their daily massacres were of businessmen or other Mafia leaders. Assassinations change the pages of history, and Russia, like the United States, has a reputation for political murders that have brought about radical reforms. Did it matter what Lee Harvey Oswald's motives were in killing Kennedy? Did it matter now? The real purpose, the real point of any assassination is what changes it ushers in.

Who did it, no one knew; why they did it did not matter. Vladimir was driving down an empty suburban Moscow street in his usual bullet-proof car. Cars heavily laden with his personal bodyguards travelled in close formation to the front and to the rear of his vehicle. There was no way anyone could get at Vladimir. The trouble was that the bullet-proof, bomb-proof Mercedes in which he normally travelled had been secretly substituted that morning. No one knew precisely how, but probably some driver or guard had been bribed or beaten up, and it had been swapped for an ordinary, similar-looking, Mercedes car. Vladimir, nursing his usual hangover, had not noticed that the doors were not as heavy as usual nor that the springs of the car bounced more lightly than they did when they had an extra half-ton of armour-plating built into the bodywork.

His convoy, or cortège, drove fast down the middle of the wide street, but not too fast for the sniper with his telescopic lens and his years of professional work in the mountains of Afghanistan. Three, five, ten, fifteen rounds of incendiary bullets were pumped into the Mercedes. The car spun out of control, hit the wall of a derelict building, and burst into a huge ball of flame that was too great to have been caused by a single tank of fuel. Much later the police found the remains of the extra cans of petrol where they had been hidden in the boot.

The assassination sent shock waves throughout Russia. The people's choice for President was dead. It was the lead item on all the news stories and, thereafter, was widely reported throughout the world. Witnesses were found who said that they saw the rooftop gunman fleeing with his automatic rifle and telescopic sight. Others claimed to have heard the shots and to have seen that Vladimir, his driver and the two bodyguards who were with him were killed immediately. It was a brazen attack in broad daylight. It was widely condemned. Vladimir had been tolerated by the other Russian political parties because he was a safety valve for the discontented of the far right. He had acted as a channel for extreme nationalistic longings; even the western powers had put up with him, since he allowed them to argue that 'Without Yeltsin, that's the sort of leader you would get in Russia'. At his most successful, Vladimir only gained ten per cent of the national vote, but he was the focal point for the mass migrations, the torrents of economic refugees that had so harried the western powers over the last dangerous months. There was no obvious successor waiting in the wings to take his place, to lead the charge, to promote the invasions, to blackmail the West in the way he had been doing.

Vladimir, drunken womanizer, mock hero, madman to some and charismatic redeemer to others, was no longer. It did not matter who killed him; it did not matter why. But without him, and eased by the additional influx of western aid that came on the coat-tails of his assassination, the crisis would fade away.

In Berlin, a small but important meeting was taking place in the ambassador's office at the embassy. Fawcett was, unusually, in his shirtsleeves. Normally, when he was working with the ambassador, he was extremely smartly dressed. The two men were sitting opposite each other across a paper-strewn table in the middle of the office, drafting a very important letter to London.

'The headache is to explain why we didn't move about this before,' said the ambassador in a low voice.

'You've every excuse, sir. The Foreign Secretary was coming, you had a new and untried head of chancery, the inspectors were on your doorstep, and you were dealing with the biggest crisis to hit Europe in decades. You can't be blamed for not having realized the cases had gone.'

'The buck stops with me,' responded the ambassador.

'What does Karen Deighton know, sir?' asked Fawcett.

'As far as I know, nothing. Only that bastard Bennett.'

'Bennett won't squeak. He's in it too deep.'

'People always bleat when they're pushed into a corner. Bennett has no moral fibre.'

'Who're you going to get to type this?' asked Fawcett.

'You. You can use the word processor, I hope. I don't want to leave this to anyone else. We have to get our words very precise before anything goes to London.'

Alex Murray had always hated blood, always shivered involuntarily at the thought of any injury. When he had fallen over as a child, he could not bear to look at the tiniest wound on his knee; he would always turn his head away and ask his mother to look at it for him, with the cry, 'How deep is it, Mummy?' Then had come that terrible day when he didn't have to ask that question; he knew how deep the wound down the side of his face must be. He had recalled his mother's anger, tears, panic, and the long wait before the ambulance came and rushed him to hospital. Every now and again, in a fit of introspection, Murray would wonder how much that one single event had moulded his life. He knew what it had done to his relationship with his brother; he knew what it had done to his relationship with his mother, who seemed more concerned, even at that terrible moment, about why Ian had behaved in the way he had done and where he had hidden, than about the lasting effect that the attack might have on her elder son. Now, many years later, he understood why. Once the act was committed, the result was with Alex for ever, whereas his mother had worried, through many sleepless nights, about when Ian might do something similar again.

Someone who dies young is for ever young in the memory. If Ian had run away from for Alex those many years ago, that day he died again. On the dreadful drive back to the embassy, with Fox beside him and Sergeant Tate at the wheel, he tried to plough back into his past and its long-forgotten relationships. He failed. Now, all he could think of was the bloody, lifeless body, blocking the turnstile at the zoo.

It took some fifteen minutes in heavy traffic to make it to the chancery. Pushing aside Fox's restraining arm – he would later blame him for having failed to provide sufficient protection for Ian – he stormed past Curran at the front desk, ran up the stairs two at a time and along the corridor to the ambassador's office. The ambassador's PA, Sylvia Watt, normally so cool and self-possessed, and in full charge both of herself and any situation she found herself in, was totally nonplussed at the sight. Though privately she was the ambassador's greatest critic, in her professional life she was the stern guardian of his office, privacy and diary, and so, briefly, she tried to stop Murray. She stood up, her usual stiff smile of welcome on her face. But when she saw his angry, tear-flecked face, she merely muttered, 'He's got a meeting on' but then said no more. Murray thrust open the door of the ambassador's office and barged straight in. The ambassador was in the middle of a meeting. Fawcett had been joined by Karen Deighton and Bobby Sofer, the commercial counsellor. They were sitting discussing some new problem, some new solution. 'I'm in the middle of a meeting, Alex,' said Sir Edward, looking up angrily at the unwarranted noise.

'Your meeting is at an end, as of this moment,' said Murray.

'What the hell do you mean?' said the ambassador.

Murray stared at Sofer and Karen Deighton; 'Get out, please. Like right now.'

'Have you taken leave of your senses, Murray?' began the ambassador, but then Fox, who had appeared behind him in the doorway, interrupted; 'Sir, it'll be for the best. Just you and Paul please, sir, otherwise all hell will break loose.'

With bewildered looks, Karen Deighton and Bobby Sofer left the room quickly, shutting the door behind them.

'What the bloody hell's going on?' demanded Sir Edward.

'If I can begin,' said Fox, with an unusual note of uncertainty in his voice. 'Alex has just witnessed the most terrible event. His half-brother, Ian, has just been shot dead in front of him. Here at the zoo,' he added unnecessarily.

'Zoo?' said the ambassador stupidly, trying to understand what he was being told. Beside him, Paul Fawcett had turned pale.

'Leave that, Anthony,' said Murray, tersely. 'That's not why I've come. Right now, Sir Edward, I'm not looking for recriminations, I'm looking for answers. I am extremely angry. The death of my brother, well, that's happened. I barely knew him and my tears for him can wait for the funeral. What I want to know is why I was spun a trail of lies and deceit, when I first arrived, about why Douglas Young had left, about the fire in my office, about why Fawcett was so intent on moving our offices around so that I wouldn't notice, for Christ's sake. Would it, by any chance, be to do with something that had gone missing that you, sir, failed to report to London? Could it be that you were desperately worried, because the inspectors were about to arrive, and that led you to a very nasty cover-up? Cover-up is a strange phrase, but there have been bigger ones than this in recent history. Would it, for example, be to do with where a second metal-bound case of stolen British passports landed up?'

The ambassador had collapsed in silence in his chair behind his large desk. Fawcett, standing behind him, was shaking uncontrollably. Fox decided, wisely, not to interrupt Murray's anger-filled flow.

'One more question before I tell you my answers,' Alex Murray went on remorselessly. 'Did Peter Bennett know some or all of this, so that you refused to send him home, even though he had contrived a false robbery, a crime for which he should not only have been dismissed from the service, but probably have had to appear in a criminal court? What are the answers to all these questions, ambassador? I'll tell you one answer. It's here.' With a simple dramatic gesture, Murray produced from an inside pocket the envelope which his brother had given him that short fifty minutes earlier. In it was a brief instruction and two keys, keys to a safe deposit box in the Moscow headquarters of the Narodny Bank. 'Could this,' Murray went on, his eyes darting accusingly around the room, 'could this,' he repeated, 'be the clue to where the missing case of British passports is? I bet you were terror-struck as to where they might have ended up? You, *sir*,' Murray paused, emphasizing 'sir' in the most disparaging way, 'knew that both cases of passports had disappeared, because Bennett had reported it all to you. I can't believe that Karen Deighton knew and had not reported it, so you've been hiding it from her too.' Murray swung round dismissively. 'Well, for the good of Britain, *Mr Ambassador*, you can relax. I'll tell you exactly where the missing case is. I am not going to let this matter rest here. It's not just the death of a brother; it is because a weak, vacillating man and his sycophantic sidekick,' Murray threw an angry glance at Fawcett, 'were so scared for their own skins, that what might have started out as a minor

lapse got so totally out of hand that there was no going back.'
Murray walked towards the door, opened it, then turned to Fox.
'I hope you remember all this, Anthony. Because if you don't tell
this whole story to London, then I can tell you, I will.' With that,
Murray, eyes red more with anger than with tears, turned on his
heel and stormed from the room.

It was a cathartic, defining moment – he would never be
the same again. He had few friends; some colleagues liked
him well enough, but indifference was their more common
reaction. Alex Murray was just there. Now came the rapid
erosion, the stripping away of the protective shell he had long
built up around him. Now, his defences in ruins, he would
have to confront his own humanity, his deeply buried feelings.
It would not be easy.

Karen Deighton, encouraged by Fox, tried to reach him, tried
to talk to him on the telephone, but he failed to answer her
repeated calls. Eventually Frau Müller found him in the dark-
ened sitting room of his flat. At first she thought that he was
sleeping, or perhaps he was ill. Then she saw that he had been
crying and, having recently noted that all Carol-Anne's things
had gone from the bedroom they frequently shared, guessed,
inaccurately, at the cause of his grief. How could she know that
she too had, with the discovery of that forbidden case, had a
hand in what had happened. Frau Müller thought of casting her
natural discretion aside by coming forward, putting a hand on
his shoulder, perhaps offering a word of comfort. Instead, she
waited for a moment, then turned and left, closing the door
softly behind her.

There was one minor follow-up to those tragic events. In
keeping with the age of democracy and a need to butter up a
fickle press, new Ministry of Defence instructions allowed the
brigadier, when he threw one of his regular cocktail parties, to
invite both Sergeant Tate and the journalist Fred Cree to it. Cree
was a dangerous man, and a duty-free drink or two might just
make him, if never a friend, then at least less of an enemy.
And as for Sergeant Tate, the brigadier was most impressed to

have learned that, with the blessing and encouragement of Alex Murray and Anthony Fox, he was about to sit the late-entrant exams for the diplomatic service.

But that was all in the future. Now, when they met at the party, the conversation between Cree and Tate went as follows:

'I hear you've been over on Poland's border with Belorussia. Just back, eh? Interesting trip, I bet?' asked Cree.

'You're well informed,' responded Tate carefully. He had done the army's media-handling course and knew that journalists were more the enemy than any enemy.

'Gather you went on to Minsk?'

Tate nodded.

'With Alex Murray?'

'You'd be better talking to Mr Murray on all this. I was just the driver.'

'So he eventually met up with that renegade brother of his, did he?'

'Sorry? Come again?' said Tate softly.

'His brother is, I think, involved with that mad Russian Vladimir, the one who was assassinated the other day?'

Sergeant Tate, having carefully noted Cree's words, 'I think', turned and stared hard at him and, without flinching, said, 'You know, Mr Cree, you seem to be doing a lot of guessing, without having much certainty to go on. Let me save you one piece of work. I can tell you as a guaranteed, one hundred per cent fact, Alex Murray's one and only brother is dead. Dead and buried.'

'Really?' said Cree, totally flummoxed. He had, until then, felt he had been on to a certainty, a big headline story for his paper. He felt its credibility rapidly slipping away from beneath him.

'Are you sure?' he insisted, increased uncertainty showing in his voice.

'Dead certain,' said Sergeant Tate, continuing to choose his words appropriately.

A little later, as Cree walked disconsolately away, Tate smiled a secret smile to himself. Perhaps that little exchange had proved what Alex Murray had flatteringly suggested when he had been pressed to apply for entry to the Foreign Office. What was that old adage about a diplomat? 'A man sent to lie abroad for his country.' Pun intended.

AUTUMN AND WINTER

There were a number of other aftermaths. Alex Murray arranged, via Fox, to move Tatiana Nabakov to a place of greater safety, which was just as well, because some days later Ian Carter's luxurious South Kensington apartment was totally gutted by a fire which expert investigators designated as suspicious. Fox's people were generous. They went to great trouble and expense to give the girl another name and identity and did not question the large sums of convertible currency that were deposited in various banks under her new name. They felt guilty at the way things had ended for Ian Carter and were as grateful to him as they as an institution were capable of, for helping solve the embarrassing mystery of the fate of Douglas Young.

When Murray returned to London shortly before his new posting as Ambassador to Guatemala, they arranged for him to go and call on the girl who had once been known as Tatiana Nabakov. She told him that she had felt very distraught for a while, and very much alone, which was fully understandable, because she had lost both her father and Ivan Katerski in the course of a few days. But by the time Alex Murray came to see her, she was beginning to come to terms with her misfortune, helped by her realization that she had inherited a very considerable fortune, and her discovery of a style of life in Britain which she found hugely preferable to her old one in Moscow or in the backward depths of a primitive countryside. She had rapidly acquired new aims and ambitions and was fully prepared to throw down strong roots in her new-found land.

Before all that, before he went to call on Tatiana, Alex Murray had one other visit to make.

The old grey-haired lady was sitting at a bay window, motionless, staring as was her habit, out over an ice-grey sea. Around her, in their silver frames, were her memories, each captured in a photographic instant in time. Neatly dressed, her hair newly done, from a distance she looked as composed and alert as she had always been. Close to, however, her eyes were vacant with the blue haze of senility's void.

On a delicate mahogany table behind her, in this, her eventide home which she would never leave, these silver-framed photographs of an elegant past were her memories, her only memories; the ones of her mind were long gone. Yet she would often stand, infirm but unaided, and go and peer closely at these freeze-framed, smiling faces, and she would smile back at them and speak indistinguishable words to herself or to them, that might once have told the listener who was who among husbands, sons and other loved ones.

Alex Murray brought her flowers and took her hand, and, for a moment, he thought he saw a flicker of recognition and of affection as she turned from the window to stare with brief curiosity at her visitor. Was there something about that faint white scar that ran down the full side of his face that briefly triggered some long-buried memory? Then she looked away again, but continued to hold his hand, her fingers gently pressing on his.

He tried to tell her what had happened, that her Ian, or Ivan, would not be coming to see her any more.

'That is sad. That is sad,' she said suddenly as if she had, by some magic, regained her sense and her memory. Then: 'Who is Ian?' she asked, looking at him curiously. 'And . . . and,' she added hesitantly, 'and who are you?'